I AM HISTORY

I AM HISTORY

J. D. Hearn

I Am History

Artwork created using AI

Published by JDH Publishing
Germantown, TN

ISBN 979-8-9946432-3-5 [paperback]

This is a work of fiction. Names, characters, places, and incidents are either products of the author's imagination or used fictitiously.

Printed in the United States of America

For my mother,

Elizabeth Ann Hearn

FADE IN:

EXT. SPACE - NIGHT

Earth spins silently, bathed in blue and cloud-
whorled white, suspended in the cosmic dark.
Music fades in: drums,percussion, and rhythm, a
driving beat as

CAMERA ZOOMS IN - CONTINUOUS

We draw closer—faster now. Past drifting
satellites as they collide. Hurtling through
the stratosphere. Dizzily moving toward the
blue-green swirl of North America.
Rushing downward—
East Coast.
New York.
MANHATTAN.
Sparse clouds part to reveal:

EXT. BROADWAY - EARLY MORNING

A once-bustling artery, now bled out. Lifeless
pile-ups choke the street. Trash flutters in
the ghostly glide, as shadows stretch across
shattered storefronts and bloodied
intersections. A war zone.

A solitary FIGURE jogs purposefully down the
middle of the street. Burgundy beanie. Boxers
and running shoes. Money belt.
Cord clipped to his shirt. WALKMAN clipped to
his hip.
From the headphones blasts the opening music:
Chicago's "I'm a Man."

He pounded the pavement like the city depended on it. Maybe it did.

Every morning, the same route, the same beat in his ears. Like ritual. Like penance. Like something he couldn't let himself forget—if only he could remember what it was.

Broadway stretched long before him, an unswept cutting-room floor. Lighted signs flared like forgotten cues. Rats scurried to eat mixed reviews. Hell's world premiere at every venue. He ran, each staggered-algorithmic step a clapperboard slap restarting his take, chasing lines that no longer made sense, this abandoned movie set folding and unfolding around him with the pulse of an irregular heartbeat—quick, uneven, relentless—one he tried to calculate, memorize, control. Somewhere in the middle of all this, he kept pretending he knew his lines and stage directions—because admitting he didn't would have made it all much worse.

Henry Thaddeus Gorestriker—bank clerk, failed screenwriter, unlikely survivor—had made this his morning ritual after days of deliberation. The jogging. The money belt. The Walkman. The music. Chicago's "I'm a Man" blasted into his ears like a stubborn anthem— nobody else to hear it, of course. But Henry needed it. The beat. The arrogance. The lie that said the world still danced to it.

He passed Times Square without looking up. What once announced a thousand advertisements now screamed splattered blood and conquered rot. Billboards half-lit. Giant LED smiles frozen in digital rigor mortis.

And still, he jogged.

He didn't know what day it was. Or maybe he did, once. But days had blurred, as had hours. The only clock that mattered now was the one in the sky.

Sun up meant safety.

Sun down meant survival.

His building had once been one of those "luxury living" places with a doorman and potted palms under the fascia. Now the doorman was a pile of mangled flesh with no palms, no fingers, arms and legs raked clean of flesh, a twisted heap of bones and shredded tissue, behind the lobby's front desk, in front of the lobby's front desk, and on top of the blood-crusted marble, where he lost a piece of his mind.

The ever-friendly thumbs-up greeted Henry at the steel door marked STAIRS. Just the thumb, of course—jammed upright in one of the displaced pots where a tropical plant used to be. On a luggage cart. Couldn't have been intentional.

"And a good day to you, too, Charles," Henry muttered. He returned the gesture and didn't look twice. Nausea shimmied through his body to his brain. Slightly disoriented, cheeks puffed, he exhaled and let some of the tension bleed out.

I've got to do something about this.

Guests may never be arriving—any minute now.

But what if they do?

I'm worn out. Never clean enough. Bodies hauled out, shoved into a moving van that can't move. That was a rough day. Not enough masks and gloves.

I guess I should be grateful most of them shaped up and shipped out on their own.

Still—exhausting, even to think about.

Henry chose the stairwell climb every time since waking up in hell that day. Not that the elevators didn't work. They did. Just no power now, not since Henry cut it in the Elevator Equipment Room. Just in case. One of them might have key access to the penthouse.

He took a deep breath and exhaled quickly, trying to ignore the foul taste of lingering death-smells, and started up the stairwell. He picked up his shirt, which was draped over the rail of the second-floor landing, and hung it around his shoulders like a towel. He was going to make this climb as easy on himself as possible. No rush. Pause on landings and breathe slow and easy. *Open each door, check each floor* —his mantra—as he ascended, fingers fondling the master key fob in his belt pocket as if to reassure himself it was still there.

By the tenth floor, Henry was already panting.

Not just winded—fighting-for-his-life panting. Sweat slid down his back in crooked trails.

He slapped the wall like it owed him something.

"Schwarzenegger!" he called, breathless.

The name rebounded off the concrete walls, a challenge to no one.

At floor fifteen, he wheezed, "Sylvester!" By twenty, with heavy exhalation: "Lundgren!" Twenty-five, pitch bouncing to the plate: "Nor-or-or-orris..." Thirty, gasping: "Ce... na..." Thirty-five: "Dolph!"—barking like a Basset Hound.

By the time he reached the fortieth floor, he was dragging himself up the final steps, a man climbing out of his own grave. Once inside the penthouse apartment, Henry staggered, head tilted back as if trying to keep his bouncing brain balanced, sweating like a blind, deserted sheikh in search of his camel, and groped his way to the bedroom, finally collapsing onto the mattress in a pile of limbs and regret.

Face pressed into the blanket, he whispered:

"Stallone."

The word hung in the cool air, settling like dust.

Stallone.

Alone.

39

I'm the only one here who can tell me what happened. Wonderful.

Congratulations, Detective Gorestriker. You're not only the best man for the job, but given the choice between you and you, you are the one to solve this.

No pressure.

"To My Star-Gazer—Happy Birthday"

I adjust the telescope—slightly off-kilter on its tripod, but still reliable.

Or is that me? Slightly off-kilter, maybe not so reliable?

It doesn't matter. There's nothing moving out there. Yet. No suspects, no clues, no getaway car idling outside a bank. Just still buildings, still streets, and still me.

And not much going on in here, unless confusion can be brought into focus and weighed like fractured light.

Even the wind has better places to be.

The city looks fake from up here. Someone left it on pause and wandered off with the remote. Broadway is empty. The park plays quietude. The Hudson just sort of lies there. I used to think the river had personality. Now it's just wet.

And I'm up here in my robe, a hermit Sherlock, staring into the silent world, and waiting for a confession that'll never come. Crazy to think I tried to find some purpose—some noble meaning—in all this. The last observer of the fall of man. A special report by Henry Gorestriker.

A.K.A. "The Ort".

A report by The Ort.

Now it just feels like I've been benched from a game no one plays anymore.

I've been running theories. That helps. Keeps me sharp.

Theory 1: Everyone died. Simple. Clean. Grim. Doesn't explain why I didn't.

Theory 2: I died, and this is hell. Also simple. Also grim. But I'm still clipping my toenails and worrying about cholesterol, so it lacks the fiery gravitas.

Theory 3: Mass abduction. Aliens. Some sort of cosmic recall.

Theory 4: I'm in a coma, and all of this—this telescope, this wine, this daily scavenger hunt—is just my brain trying to keep the lights on.

Theory 5:... pending.

(Foghorn Leghorn: "That boy's about as sharp as a bowlin' ball." Cue laughter. Merrie Melodies music. Fade to black.)

Sometimes I add new evidence. Like this morning, I found my old Trader Joe's loyalty card tucked in a crack in the pantry floorboards. I held it up like a relic. EXHIBIT A. I don't even shop there. Did I imagine it? Or was I just trying to make the world feel normal by inventing something unimportant?

My mind is trying to gaslight me, and frankly, it's doing a bang-up job.

Here's the real truth: I don't remember the end. Not really. I remember some of life before—lines at the bank, clinking glasses, a woman with red shoes. Life after? Waking up, climbing forty floors on legs that forgot how knees work, and listening to my own breath, filling me in on what I missed.

There's a hole in the middle. The shape of an answer.

So yeah, I'm the only one left to ask. But I'm also the only one lying to me.

That's going to make this tricky.

I pour another glass of wine. Stare into it like it's going to ripple with some ancient truth.

It doesn't.

Case file remains open. No leads, no witnesses, and the suspect won't stop making bad jokes to distract from the fact that his memory's Swiss cheese.

Am I being drugged?

Something in the air?

"Mister Gluesniffer."

Who said that?

I sit on the edge of the balcony with the wind barely tugging at the hem of my robe. No movement in the city. The world holds its breath.

I take another look through the telescope.

Nothing.

But not a normal nothing.

Because nothing is normal anymore. So, if nothing is what I find,

then something abnormal is at work that I'm just not seeing.

And that something is nothing I'd know when I do.

38

"Henry, did you hear me?"

Henry was at the telescope again. Through a thin patch of broken cloud, a strange mass had begun to drift into Earth's upper atmosphere.

"What—what—what?" Henry adjusted the focus wheel slowly, watching a black smear curl like oil on moon-reflected water, roiling with faint green discharges beneath its surface. He pushed his glasses higher on his nose, squinting until the image steadied—the lenses already smudged from the last hour's breath and fingerprints.

"It's still up there," he said, without looking away. "*Bigger.*"

From inside, a woman's voice replied, "What is?"

"This thing. This—*cloud*? It's not—right."

"If I wasn't running late, but I am, late." She cleared her throat. "Will you wait up for your surprise?"

Henry didn't answer. The expanding mass in the night sky scintillated like something unreal.

"It's probably something to do with that solar flare thing. Didn't you say there was one this week?" she offered.

Henry mumbled under his breath, "What *are* you?"

"Are you sure you don't want to come?"

Henry finally pulled away from the telescope. "It's not my place."

"Marcus asked about you."

Henry glanced back at the stunning figure just inside the opened glass frame, silhouetted in kitchen light. "Did he?"

"Okay. He didn't. But Dimitri said it was fine."

Henry scoffed faintly. "That means a lot."

"Okay. Yeah, um, he didn't, either… *Neither.*"

"Well, what is it? Either or neither?"

"Neither one did, say anything. Okay. But, Marcus did make a face when I mentioned your birthday."

"Ah," the sky observer concluded, "clearly I need to be there."

She said softly, "I don't want to leave you and not tell you, but I don't want to tell you and leave you."

"Are you telling me that you're leaving me?" He glanced back with a fake wince, unable to interpret her meaning.

"I'm not telling anyone but you. But not until we unwrap each other."

"Okay. This is where I'd give it a beat... just let it hang." He paused—quietly counting with small nods, lips puckered—then continued: "Careful. Once you unwrap me, I'm nonrefundable."

"Hmm. I see what you did there… I just might keep you after all."

Henry felt her move over him, as he leaned back into the telescope. She whispered close to his ear, softly, "You can still change your mind. It's not like I need a date. It's just... I want you there."

"I'll be here when you get back." He managed a half-smile. "I'll be better here. I'll take a shower and decorate myself, with petals—red peonies—awaiting your return, wrapped in silk."

"Just let it hang, huh?"

Henry grinned, a little sheepishly, letting the moment linger like a shared secret.

"A long beat?"

She hesitated. He felt her lipstick on his cheek, and a hand lightly patted his shoulder.

"Suit yourself."

He heard her go back inside. "You know the rules: don't touch the wine fridge, don't reprogram the thermostat, don't fall asleep without the CPAP—and maybe something besides *Planet of the Apes* tonight? Netflix? Hulu?"

Henry raised a hand in a lazy salute—forefinger tapping his temple. "Remember? Dumb TV. And no laptop, *kemosabe*—it's gone with the geeks."

"It's not too late to go get a new one, is it? You have the car keys."

"Listen—my old Best Buy buddy, Butch—he said I should have it back tomorrow. And, no charge. Now that's a pal. I'll pay him something, of course."

"A long beat?" she jabbed playfully.

"Aww. You're hitting below the belt now." He laughed, leaning back, letting his telescope eye rest. "Yes, it's too late. Store's closed. But I'm good. I can wait, I'm a great waiter."

"I'm sorry to rush in and out like this. They're downstairs."

"Babe—relax, enjoy being with your son. Be safe. Come back to me."

"Timing is terrible," she continued, "but you'll have my full attention when I get back. And I need yours, too. You get your peonies on, I'll slip into my cherry blossom."

"*Ooh la la*." He turned toward her voice. "Deal. I'm looking forward to celebrating. And thank you—for the gift. And the gift to come?"

He felt her smile, first easy, then forced. She stepped into the hallway, heels sharp on marble, her silhouette framed by the door as she gathered her bag, keys, and jacket.

"Love you."

The door shut quietly behind her.

Henry turned back to the telescope. The cloud had grown even wider—blacker—alive with green pulse.

He whispered, "What a mystery you are."

I sit there like a fool, watching the sky, ears tuned but body still, holding myself against the pull of the door. Listening. You know, the way you do when you're trying to memorize the sound of someone leaving—which, by the way, is the worst possible sound to try and memorize. It's not romantic, it's tragic. A door clicking shut? That's what people remember in horror movies right before the monster gets them.

She said it. "Love you." And not in a distracted way, either—like when you hang up the phone with Mom to take another call. No, this was the real deal. At least, I think it was. Unless she's just very good at saying it in a way that sounds real, which, frankly, would be cruel. But she married me.

Mysterious? Yes. Slightly too good to be true? Definitely. Intentionally cruel?

Am I thinking this way because I think I don't deserve the winning hand of love?

And yet my brain immediately jumps into algebra. How does love actually add up? How can I be a part of this formula I don't even comprehend? If she loves me, and I love her, then shouldn't that equate to... something? Providence? Harmony? But I feel like I'm short-changing the equation. Like she's bringing advanced calculus, and I'm showing up with an abacus.

Which makes me wonder: what happens when she realizes? When she looks at me one night and thinks, This guy? This is who I said "I love you" to? And then the door shuts—only this time it doesn't reopen. Would that be the end of the world?

Sometimes I think I'm too self-consciously self-aware for my own good, secure in my ability to make myself insecure.

Of course, then I hate myself for even thinking like this. Because self-loathing, I've been told, is very unattractive. And if I keep it up, I'll become that guy who spends all day apologizing for existing. "Sorry, sorry. Do you still love me? If I try to be someone I'm not, but in a better way, will you accept me for who I am?"

Wow, there's that Kindergarten Henry voice surfacing from fifty leagues under the sea.

So I snap out of it. I tell myself: she said it, she meant it, you heard it, now shut up. Be grateful. Enjoy the miracle. Because it is a miracle. And if I can't enjoy it, then what am I even doing up here on the fortieth floor, occupying the house that Jack built? Honestly, I'm not supposed to take any comfort in that. What kind of man would I be if I did?

But it is an amazing view up here. I mean, wow!

Still, I can't really take full credit for being where I am. My brain doesn't operate that way. The guilt part keeps tripping me, but she keeps helping me back up, whether she realizes it or not. She got me here. I'm like this passenger who was told to change flights because of mechanical issues. And, voilà.

Voilà. There's a good name for the wine. The wine talking in me again. Guess that's why it's called wine.

Voilà.

37

Before the shower, the mirror was lightly smeared and speckled with grime. After the shower, the steam hid most of that. He wiped a semi-circle into the fog with the heel of his hand and leaned in. Gaunt face. Wiry grayish-brown or brownish-gray hair. Eyes like ashtrays.

He cocked his head and stared.

"Well, we're still here," he said, voice barely audible.

His eyes dug in, searching for that faded everyman charm someone once told him he had—buried now under the layers of collapse staring back. He couldn't find it. He slipped his glasses on, nodded insightfully at the upgraded fog, then slipped them back off.

He tried a smile. The muscles didn't cooperate. The grin landed somewhere between exhausted and deranged.

"What am I doing to myself? Any ideas? Anyone?" He frowned. "Anyone? I won't complain anymore, promise. Period. Period, with an exclamation mark. Just anyone, speak up."

Punchline? "And you can't eat me. That's the deal."

Silence. Well, silence and the soft drip of condensation into the sink.

He chuckled. Not because anything was funny, but because that's what you do after a line like that—even if no one was there to hear it. The sound startled him, like a cough that took a detour through his digestive system and reemerged as a lonely parade of eructations.

He opened the mirrored medicine cabinet.

Inside: three dead AA batteries, a well-used toothbrush—its bristles bent like grass in the wind—and a single grape cough drop melded to its wrapper. He stared at them as if something were missing, as if there should have been more.

"Used to be crowded here," he muttered. "Well… used, it seems. Well-guarded secrets, you." He paused, frowning. "I don't remember you, but I feel you. Something in the air? Something in me?"

He took the cough drop and held it in his palm like a keepsake from a better world. Then he shut the door. The mirror winked back his face, tired and warped.

Outside the bedroom, the penthouse greeted him with silence and sunlight. Wall-sized windows bathed the room in brilliant gold, with the curtains pulled back—light so pure, Henry shivered briefly with the chill of delight.

No creatures enter this place.

Books were stacked like barricades. Pots of parsley and basil flanked the doors like green, leafy crucifixes. A wicker basket filled with apples and oranges sat on the counter, cheerful and absurd. Taken from a grocery store. Or stolen. Apples and oranges. The air smelled faintly of citrus and fear.

In the kitchen, Henry pulled a bottle of water from the dark fridge —a non-functional fridge since the first outage occurred—and closed the door with mechanical precision.

"Gotta keep it cool," he said to no one, and took a sip.

INT. / EXT. HENRY'S PENTHOUSE — LATE AFTERNOON

The light had shifted—amber now, slanted, soft.

Henry grimaced, still sore. He scratched his chest absently, closed a photo album, stood up from the table of assorted memorabilia, wandered barefoot across the rug, and slid open the glass door to the balcony. A nice breeze met him.

He stepped out with the bottle of water. The cap was off. He didn't remember opening it.

He sat on one metal stack chair next to the positioned telescope and swished and swallowed another swig of tepid purity from the upturned bottle, the plastic crinkling and popping from suction.

Before him, a view worth the price of admission. Or, at least, from a distance, a semblance of the previous world. His eyes could fly much further from this height, and he could close them then and chase the dream.

There's something about climbing forty floors that makes you think deeply about your life choices. Especially when the stairwell smells like sautéed doorman and mildew.

I used to take elevators. I used to wait in line for coffee and complain about bad Wi-Fi. Now I drink warm water, talk to herbs, and give motivational speeches to my reflection.

They say humans are adaptable. I guess that's true. I've adapted to the quiet. To the ghosts. To the sound of my own breathing being the loudest thing in the room.

Every morning, I jog like it matters. Like someone is watching. Like if I stop, the world will notice and say, "Ah. Finally. He gave up."

But I haven't. Not yet.

There's no reason I should still be alive, but I am.

And maybe that's the joke. The universe saved the least prepared man on earth. A bank clerk with a screenplay in a drawer and knees that click on the stairs.

Sometimes I wonder if anyone else is out there. If someone else is watching the sunset from a rooftop, sipping from a bottle, whispering old movie quotes to the wind.

But mostly... I wonder what the hell I'm still doing here.

And if it means anything that I haven't stopped.

36

Young Henry stood in the entrance hall—his stage—wearing dark-blue space pajamas stitched with white stars and yellow rockets. His bony knees poked out where the fabric was thinning, and in both hands he gripped a flashlight like a laser blaster. The NASA patch on his chest itched, but he refused to scratch—it broke character. The air smelled of popcorn, sweet and buttery from the old stove-top popper.

In the living room, the audience sat, waiting.

Shapes on the aligned fold-out chairs: Mom perched on the edge of hers, smiling into the steam of her mug of hot cocoa, her white house robe bundled tight as if she were attending a Broadway premiere; chubby brother Bart slouched beside her, elbows out, one hand buried in a bowl of popcorn, the other holding a can of Coke; present-but-absent sister Jane, the smallest, legs swinging, her chin resting on the seat back in front of her, as if she were floating in space. Even the dog, rusty brown and obedient, curled beside the piano stool, tail tucked over its nose, expectant. A family, gathered for the mission briefing.

And in the corner—towering, awkward—stood Zorton the Destroyer. Or rather, Dad, half-hidden in the hallway shadows. He wore a crumpled bed sheet tied as a cape over his Beau Brummell pajamas, reading glasses low on his nose, beige slippers drooping at the toes. Henry's script was clutched in his hand like it was state secrets. Slightly amused. Slightly embarrassed. But here. Playing along.

Henry stepped forward, flashlight shaking just enough to make the hallway look alive.

"I am the last astronaut," he declared, voice cracking with bravado. "Earth is gone."

Bart punctured the moment with a loud slurp.

"Why?" Henry cried, dramatic as any seven-year-old Richard Burton. Bart exploded with laughter, spitting fizz out of his nose. Mom quickly hushed him with a glare that promised dish duty for a week.

"I am Zorton," Dad intoned, lowering his voice to an ominous gnarl. "You are my prisoner."

"Where am I?" Henry gestured with Shakespearean flourish. "What have you done with my ship? Who—are—you?"

"Um..." Dad blinked. "I am Zorton. You are my prisoner." A turn of the page. "You were rescued from our... galactic sewage spill? You are the only survivor."

Henry batted, his focus slipping out of range. He forgot his line.

The room fell silent.

Then Bart belched.

The sound deepened. Warped. Rolled into a low, monstrous croak.

Henry's stomach clenched. He looked up.

The faces watching him were gone. Faceless figures were rising up.

The flashlight slipped slightly in his grip.

"I'm—" he stammered.

The faceless shapes were somehow laughing now.

The dog lifted its head. Its jaw cracked wide—rows of teeth. Too many teeth.

From the corner, Zorton moved.

One step. Two. Not Dad anymore.

Too tall. Neck elongating, face stretching, contorting, hands curling into claws.

Henry stumbled backward, throat catching in little squeaks. The beam trembled, skittering across the converging shapes. The air smelled like popcorn still, but burnt now—acrid, like frying wires.

"I'm—" he tried. Nothing came.

The laughter was grotesque—inhuman.

A wet, gargled cackling—rhythmic, endless—drumming in his ears.

The flashlight flickered once, twice—

—and the shapes leaned closer.

Henry bolts upright in bed, hyperventilating under the bright room light. He yanks off the CPAP mask, then tears away the black sleep mask. His chest heaves. The CPAP machine hisses a steady stream of air beside him, a soft exhale like something alive. Dawn is just a faint bruise at the edge of the tall windows, gray light hinting at the city beyond. Henry sits there, gulping breaths, sweat slick on his forehead, the echo of onerous laughter still crawling in his ears.

35

Returning from the kitchen, letting his glass of Chardonnay breathe, Henry stood for a moment in the stillness, contemplating the heavens. Eventually, he sat and looked back through the telescope.

Even now, the cloud was there—dark, impossible. It pulsed faintly, and for a moment, he thought he saw shapes moving just beneath its surface. Something vine-like. Or electric.

How fast could it be approaching?

He let the lens go. He was tired. Tired in that way that filled the spine and shoulders first.

At the entertainment center, Henry pulled open the cabinet to the left of the OLED screen and powered on a small DVD player. On top of it sat a lightly-scratched copy of Planet of the Apes. He slid the DVD into the tray and sent it in to play.

He lowered himself onto the couch with practiced care. The wine glass went on the coaster—always the coaster, he had the memo—on the end table to his right. He reclined, lifted his legs, and reached, without looking, for the Bravia remote. The TV lit up. Ritual complete.

The pillows behind him were arranged with ceremonial precision. So comfortable, he considered the possibility of dozing off—and remembered the CPAP machine on the bedroom nightstand.

He settled back, pressed play on the DVD remote, and sighed, "Fuhgeddaboudit," in his practiced New York accent.

As the ship crashed-landed while Charlton Heston's character slept, Henry felt his thoughts drifting.

Popcorn goes well with wine, doesn't it?

Henry got up and headed to the kitchen. There his eyes popped open.

The camera.

It had been left on the counter—the small, professional one she used for Marcus's recitals and debates. Never just her phone.

"She's gonna be pissed." Henry snatched the compact device and hurried out the door, down the hall, to the elevator.

The lobby wasn't far.

34

DING!

The elevator doors slid open with immaculate timing, revealing a single yellow bucket and a mop leaning dramatically inside like a forgotten stage prop. Next to it, a container of some industrial-strength cleaner and a stack of bath towels on a luggage cart. For a moment, it looked like the tools had summoned themselves from the depths of the basement janitorial storeroom.

Climbing up from the basement, Henry, adorned in confiscated janitorial gear—gray coveralls and worn-out boots with smooth rubber soles—emerged from the stairwell into the lobby, panting like a pensioner in a sauna. He winced as the sour air hit his lungs. The lobby looked worse today in daylight. Or maybe that was just optimism giving up the fight.

The floor was carnage. A wide brown-red smear led from the shattered revolving door to the elevator banks, like someone had tried to drag a marinated side of beef across marble.

Henry shuffled toward the elevator, perking up like a haywire kook, ready to pluck the mop out like Fred Astaire removing a cane from a coat check. That's when his left sole crunched down on something slick, and his rendition of a chorus-line kick sent him flailing back—like that sliced detective from *Psycho*, stumbling on heels down the stairs, half dancing, half dying, rubber soles squeaking in terror instead of tapping. He caught his balance against the marble counter of the front desk, gasped with stunned relief, and immediately bent to inspect the bottom of his boot.

"Cheez-Its," Henry muttered, peeling off the half-decimated snack bag that had fused to his sole with dried blood. He studied it like forensic evidence—a twinkle of madness in his eyes, briefly considering the taste of one—then flung it into the wastebasket behind the desk.

He eyed the bucket.

The bucket eyed him.

"I don't like your tone," he said, and splashed in a little of the Citrus Sunshine cleaner, which had congealed into something the consistency of syrup and the scent of urinal cake soufflé.

He fished his earphones from a pocket, plugged them in, and pressed play. INXS poured into his ears, crisp and urgent.

With a showman's beckon, he pulled the mop from the elevator. It sagged in his grip like it already knew this would end badly. He dipped the mop, gave the cleaning cocktail a gentle swirl, and launched into the mess like he was scrubbing a crime scene for karma points. The bucket spun on its wheels, squeaky and slow, but ready to dance.

The chaos, the smells, the sticky floor—all faded into the beat. He moved, a dancer now working in the groove, letting the rhythm guide him. Each mop swipe became a drumbeat; each twist of his torso became a guitar riff. He swished, spun, and leaned into the chaos, moving in time with the music, each motion part of an invisible performance. One slide-step away from an accident happening, but each unintentional skid and pivot seemed choreographed.

A chunk of something—maybe upholstery, maybe scalp—stuck to the mop head like it wanted to be reborn. He gagged but didn't stop.

An arm bone rolled out from under the front desk as he worked. Henry gave it a tired nod, nudged it aside with his foot, and kept scrubbing.

The mop hit a patch of old rot, Henry skidded in a stretch of blood, and slid sideways like a runner stealing a base, then went down in a graceless, wet-bodied sprawl. The bucket keeled over with all the loyalty of a deserter, soaking him with a lukewarm wave of grime-water and lemon shame.

He lay there. Squinted at the vaulted ceiling and grimy chandelier. "Need You Tonight" still thrummed in his ears.

How do I feel?

Henry's eyes welled, the blood-drenched mop useless in his hands now, the absurdity of the day pressing down on him, as he achingly cheered aloud:

"Yes!"

Yes… yes… yes… I'm… lonely.

Henry stepped outside. A light mist drifted down, clinging to his arms, his face. He wiped at himself with one of the stolen bath towels, streaking gray water across his skin.

Some men star in French films, smoking on balconies, tragic and romantic. Me? I'm dripping mop water on concrete, clutching a towel like a surrender flag.

He paused, his gaze softening, as a melody tugged at the corner of his mind. A commercial? A detergent ad? Something about towels staying "Lighter than—?" No, not quite. "Brighter than the moon?" No… "Whiter than yesterday's mashed potatoes?"

The tune twisted and fractured as he tried to pin it down, becoming nonsense words that sounded like promises he didn't understand. He hummed along anyway:

"Whiter, brighter, Lemon Sunshine fight-ah…!"

The tune slipped away before he could catch it.

That's when the sound broke through: high, electronic, stuttering across the distance. A car alarm, faint but undeniable, echoing from somewhere far off in the city.

Henry froze, towel pressed to his cheek, listening.

33

As Henry sidestepped a collapsed pyramid of black trash bags, rats scattering like bargain hunters at a Black Friday sale, the batteries died on the Walkman.

Henry slowed near Ninth Avenue, letting the stillness catch up to him. The air was clean enough today. Less of that sweet rot smell. He wiped sweat from his temple and looked up at the half-cracked windows of a sushi place, the red lanterns swinging gently inside.

From time to time, in moments of calm, Henry's mind latched onto textures, fluctuating currents, sensations of his surroundings—the realization of time and place—as if he'd been sleepwalking forever, waking to find his bed no longer existed, and that the warm, snugly comforts that had lulled him to sleep were only a dream. Left in a world he didn't know, where he didn't belong.

Periodically, he gathered the city's pretense of wanting to wake, to be familiar again. But it wouldn't—as if it knew what it would wake up to.

Often Henry felt the city speaking to him in a way only the dead hush can. *Of course, this is New York silence: pigeons cooing, scaffolding tarps snapping, rats auditioning in the wings.*

Sometimes, silence wasn't silence.

Sometimes, it was the pause before laughter. Sometimes, the pause before slaughter.

No worse nightmare than a city without sound.

A sudden scream—shrill, inhuman—pierced the repose. Somewhere high, it bounced off steel and glass like a bird-call from hell. Henry stiffened. Then another, further off. Then a third, impossibly distant, rising and falling in pitch. Hunger cries, flung between the buildings like bats in conversation.

Or maybe not.

Then, just as suddenly, silence again—

A silence that wasn't silence.

He turned the corner and saw the café.

Still powered, up and running and open for fictitious business.

Passing the shattered hostess stand, he walked into the once-busy patio. Plastic chairs with faux-metal curves. Umbrellas faded green. A birdbath cracked down the center, yet still caught the light.

His first stop—his cause for pause—a can of orange soda and a sealed bag of frozen donuts from the functional fridge inside. It buzzed like a tired beehive, but it worked. Barely. He didn't know how long it would keep running, but so far, every day he came by it still hummed.

Funny—I still treat it like a reward, like I actually ran somewhere worth getting to. Not exactly my old post-run Gatorade, but I guess it counts as a recovery drink—vitamin C, right? And electrolytes for the emotionally dehydrated. I can believe it if I pretend hard enough.

He pulled the tab's ring up and caught the spewing pop from the opening with his lapping tongue and sucking lips before it could reach his hand. Then he sat at the third table from the left—always that one —where the shadow of the awning made him feel like he was being shaded by something alive. He pulled off the beanie and earbuds and let his ears breathe.

He took another sip, then opened the freezer-safe bag and surveyed the variety of still-eatables. Chocolate glaze, maple ring, strawberry jelly, powdered cream. He bit into the chocolate-glazed one too soon, his teeth scraping off fragments.

"Come on, baby, don't be so cold. Let me take you home."

And then it came.

First, a wobble in the street corner to his left.

Then, a warble, like heat rising off pavement, but it wasn't heat—it was his constant imagination grappling with something that maybe never happened. Haunted by reality, not actually witnessed but easily surmised, it stalked his thoughts at every turn.

Nice of my brain to play this little trick. "We interrupt your gargantuan craving for a reminder that you are wanting to devour donuts at a crime scene so vast there's not enough yellow tape to cordon it off." Forensic markers would look like confetti after New Year's Eve.

Maybe it hadn't happened the way he imagined it. More likely, it was far worse—something he couldn't imagine at all.

The patio, the chairs, the cracked birdbath—all remained. But the scene changed.

People began to fill in. A man in a leather jacket arguing with his date. A woman in a sequined dress laughing too loudly. The hostess—Jules? No, Julie. She welcomed guests with a practiced smile and a subtle eye-roll that Henry had always admired.

And then—

Darkness descended.

Screams.

Something lunged from the blackness. Fangs. Claws. Eyes red as open wounds.

Henry didn't move.

The scene played on like a film, fast-forwarding through carnage. Julie's smile became a scream. The man in the jacket fell backward onto broken glass. A woman with a violin case tried to use it as a weapon—failed.

The images blurred and blinked out.

The patio was empty again. Quiet. Only the buzz of the fridge remained.

Henry took another sip. Still cold. Still carbonated.

"What came down?" the detective inquired. "What happened here?"

World slipped on a banana peel and cracked its skull.

Sitting at the opposite table, Sherlock Holmes puffed his pipe. No words. At the newsstand, Batman pretended not to hear the question, his nose in a comic book. Hercule Poirot kept touching his nose and waxed moustache with a pleasant-scented handkerchef. And Philip Marlowe sat with a glass of beer, staring down at the chessboard on the table, waiting for Holmes to make his move.

"Nice little lunch spot you picked, kid," Marlowe jabbed, with a slight snarl of disgust. "Blood on the cobblestones, chairs tipped like a brawl at closing time, and the smell of yesterday's fear still hanging in the air. Now that the world is over... makes a man wonder if the world ever really changed."

Holmes (sniffing the air, disdainful): "The evidence is clear. Blood spatter to the east wall, drag marks to the alley. Primitive creatures, but methodical. They hunt in packs."

Poirot (fussing with his mustache, regarding the carnage): "*Mais non, monsieur*! There is order even in chaos. The angles of the stains—they form a pattern, a signature, *oui*? Someone wishes to be noticed."

Batman (voice low and gravelly, from the shadows of the awning): "They don't think. They don't plan. Monsters don't reason. They only react. They strike. Fear is their only weapon. The only language they understand. And you, Henry, are fluent in it—whether you like it or not."

Henry's chest tightened.

"Why do I have to live like this? Why doesn't it all go away? I keep cleaning my contacts like they're the problem—like there's enough saline in New York to wash these visions away."

Batman closed the comic book. His cape whispered softly, trailing his turn.

"I've got bat-blinders you can have.

"But you've got to find yourself, Henry.

"No one else here.

"This is you.

"You've got to be your own hero.

"See it. Get it."

Henry put the donut back in the bag. The comic book, fallen open on the sidewalk, fluttered a tear in the breeze.

A sudden burst of laughter overtook him.

"We'll have fun later, sugar. Gonna get messy, too, frosting everywhere," Henry whispered to the smiling dunker.

Then, a shift of wind, carrying a whiff of rot. Another smile stolen away.

Across the street sat a delivery truck where it had died weeks ago in a panicky U-turn. Behind the windshield, a long-dried stain stretched across the glass like it had tried to crawl away.

Henry turned his head. Another remnant of horror he wished he hadn't glimpsed.

The soda was too sweet now.

He sighed, with that loss of appetite happening again. He zipped the bag shut and set it on the table.

"Stay here, ladies, enjoy the sun. Don't fall asleep. Wouldn't want you to burn. Stay soft. Stay sweet. Lickety Lips will be back."

He stood, stretched his legs, and decided to walk it off. Appetite would come back.

Like it always did.

Just have to find those mental blinders once more.

"How can outdoor cafés continue under these conditions? Where are the sanitation crews?" Henry feigned protest, raising his voice to the empty street. "I am writing to the governor!"

32

The rooftop air was still and hot above the dead city. Henry stood near the railing with the telescope already locked in place, angled across the East River.

He looked through the eyepiece and slowly adjusted the focus. The bridges came into view one by one, and with them, the reminders.

The Queensboro Bridge: cars jammed at the entrance, doors open, scattered belongings baked in the heat. Not abandoned long enough to rot, just long enough to feel forgotten. But what turned him away last time wasn't the blockade—it was the growth.

A black splotch along the sidewalk had split open. From it, a network of thin, glossy strands had emerged, winding upward along the nearest rail post. They pulsed faintly in places, like veins twitching under the surface.

He hadn't gone anywhere near one of these alien membranous hair-growth sightings to get a close-up analysis. Only through his telescope. Ideas came to mind, all of them bad, and, if not bad, then worse. *Mutated giant alien amoebas? Demon semen? Hell's hemorrhoids? Satan's scrotum? The defecation invasion?*

Somewhere in there is a joke I shouldn't miss.

Nothing visible in his neighborhood, though. At least not yet.

He shifted the lens.

The Manhattan Bridge had a silver sedan teetering at its midpoint, trunk open, as if someone had once tried to unload and run. Near it, what looked like another patch of that strange development, filling in the seams between the concrete panels. It hadn't been there the week before. Nothing noticeable, anyway.

He noted the spot. Crossed it off mentally.

Brooklyn Bridge. The far side showed a scorched barricade—burned cars, slumped obstructions, and no movement. But in the far corner of his field of view, more black tendrils curling from a ruptured van door. They clung to the chassis, thin but growing outward. *Searching?*

He stepped back from the scope.

"How long did anyone survive?"

They weren't everywhere. Not yet. But they were spreading. *Spreading? Something growing and spreading?* Or, could it be, he was seeing things through a window to another dimension?

Aha! Now that I can live with!

He turned west now. The Hudson River reflected harsh sunlight. No boats. Nothing floating. No smell of rot. Just stillness and that same thin haze that hung over the entire skyline. When he aimed the telescope toward New Jersey, he spotted a toppled billboard near the waterfront—its back face ripped open. Something slick and pale had pooled underneath it. He didn't look long.

Henry didn't know what the substance was. No one in Popular Science had explained it. It wasn't recognizable, at least not in any Star Trek episodes he remembered. It didn't belong to anything earthly.

But he knew one thing: it liked blood.

The first time he saw it was after a scavenging trip gone wrong. A dog—or what had once been one—had bled out behind a diner door. A week later, the floor under the stain had cracked. The tendrils grew outward in quiet loops, as if following a pattern only they understood.

He avoided those places now.

From forty floors up, he could see how some intersections remained untouched. Others were marked—crosswalks with strange discolorations, the faint glint of something wet even days after the rain had passed. And near the base of the Queensboro, the substance had begun to thread through a crushed bus's windshield, like roots searching for something.

Henry rubbed his eyes and looked away from the telescope.

It hadn't been long—eight, maybe nine weeks—but the city was already changing. Not collapsing, not rotting. Changing.

The bridges weren't just blocked. They were unwelcome.

"Not that way," Henry said. "Not anymore."

He picked up his notebook and scratched out a route.

31

DING!

The elevator doors slid open with a mechanical but cheerful hiss, a sound vaguely like canned laughter—tinny and artificial. Henry stepped inside, feeling at once like he wasn't entering an elevator but rather a rigged set-piece on the stage of an old sitcom. A light shower of music drizzled from the ceiling.

With black socks in slippers on, his hair askew, Henry stood facing the panel. In his hand, he held the compact digital camera—sleek, black, and professional-looking, with a sturdy wrist strap and a ghost-smear of touch on the screen.

He regarded the camera and shuddered. "Why do I always end up holding the important things after people leave?" A thought that didn't sound out right but helped him yawn with a chuckle.

He selected his destination and stepped back. The elevator began its non-stop descent. He leaned back against the mirrored wall and regarded his reflection—slouching, graying, pajama-clad, holding a very expensive piece of equipment like it was a granola bar. As Air played "La Femme D'Argent," Henry began to sway, winked at his reflection, and blew himself a kiss.

As the digital numbers decreased steadily on the screen, Henry cleared his throat, closed his eyes, and attempted in his best Casey Kasem voice: "And now, welcome back to American Top Forty. And coming in at number one, for its tenth week in a row, a song that tells it like it is. Here is—"

DING!

"Ruh-roh," his Scooby Doo impression cut in.

The laugh track was delayed this time. Late. Awkward. Like a laugh that came after a cruel joke.

The doors opened; so did Henry's eyes. He stepped out, gliding through the private alcove, past the adjacent elevator banks, and into the lobby's spread. No one here but the paid loiterers: red-haired Charlie and the Filipino King, gabbing at the front desk. The doorman noticed Henry seconds slower than he should have, and with a delayed nod and smile, acknowledged him and gave his customary thumbs-up gesture. Henry tossed up some friendly fingers in a twiddling howdy-do, then pondered the rest of the lobby and the traffic beyond the glass. No limo.

"I, uh, saw your wife head out a few minutes ago," Charles mentioned, as Henry shuffled quickly to the front entrance and stepped outside. He knew he wouldn't find her.

The night air was... strange. Not cold. Not warm. Faintly odorous with a different scent he couldn't recognize. Like bad breath from a sleeping god. Something in the distance rumbled. Not thunder. Lower. The sky was dark between the towers of lights.

Henry turned in a slow half-circle, then shrugged. "She's gone." He gave the camera a small, apologetic nod. "You missed your big day, little buddy."

And with that, he walked back inside and shuffled back to the elevator.

DING!

Laughter again. Louder this time?

Inside, the calm, soothing ambient music of Zero 7—breathing sultry vocals—was "In the Waiting Line," in the elevator, in Henry's reflection, in how to move while waiting.

Guess we'll be waiting in.

The great room was still and warm, lit by the blue glow of the television. Charlton Heston dangled in a net on-screen, patiently waiting—for Henry to release him, for these close-minded simians around him to hear his rage vocalized for once—for "Action!"

Henry set the camera on the kitchen counter next to an unwrapped package of popcorn.

Dr. Redenbacher, I presume.

He ripped off the plastic and shoved the bag into the over-the-stove microwave with the reverence of a priest lighting a candle. Pressed the timer. Glanced down, to the right. In front of the toaster, a plush purple-and-white monkey sat, slouched like it had been up all night. A flash drive on a handwritten note lay between its bowed legs. As the kernels commenced popping, Henry set the flash drive aside and picked up the note. It read: "Our Memories. Saved. Go light the corners of your mind."

Saved. Excellent. He grinned. "That's my girl."

Amused—not musing over her choice of placing the monkey there, his gift to her last Valentine's Day—Henry poured himself another glass of cougar juice.

When the timer beeped, he poured the popcorn into a red bowl big enough to bathe a toddler and plopped onto the couch, not a drop of wine spilt, glass centered on the coaster, this should certainly get him a raise and maybe even a promotion. Heston, still set in pose, appeared to be suffering more, staring right at Henry, who was stuffing a fistful of popcorn into his mouth before proceeding to the play button. Henry smiled and chewed like a man who had won something. He reached for the remote.

Then came the twitch.

The sneeze erupted with the grace of an industrial explosion. Half-chewed popcorn flew across the room like buckshot. Henry curdled, mortified. Another sneeze detonated, peppering the astronaut's face onscreen with slimy shrapnel. Two more sneezing-grenade volleys streaked through the air in rapid succession.

"That's it!" Henry roared, rising from the couch, nostrils flared and bubbly. "This is not going to happen! I'm stopping you—right now!"

In the bathroom, her Naväge machine glistened under the light. It looked smug. Predatory. Henry hesitated, hands on his hips, studying it the way gladiators must've studied lions.

"All right," he said, lowering his voice. "Look. I know we've had our differences. But we're on the same team here, right? You and me. We're… friends." He gave it an awkward pat, as if that might help. "Come on, compadre. We can do this together. You're on my side, I know you're on my side."

He filled the tank carefully with distilled water, talking the whole time like a man diffusing a bomb.

"I respect you. You're a powerful little contraption, aren't you? A real beast. But I'm not your enemy. Sinuses—that's our enemy. We're just two guys trying to clean house."

As if in response to the threat of nasal exorcism, a demonic sneeze —furious and full of spite—blasted through his passages and sprayed the room. The foreign-substance expulsion triggered a tremulous reaction with a shuddering neigh. Henry's grimace showed a soul in torment. The repeat offender attacked again, and this time Henry's scream was a roar.

After wiping and growling down his anger-knob from a boil-over to a controlled simmer, he steadied the machine. Shoulders squared, he steadied himself. "All right. Let's do this. Gentle. Nice and easy." New twitches, facial muscles flexing, Henry knew he had to hurry.

He jammed the nose pillows into place and pressed the button.

"Nice and easy. Ah, yes." He tried to stifle his laugh at the pinched nasal voice and snorted.

The NavÄge responded with an elated *whirrr*, which Henry decided sounded more like a battle cry. A saline torrent slammed through his nasal pipes with all the grace of a fire hose.

Too much salt! In my brain!

"You're not *NavÄge*!"

His eyes bulged. He gurgled and gagged. What came out next was not language—it was something between a blender full of spaghetti and a coffee percolator.

"*Ghhhaahhh-bbrrhhh-pphhhfftt!*"

Then it happened. The rogue popcorn kernel, perfectly timed, lodged in his throat. Henry coughed mid-rinse, a coughing fit with an added sneeze, choking and spraying water from his nose like a possessed lawn sprinkler. He staggered backward, slapping at the Naväge as it continued whirring happily, oblivious to his suffering.

This—ggguhhhkkk—this is how it ends! his brain screamed.

He ripped the machine from his face with the panic of a drowning Houdini who suddenly knows the trick has gone wrong. Gasping and dripping, he collapsed over the bathroom counter, shirt plastered to his chest. The Naväge gurgled one last time—mockingly, Henry was sure.

Ten minutes later, pajamas in the dryer, Henry sat on the couch in a fresh T-shirt and khaki shorts. Heston's face was wiped, and he finally got to express his appreciation.

Halfway through the bowl and starting on his third glass, Henry felt the nudge of sleep on his relaxing neck, and a slight shudder followed. His eyelids were weighing heavy. With effort, the clean-up chef rose and dutifully returned his gourmet snack to the kitchen.

After washing and wiping the butter off his fingers, he grabbed the monkey and carried it to the bedroom. A gentle toss landed it on her pillow, then a quick decision took the CPAP machine from his nightstand and carried it out to the couch. After he had the hose uncoiled to the mask on the cushion, he plugged the cord in the outlet behind the stand. Afterwards, he sighed, poured one last quarter-glass of wine and swallowed it down quickly, then put the bottle back in the wine fridge and the glass in the sink.

Henry wandered to the bathroom and flipped on the dim vanity light. He splashed cold water on his face and met his own bewilderment.

"Whew. All right. That was cold. And why did I want to do that?"

He opened the mirrored medicine cabinet and scanned the contents with narrowed eyes.

Toothpaste. Ointments. Contact lens case. A pack of cough drops. An old bottle of aspirin. And something else.

He reached for the aspirin, popped the cap, shook two tablets into his hand.

The pregnancy test was tucked in the corner of the shelf, mostly obscured behind the box of band-aids. Faintly pink. Faintly positive. He returned the bottle of aspirin, moved the box of band-aids aside, and picked up the plastic casing.

"Oh boy." He smiled. "Or, girl."

Something she wanted to tell me. Mmm. Or did she leave it here for me to find?

"Years from now, if I'm still here, if she hasn't thrown me off the balcony... she will *not* know our secret. I will still be guarding it. I will. I will be surprised like hell for her, and we will celebrate." He studied the test, replaced it carefully, reset the band-aids box, and let out a nervous huff, shoulders tight.

He closed the cabinet with a soft click, palmed the aspirins into his mouth, cupped a swallow of water from the faucet, and wiped his chin with his thumb. Then he paused, blinking a tear and letting a flicker of a smile cross his face. Another flicker followed—a frown, and an *oops* jumping onto it.

"She's going to know I've seen it. I've got to be surprised... And I am."

He studied his reflection, practiced his startled gaze.

"Oh boy... Or girl."

Returning to the great room, Henry shuffled to the couch, lowered himself with a slow exhale, and pulled the CPAP mask over his face like a diver descending into deep water.

"She's gonna be pissed," he mumbled, resuming play and flipping the switch on the machine. It hummed, and he let the tension roll off with each measured inhale. He watched the screen until he didn't.

And he didn't snore.

Outside, the stars began to go out.

30

The sun wasn't warm—it was white. Bleached the sky like old laundry and made the ruins of midtown glimmer like cracked glass. Henry walked with the studied casualness of someone who used to pretend to be busy on sidewalks. Old habit. He passed department stores with shattered mannequins, a wall of fliers announcing bands that never got to play, and one pizzeria overrun with alien vines and dead rats. He steered clear and began his alternate route.

He stopped beside a row of yellow cabs. They sat like wilted wasps, front wheels turned at odd angles, doors ajar, city grime thick on the windows.

He tried the door on the first one—locked. The second had been stripped of anything useful. The third—

Bingo.

The driver's door opened with a creak. The keys weren't in the ignition, but the glovebox yielded a handful of peppermints, a pocket Bible, and a MetroCard that now meant nothing. Still, he checked the floor, under the visor.

Then he noticed the back seat.

A lumpy black shape. Covered. Like someone had thrown a tarp or trench coat over a duffel bag and forgotten it.

Henry frowned. Glanced at the sky—morning still held. No clouds. He stepped around to the back window, already halfway down.

The fabric looked thick—pleather, maybe? His fingers pinched a corner of it. Pulled.

The tarp fell back.

Beneath it, a curled, waxy creature twitched. Its skin blistered instantly, eyes sealed shut, limbs coiling inward like a spider touched by flame. It made no sound—just a shuddering inhale of death.

Henry leapt back, missing the swing of the door, as the creature awkwardly, blindly spilled out of the cab onto the pavement, dragging the tarp with it.

Henry laughed in a way to keep back the scream. Not a laugh of shock or relief, but one of those lonely, ironic chuckles that echoed weird in the silence. He stepped away as the smoke puffed strange signals. The tarp, like a turtle's shell on extra-fried legs, crawled weakly with its inhabitant.

"Not too bright," Henry said. He carefully stepped on a corner to pull the tarp away. It slid off easily. "But bright enough for me."

Let the sun finish what evolution hasn't.

Henry tapped his Walkman's play button. Drumsticks cracked against cymbals—Danny Seraphine's manic solo filling his ears. He let out a breath. "Should've taken the subway," he muttered, turning from the cab.

But the wind had other plans.

The tarp lifted, flapped once, and settled again—dropping squarely across the frying body. The shape stirred. Twitched. Rose.

The creature staggered upright, swaddled in filthy fabric, a blind magician in a weathered costume. It turned toward Henry's retreating footsteps.

"You've got to be kidding me," Henry whispered.

It lurched.

He bolted.

Across the empty intersection they ran, zigzagging like dancers in a grotesque routine. Henry vaulted a fallen traffic sign, the music propelling him forward. Behind him, the creature stumbled and veered, smoke leaking from its shroud as it fought to keep up.

It smashed into a mailbox, reeled sideways, but kept on. Henry swerved around a toppled hot dog cart. "No relish, thanks," he puffed. Cymbals hissed in his ears, mirroring the creature's scorched skin.

Both slowed at once—Henry stumbling over a garbage bag, the creature pawing it blindly. For a heartbeat, the absurdity suspended them. Then Henry darted left; the creature followed, shrieking through cloth.

Finally, Henry ducked into a doorway, chest heaving. The thing thundered past, trailing melted tarp like a burned banner.

The drum solo sputtered out. Silence returned.

Bent forward, hands on his knees, sweat dripping, Henry let out one sharp, breathless laugh.

A gust caught the tarp, peeled it free. The creature collapsed into ash mid-intersection, scattering like burned laundry in the bleaching sun.

Henry didn't move for a long time—not until the sweat had cooled on his scalp.

29

Unbelievable. How many pigeons in this city are still alive? So few pigeons, by pre-apocalyptic standards, of course. This city probably holds the record of most pigeon droppings of any city in the world. Certainly an exaggeration, right? Maybe? But now, the scarcity of pigeons, it is freaky. To go from millions to just a few. Literally, a few. And how did they survive?

Then again, I can't explain me being here either. The ultimate pigeon? I guess, because I'm completely duped. But I am trying.

"Keeping it cooooo—cooooo."

At street level, it's easy to find the hints of remains—pigeon feathers clumped with alien grease and blood, dark stains on the sidewalks like someone tried to mop up an oil spill with a bird. The fallen crumbs. Maybe the ones I see fluttering overhead are out-of-towners. Wrong time to come visit. I don't know what I'm seeing, but they're here and there, and once in a while I'll see one just drop from the sky, and D.O.A., like something else besides the air up there got to it.

The sound from below—it's not trains, not rats. Too heavy, too synchronized. Something far, far larger is shuffling through the tunnels. Maybe the whole population is crawling over itself down there. I don't intend to ever find out.

I don't know what to call them yet... Zompire, maybe. Zombie? Vampire? Both? Zombie, because, I mean, they cannot possibly still be alive in that condition. Surely their souls have skedaddled. And they seem to have trouble walking, stepping over things. Vampire, because they only come out at night. (Of course, it is New York, the city that never sleeps.) Zompire. Naming it makes it feel smaller—yeah, right. I whisper the word to myself, and it feels strange on my tongue, like what has happened to us? I've been avoiding this without realizing it, but what the hell am I going to do? What if they—evolve, even more?

The rats, though—they've thrived. They seem to appease these midnight snackers.

As long as the zompires won't bother so much with me, I can survive. Let the rats thrive, keep the zompires supplied, and I'll stay up high and survive. That's my working theory, anyway. I haven't really put music to it yet.

Zompires. They hate the light. But the way the tunnels shift, the faint vibrations through the pavement, the darkness that seems to slither between buildings—they're not just hiding. They're learning. Watching. Gathering.

And cockroaches—can't forget them. They might be the real champions of this whole apocalypse. Scuttle across the kitchen tile like they own the place, and big ones, too. I swear I saw one dragging a potato chip bag twice its size up a stairwell. I should've applauded. If anyone deserves applause these days, it's the cockroach. "Tenacity award, ladies and gentlemen—accepting on behalf of the insect kingdom... Chip Bag Coley."

The water still runs. Don't ask me how. It seems normal enough, though the taste is different—like licking a penny. Or maybe that's just me. With all the doctors gone, who do you ask about astringent tap water? Better question: with all the doctors gone, who do you ask about anything? Dr. Google's not taking patients anymore.

I used to picture the important ones being hidden away somewhere. The surgeons, the scientists, the clever types, the people who could actually fix this mess. Maybe they've all flown to a secret bunker in the mountains. But no. If they were still around, I'd know. This city would look different. Safer. Brighter. Instead, I've got pooped pigeons, rats on the run, cockroach landlords, and, of course, the zompires. Zompires. And me, always there in the mirror, looking at myself and trying to figure out what I'm going to do about... any of this.

Some buildings still have power. I'll stand on my rooftop and stare at them sometimes, wondering if anyone's inside. Or if it's just electricity running on a timer, powering empty rooms. That's almost worse. I try to map them accurately for my daytime scavenging. So far, the ones that have lights on have been safe to go into. Not that I would ever go in unarmed.

But here's the thing: the darkness is spreading. Lights are being knocked out. Even from my rooftop, I can feel the city dimming, as if something down there is testing its reach. I've noticed distant buildings that once were lit, that I had ventured into once, now have lost their lights. The zompires—whatever they are—could they be doing this? Which makes no sense. Their hatred of light is so extreme, so instinctive, I thought that was the one rule that never broke. Light burns them. Always.

Now I'm not so sure.

I try to keep myself occupied. Moving cars around, clearing some paths, figuring out which vehicles might come in handy later. The ultimate game of Autosokoban. Push, pull, shift, shuffle. A puzzle with no ending. I didn't have much energy before I started this project, but now it's sort of my nine-to-five. Rules matter. One is: keep working.

Something else I've thought of doing while moving vehicles around: scarecrows on the corners. Mannequins, in uniforms. I know, I know, crazy, and I'm not really there yet. Something about trying it— or not trying it—makes me want to cry.

Another rule: keep your eyes on the sky.

There's this one building entrance I pass sometimes, the kind with an old gargoyle face carved in stone above the doorframe. Used to creep me out. Who would want to walk in with that thing staring down at you? But now I stop and talk to it occasionally. I call it Chadwick. Chadwick's a good listener. Doesn't interrupt. Gives me the same look every time—judgmental, but hey, that's New York for you. (Told me to call him Doctor Grimby.) My therapist takes granite, but the sessions are free. Somehow, this ridiculous therapy session helps me feel braver, and I need that. (Still creeps me out, got to be honest. But then, really, what wouldn't at this level of the game?)

Sometimes I even say hello to fire hydrants. Not out loud, but in my head. Just a nod, like we're neighbors. Keeps the city from swallowing me whole.

Because without rules, without games, without Chadwick—or Chip Bag Coley—it's just the silence. And silence is when the nightmares seem loudest.

28

Henry jogged with his usual, obstinate rhythm. Not quite a sprint, not quite a shuffle. Just enough to feel alive. Just enough to remind his joints they still had something to prove. He did it because his bones told him not to, and because it made his heart pound in a way that reminded him he was still in there somewhere.

He stopped near Forty-fifth and crouched near an abandoned flower stand to strangle the annoying flap of untied shoelaces. The double knot had come undone again. *Dammit.* The laces were soaked and frayed, full of city grit.

Time for a new pair.

Calming his anger, he finished retying the double knot, then stood and readjusted his black-and-white NY cap and refitted the earbuds. And that's when he heard it.

CRACK!

A brick slammed into the side of a long-dead Uber, caving in its passenger-door with a hollow clunk.

Henry's head snapped up. "…Hello?" He turned off the Walkman.

Silence.

Another—THUNK-A-BOOM!

Like a giant gong-banger slamming his hammer against bronze, this larger concrete brick plowed into and even cracked the sidewalk with a collision of resonating reverb. Pieces of it skittered past Henry's dodging feet, and the sound wave had weight, brushing him.

Henry ran with the over-the-top performance of a horrible Fosse audition. Raw choreography: bent-in limbs, jerky hip rolls, curved shoulders, body swerving, legs cutting, crossing, kicking, and facial gestures: shock and fear, interpreting his own dance of panic with some sort of befuddled rhythm. For it all, a gain of five yards.

Behind him: a faraway grunt, the whistling of air, then— WHACK!—a smaller brick clipped the side of Henry's head. Not a full impact. Just enough. His cap took flight, and Henry staggered. His ankle twisted on a curb and he collapsed forward, arms pinwheeling. Balance off but continuing, his teary eyes viewed the passing pattern of concrete below as if looking through the window-seat of a descending seven-forty-seven for the landing strip. Instead, the plane hit a mountain. Henry caught the side of the bus bench with his right shoulder and climbed over it, like a running back pushing past the tackle and fumbling. Taken down. No score.

The bus bench had been knocked loose by an old yellow taxi that had collided with it on hell-day—its front hood crumpled like a frown, windshield long gone. The bench now sat askew, halfway into the street. Henry fell face-first across it, sprawled awkwardly, and his left arm dropped and dangled toward the curb while the rest of him was crumpled and twisted against plastic-covered metal.

Just before it closed, Henry's right eye caught an impression of the horrendous face his mouth seemed to be kissing. The bench ad stared back through smeared plexiglass: a cartoon man in a dentist's chair, mouth stretched wide in agonized laughter, eyes full of tears. The rest of the sign, flowing from this image, read: "CRACK-UP COMEDY CLUB Where Cackling Fills The Air Like Spackling In The Crack – And The Filling Is Killing!"

Henry's mouth opened and a sound escaped. Half a rag-wrenched laugh. Half a gasp. Then—darkness.

<h1 style="text-align:center">27</h1>

He woke with a jolt, the DVD still spinning in place, the dissonant loop of primitive ape sounds replaced by a blaring pulse. At first, he thought it was part of the movie. Maybe the DVD had glitched. But the sound rose sharp and shrill, not cinematic—real. The fire alarm was going off. Loud. Everywhere. A bone-rattling strobe of noise that drilled straight into the center of his skull.

He ripped off the CPAP mask and stood. His socked feet found the slippers, his body moved, but the alarm whacking his ears was a jackhammer on his head he couldn't shake off, and his cranium felt crushed by a hangover on steroids.

Instinctively, he stumbled toward the balcony door, shoved it open, and stepped outside. Closing it behind him muffled the shrill noise just enough to ease his headache. He took another step and slipped—his heel skidding across what felt like a patch of ice. He looked down.

Black ink, or something like it, scattered across the porcelain pavers—darting between the planters that ringed the balcony, where jasmine tangled with basil and thyme, and petunias brushed against lavender, still somehow alive, glinting faintly under the city's dim glow. The dark liquid skirted the pots, veering away as if avoiding them, then spilled under the rails and over the edge. A cool breeze moved through the greenery, carrying a faint, clean scent—sweet and herbal. It cut through Henry's haze, the stale wine and panic still clinging to his tongue.

Henry's eyes followed the black streaks downward.

"What the hell—?"

Below, a vast, sinking mass of darkness sprawled between the buildings—a strange, descending veil drifting lower through the city canyons. Its surface rippled faintly, as if disturbed by distant motion. Then it began to dissipate—slowly unraveling into the muted illumination of rooftops and upper windows, reappearing one by one. The lower depths remained buried in shadow, a black ocean swallowing its own tide.

From far below came faint, indistinct screams—drawn-out, then cut short—swallowed by the wind and the distant hum of the city that never really slept. Henry's breath caught.

This was no ordinary alarm.

Leaving the penthouse, crossing the private vestibule, Henry discovered the elevator was disabled. Of course it was. He took the stairs.

Forty floors.

Residents from the lower levels were ahead of him and moving in behind him as he descended.

Someone yelled, "It's not a drill!"

Ahead of Henry, a young blond boy, being carried by his father, glanced at him, then whispered to his mother, "Are we going to die?"

Others, stumbling, grumbling, mumbling: "Should we smell smoke?" "Who said it's not a drill?" "Anyone know what happened?" "Wasn't there a false alarm last month?" "Remember? O.J. Simpson—he was in *The Towering Inferno*?"

By the time he reached the lobby, Henry was clearer-headed and shorter of breath and feeling a certain edginess growing inside. He leaned against the pillar near the desk, observing while letting his lungs power up. The crowd dispersed from the lobby into the surrounding atrium. He overheard a few residents near the front desk:

"Yeah, I was told some poor bastard on the fifth floor pulled the alarm."

"He came down, freaking out, took off outside like he'd lost his mind."

"Second floor. He was on his balcony, and started freaking out."

Stepping toward the front desk. Henry saw Elvis, the Filipino desk clerk, and Charles, the freckled Celtic doorman, were huddled around the fire panel just inside the open door of the back office.

Charles thumbed his walkie-talkie. "Just some crazy a-hole on two. Flipped out, like dude's on some bad acid trip. Said something was after him."

A crackle of static, then a voice in a broken British-Nigerian accent:

"Wetin dey make all these people dey craze like this sef?"

Charles laughed. "Good question, bro."

The radio replied: "Na dat one make I carry my shoko. I no get time for all dis wahala."

Charles made a face. "It's cool, Imani."

The crackling deep voice decided: "Ah'm orready hee-yah. Ah go check am. Dis boolah sheet."

Charles cut in: "Glad to know you're down there, man. We got it up here. Fire department's in touch. Don't sweat this. You got enough on your plate."

Elvis came back out, ignoring Henry, and picked up the receiver to the PBX switchboard. "Zone three. Smoke detector 4102. No smoke, no flame, no heat rise. Copy that."

Elvis blinked at Henry with the kind of look you reserve for a turd that talks. "Okay to silence, not reset. Fire Chief en route."

He glanced at the doorman. "Kill the audible."

Charles took his orders. He keyed in a code and pressed a softly lit button. The shrieking stopped. The red strobes kept flashing. A unified sigh of relief rippled through the crowded room.

Elvis put the landline on hold, the receiver still on his ear. "Yes?"

Henry glanced at the open express elevator. "Can I, uh—? It's forty floors." He tried to say *please* with his face, the word stalling somewhere behind his teeth. "Can we activate the express?"

Elvis released the hold and continued on the landline: "Yes. Got it. Very good, sir. Thank you."

He hung up the phone and considered Henry reproachfully. "You too good for stairs now, Mr. Gluesniffer? Penthouse living. More than a free magazine subscription."

Henry felt muscles tighten as he forced a smile. "Gorestriker. Forgot my phone. Caught off-guard, just in a hurry. Forgot. Trying to do the right thing. But I need my phone, kind of urgent. Be a pal." *My pal, not Dominic's.*

Elvis shook his head. "You may not know this, but I'm not supposed to activate that thing until the Chief gives the all-clear."

"You just silenced the alarm."

"That's not the same thing. Silence is a courtesy. Reset is a liability. Elevator's locked for a reason. No elevator use until it's cleared by the responding unit." Elvis glanced toward the lobby doors and the loitering crowd. "They're five minutes out."

"Look—there's no fire. You just said that. I just need five minutes. I'll be back down before they arrive. I mean, come on. No smoke, no fire. You just said so. I'll come right back down. No one has to know."

Henry couldn't explain his sudden panic attack, not to this guy. Not even to himself.

"Protocol."

"Tell you what, Elvis—if I die in there, you get bragging rights. That's something, right?"

"More paperwork."

Henry patted his back pocket and felt something soft. He reached in and pulled out a wadded-up twenty-dollar bill. He held it up like a used tissue.

"For your next pack of menthols."

Elvis looked at the bill. Then at the private elevator in the separate alcove.

Charles raised a ruddy eyebrow. "Don't do it, E."

Elvis took the twenty. "We were never friends," he muttered.

"Still aren't," Henry replied, stepping toward the lift. The elevator stood open, welcoming Henry—like a special friend invited to a bad idea.

"E." Charles shook his head, stepping up to receive the ring of keys Elvis pulled from his jacket pocket and held up. *"Eeeeeeee."*

"Elevator Equipment Room. Phase 1 recall switch. Insert the red key, turn to the 'Bypass' position," Elvis instructed the doorman.

"Understood," Henry added, clenching a tight grin.

Charles slipped away to the Elevator Equipment Room.

"I'll be fine," Henry promised. Then, with his best snarling Presley grin, he added in a wavering baritone lilt: "Return to sender!"

Elvis folded the twenty, slid it into his shirt pocket, and replied, more to himself: "Only fools rush in, Mr. Gluesniffer."

Henry winked at the returning doorman passing by.

"Thank ya, thank ya ver' much." He gave a thumbs-up to Charles, who let out a deflating sigh that suddenly caught a shifting wind in the sail and lifted a half-smile. He returned the gesture.

Henry waited. The doors didn't close.

Henry stepped over to the panel and tapped the scanner with his card. No response. He pressed the CLOSE button. The doors didn't move. The button flashed red and went dark again. Nothing.

He waited. Then jabbed it again. And again.

Charles snorted. Elvis broke first, a quick and high nasally bark of laughter escaping before he could stop it.

Henry looked out at them, jaw tight.

"Five-star operation you're running here."

Outside, the flashing red lights of the FDNY arrived. Seconds later, four uniformed firefighters, including the Chief, entered the lobby.

Elvis wiped his eyes. "Five minutes, Mr. Gluesniffer? Guess that's how long it takes to realize you've been had."

Henry stood there another beat, his milk of human kindness turning quickly sour. Finally, he stepped out.

It didn't take long. Henry stayed next to the express elevator door while the rest of the residents lingered in the atrium and lobby or hung around the other elevator banks, caught up in conversations, taking advantage of complimentary drinks being handed out at the treat shop.

After the reset, and the elevators were restored to operation, as the Chief concluded brief banter with Elvis, Charles came over to Henry, apologetic. "I felt bad about that."

"Thanks. A lot." He meant it, though his tone didn't know how.

"Try it now."

Henry stepped back into the private elevator, waved and tapped the card against the scanner. There was no response.

"I don't understand."

Charles frowned. "I don't, either. Must have to do with the reset."

Not understanding, Henry masked his panic with impatience. "Come on, friend?"

Charles quickly ushered Henry to the upper-level elevator bank— no one noticing—and reached over to the panel of the first car Henry stepped into, where ongoing familiar music was like a peace offering. He tapped his master fob on the scanner, jabbed the CLOSE button for Henry, then stepped back out.

"You deserve a first-class non-stop flight to the top. You paid for it. This will get you almost there, anyway."

Henry smiled at Charles—friendship on probation—found the panel of 28 to 39, and poked 39. The button lit up. The music already beginning to massage hips and shoulders, Henry lit up, but kept a shade on it.

It only cost him twenty.

Charles gave Henry the thumbs-up, as the doors converged. That big, rosy thumb.

Beyond the thumb, near the Fontaine's entrance, a man's silhouette caught Henry's eye, head tilted toward the glass ceiling. His gasp cut over the crowd. "What is *that?*"

An unseen woman's voice called, "Hold the elevator!"

And the doors closed.

Yeah. Sure. Twenty dollars, ma'am.

"Winelight" was playing overhead. Grover Washington, Jr. Yep. Owned it, he did, once.

The elevator began to rise.

The machine hummed as Henry stared at the digital display floor-counting.

... 3... 4... 5... 6... 7...

A faint scream drifted up the shaft from the lobby far below—then another, and another—long, ragged, fading as the car carried him higher, dissolving into rhythm. He frowned, listening hard, but the sweet saxophone buttered his ears, smooth and protective: *"Shh. Nothing. Enjoy the music."*

10 seconds.

The hum steadied, the echoes gone. He let the music wash over him, tried to relax his shoulders.

15 seconds.

The ride smoothed out, Grover's horn oozing calm.

22 seconds.

The power failed. The lights snapped off. The car jolted to a stop too hard, and Henry's buttocks clenched as his body sagged.

"Oh … *noooooo.* Come on, Elvis. *Caught in a trap.*"

He stood very still in the darkness, his eyelids straining to hold the dissipating smoke-print of his vanished reflection, one hand braced against the panel, breathing loud enough to hear his own echo bounce

back at him. The panic was returning.

7 seconds.

26

Thump.

Shhh ...

Thump. A soft impact.

"Arrruuuhhh ..."

Thump.

Shhh ...

"... uuuhhrrr ..."

A scraping noise. Henry half awoke. He opened his eyes, slowly. Slats of cold bench seat pressed against his face. Dirt under his nose. He squinnied. Through the narrow slats of the bench, light was diminishing. Something moved under the yellow cab's frame, just beyond his dangling left hand. Something emerging, so slowly. A face. Twisted. Pale. Slack. A creature, dragging itself forward by its elbows. It had no legs—half its body gone or ruined—but inched along on bony forearms, toward the curb, toward Henry's baited fingertips. Its pitiful slowness seemed to sedate his panic, but did nothing for his throbbing dizziness.

Henry flinched, pulled back his left hand, and rubbed his eyes to clear the sting.

It must've been a long clear, because, when his eyes opened again, he saw—just beyond the bars—

BOOMP!

The creature, its brutalized head twitching. One eye milky, jaw broken sideways. It rammed the underside again with the mangled, veiny clay of its leaking scalp, and Henry pulled his face up in time to avoid a mouthful of undead hairy flesh. "Shhhheee-itt!" This reaction seemed to excite the creature, whose head started banging harder, trying to find him. It hissed.

More awake now, Henry scrambled to sit, but the dizziness pinned him briefly. The creature's flayed, broken right arm swiped at Henry's feet. Its gnarled fingers grabbed hold of the sagging loop of cord to the Walkman. The earphones peeled away from Henry's yanked head and unplugged from the device.

Henry pulled himself upright and finally looked around.

Shadows were moving. Figures—blurry and slow—emerged from alleys and basements. Across the street, something long-limbed and thin climbed out of a busted subway entrance.

Dusk had passed. It was night.

Henry stood and limped into motion, sidestepping the legless thing swiping still. He turned and ran. The wrong way first, then corrected — veering down a shallow hill. The only visible light on the block came from a low building ahead—cracked stucco, a faded awning—CRACK UP COMEDY CLUB, buzzing in surging neon. The building's entrance was bathed in hard-white light—industrial flood-lamps on rusted brackets. The sidewalk in front glowed like a stage. Behind Henry, the creatures gained speed. He could hear their scraping feet, their wet breathing. He reached the pool of light, crossed into it—and the sounds stopped. He turned.

They were there. Just at the edges. Dozens, maybe more. Not entering. Just watching. A few were pacing the border where shadow met light. Some hissed softly. He could see grotesque faces hovering in the dark, drifting, alien-like with projected foreheads, jaws clicking, retracted lips where snake-fangs glistened, and glaring eyes softly boiling behind viscid layers of membranous lids.

Henry turned and stumbled through the comedy club's front door, slammed it behind him, and twisted the manual bolt lock. He stood under dim lights, doubled over, panting. Legs, overworked already, trembling. Then he noticed the soft hum of a generator somewhere deep in the building, and black steps that led down to the subtle spill of stage lights through a curtain. He took a cautious step forward.

Henry pushed through the curtains and stepped into sub-level darkness, darkness that swallowed details and smothered corners. The air was still, faintly sour with mildew and old spilled beer, but beneath that hung a sharper note—dust baking under heat lamps.

His eyes adjusting slowly, Henry started forward down the center aisle, cautious at first, then more quickly, drawn. His footsteps echoed on the sticky floor, clapped back at him like weak applause. He passed between the empty tables, their tabletops filmed in a coat of dust except for odd streaks where his fingertips trailed.

Booths hunched in rows like crouching silhouettes. The bar stretched out to his left, bottles dulled to shapeless glints, mirror behind it reduced to a smudge. Chairs sat overturned or broken, little islands in the gloom. The room felt abandoned but not dead—like it had been waiting, holding its breath.

Then his calibrated gaze returned to the stage.

Light. A square of brilliance so clean it seemed impossible after all the shadows. Spotlights cast it in sterile white, every inch an island of clarity in a black sea. The back curtains were open just enough, their black folds painted silver at the edges.

With each step, the light grew harder, sharper. By the time he reached the lip of the stage, his eyes pulsed with tears. The shadows behind him seemed to recede, and for a moment he felt like the entire city outside had vanished, replaced by this stage, these spotlights, this pull.

He set his hand on the edge of the stage, the wood surprisingly warm, and muttered to himself—half awe, half disbelief:

"So this is it."

A wave of dizziness washed over him, as he found the stairs, then climbed up onstage. Spotlights hummed above, warm and indifferent.

He weakly stood in them, vision flitting. Lit. Alive.

Blood traced a sticky line down his neck, now dried at the edge of his collar. He turned toward the empty room and said, to no one in particular, something witty that came out as: "W-well, looks like I ..." The words faltered.

I'm the punchline tonight.

Henry swayed. His eyes rolled back slightly. Mouth open, breath hitching. Then, almost peacefully, he slumped sideways onto the stage, half-conscious, the spotlight holding him in a quiet halo. Outside, the creatures paced. Scraped at walls. Watched. Inside, Henry slept under the lights. And lived.

He stepped out into the morning like a man surfacing from a shipwreck.

The front door of *The Crack-Up Comedy Club* swung gently behind him, creaking once before settling shut. He squinted against the sunlight—unfiltered, unapologetic. The city lay around him, a crime scene now tampered with by clean sunlight.

Silence.

No hiss of creatures. No scuttling. No brick-shattering violence.

Just air. Wind. Sun.

He stood still on the sidewalk, breathing through his mouth, as if afraid the scent of last night might still be hanging in the air. The sweat had dried to salt on his shirt. His ankle protested every shift in weight.

Above the street, several floors up, a mast climber hung motionless on the building's facade—the same side as the crushed bus bench. Its modular platform swayed slightly in the wind, ropes and cables whispering against glass. Shading his eyes, Henry tightened his scrutiny. Could a brick have been thrown from there? Maybe. The angle worked. The distance didn't. He couldn't picture a zompire clambering that high; they could barely handle stairs. Probably just debris shaken loose. Or maybe divine intervention with poor aim. He let the thought go, as the strain on his eyes and his brain might start whistling at any moment from the pressure.

Across the street, just beyond a dried trail of blood and shadow, something glinted beneath the bus bench—a thin white cord trailing from under it like a trapped vein.

He limped across, bent down carefully, and tugged the wire free. The right earbud dangled loose, crusted with grime; the left was torn clean off. He ran the cord through his fingers, as though touching a relic, a lifeline from another era, then wound it carefully around his palm. For a ridiculous moment, he considered going out to shop for a new pair—easier to search than find.

He turned. There it was.

The bus bench.

Twisted. Tilted off its bolts.

Pressed halfway up onto the curb by a wrecked yellow taxi, its hood still bearing a crater from whatever it had struck—or whatever had struck it.

Beneath the bench: blackened scraps. The creature he had half-seen, fully feared—now fried brittle by dawn. A grotesque slush of charcoal and sinew. Its fingers still hooked toward where his hand had once dangled.

Henry stared. The blood on the sidewalk, his blood, trailed from the taxi's shadow to where he now stood. He followed it with his eyes, then turned forward again, blinking hard.

He had survived.

He had escaped dark hell, found sanctuary in a spotlight—and lived.

And now?

He started forward down the empty sidewalk, staggering slightly.

The earphone and cord coiled in his hand, the street yawning open ahead of him.

No map yet for today. No destination planned. Home first.

Just a comedy club behind him—and the first real silence he'd heard in weeks.

25

The stage lights hum. A single stool at center stage. Henry sits, mic in hand, gazing out at a few mannequins seated at tables. A faint speaker hiss. He clears his throat.

> HENRY
> You know you've had a strange
> night when your concussion
> starts to feel like the least
> alarming thing.
>
> *(beat)*

"I mean—yeah. I got hit in the head by a flying brick. Not metaphorically. A real one."

He taps the mic lightly against his temple.

"Still hurts. Something shook my Etch A Sketch a little too hard. I think my head's leaking aluminum powder. Every time I draw a conclusion, it comes out looking like a scribbled, misspelled delusion. My dream cuts its signal, the screen goes to static, and white noise starts jamming on the dark fiber line.

"Then I wake up to a zompire taxi driver headbutting a bus bench, trying to get to me.

"But that's not the part that really bothers me."

He glances around the room.

"What really hit me over the head was this place. The Comedy Club.

"Because I think I like it here.

"So... here I am."

He shifts on the stool, looking out into the dimly-lit room.

"That night… maybe I told a joke to an empty room here? I don't recall.

"Maybe this wasn't empty.

"Maybe my angels were laughing.

"Or maybe the monsters found a way in?"

He shudders, goes still. A long pause.

"I—I can't think about that.

"But I am still alive.

"I'm still here.

"That means something, right?"

He forces a small chuckle, glances at a mannequin as if waiting for a nod.

"You ever wonder if they can laugh? These things? These zompires?

"Maybe they can.

"Which means—I think—maybe I've got it.

"And they—they just want to eat it."

He exhales, soft and uneven.

"I could use some human laughter again.

"Something real.

"My ears are itching for it—for music, singing, laughter—anything but that hideous hiss… that disconcerting click… those… nerve-shredding shrieks."

He lowers the mic. The feedback hum grows, then fades, as Henry steps down.

INT. NBC STUDIO — MORNING

Laughter and applause.

A wide shot: empty audience seats, half-covered in dust. Faint echoes of the city's silence seep in through broken windows covered in blackout curtains. A single spotlight hits the stage. A big "HENRY LIVE!" banner (clearly handmade) hangs crookedly.

At center stage stands HENRY, wearing a suit two sizes too big. His hair is combed, barely. He adjusts a tie with cartoon cats on it. He holds a microphone like it is Excalibur.

```
          HENRY
       (to camera)
  Ladies and gentlemen... welcome
  back to "Henry Live!"
```

He bows.

Music and applause.

"It's good to be here. Mostly because it's better than being out there."

Behind him, a fake set of New York's skyline leans to one side. A mannequin in a dress sits in the guest chair. Her name tag reads "Madeline." Henry leads the imaginary applause, turns and trots over to join his guest. He sits behind the host's desk and pulls a cue card

from his pocket.

<pre>
                         HENRY
          Tonight's guest has traveled
          the world, modeling for some of
          the biggest names out there.
          She once asked Barbie, 'What's
          the Mattel?' And now they don't
          speak to each other, or anyone
          else. Please
          welcome... Madeline!
</pre>

He waits for applause, nods solemnly.

"So, Madeline—I understand you keep that figure on a strict fiberglass diet?"

Laughter erupts. Henry leans in, listening.

"Yes?—Interesting. And if I want to purchase this product, do you accept plastic?—Wow. Really? I did not know moisturizer was necessary in your line of work.—Oh? K-Y Jelly?—Okay, why?—

"My dear, I am truly shocked.—That's even worse than eating brunch at Sorbet's. And nobody refills the mimosas.—

"What's that?—What do you mean, what do I mean?—

"We'll be right back after this message."

More laughter and jazzy bumper music.

He kept talking long after the tape ran out. The silence didn't bother him anymore. It was honest. More honest than the audience used to be.

Henry sat at the host desk and spun his pen. He stared into the darkness where the cameras had once been, pretending there was someone—anyone—on the other side.

He pulled out a photo. A cut-out. From a French magazine cover, wasn't it? A model's face. She even had a name... not a French one. Forgotten. Regardless, she was now his cue-card girl.

"I keep thinking you'll laugh," he said to it. "But maybe I'm not your type."

He looked toward the sound booth, where an ancient ON AIR light flickered.

CRASH.

A loud bang from backstage.

Henry became a statue.

No punchline this time.

Slowly, he thawed and flinched and flexed.

He reached under the desk, pulled out his flashlight, and flicked it on. The beam was shaky, like his hands. He aimed it toward the dark wing.

"Delivery's late," he muttered. "Hope it's not cold blood again."

Nothing moved.

He waited. Nothing.

Then, slowly, he smiled.

Back into character.

"HENRY LIVE!" (CONTINUED)

                    HENRY
                 (to the air)
        Folks, that's our show for
        tonight. If you liked what you
        saw, don't forget to set your
        DVR. And subscribe to the
        channel. And be sure to scan
        that QR Code, somewhere on the
        screen.

He bows again. The lights buzz. A long, low groan sounds in the pipes above.

INT. STAIRWELL – MOMENTS LATER

Henry exited the studio, flashlight bobbing ahead of him, the studio stage left behind like a grave.

Henry (to himself): "Killin' out there, Henry. Or... maybe not yet."

24

EXT. CONEY ISLAND – AFTERNOON

By the time Henry reached the boardwalk, the air had turned syrupy and strange—like carnival candy left out too long in the sun.

He stood at the gates of Luna Park, hands on hips, staring up at the faded sign like a man deciding whether his inner boy would survive a haunted funhouse or a hall of mirrors. Both seemed likely. Probably.

"Well," he said. "If this place isn't closed, someone's getting fired."

The gate was already open. That made it easier to pretend he was welcome.

At the edge of the boardwalk, he found an old popcorn cart. He pried open its drawer and scooped out a handful of stale kernels, tossing them toward a family of rats picking through the sand. One stared back at him.

"Hey," Henry said. "Can't have Thanksgiving without a fat turkey."

From somewhere beneath the planks came a faint scraping—nails or claws, slow and deliberate. Henry straightened. "Nope," he said aloud. "Not today."

He reached into his left cargo pants' pocket, pulled out a garland of dried orange slices, and slung it around his neck like a talisman. "Vitamin C," he said. "Courage."

He left the boardwalk behind and wandered inland, past tilted rides and sand-filled arcade booths. He circled it once: the carousel hung crooked, horses bound to mid-gallop, their glass eyes wide in eternal surprise. Climbing onto a chipped white horse, the tired knight straddled the hand-carved antique and fished a kazoo from his burgundy windbreaker, as if preparing for battle.

He blew a short fanfare—the music of royalty, if royalty lived in a dollar store. He gently spurred the wooden flank with his heel's rubber outsole and then pretended to be riding at full gallop, bouncing up and down.

"Whoa, boy! Whoa, Thunder!"

Henry glanced around the park, acting embarrassed, then laughed and dismounted. The kazoo slipped from his fingers and landed in a puddle with a sad little dying wheeze.

Wiping a tear off his face, he muttered, "Live on, my sweet music."

He gave the horse a gentle pat on its peeling flank.

The painted floorboards blurred underfoot—colors bleeding together, sand into marble, salt air cooling and thinning into silence.

Henry stepped down from the carousel—

—and his Brooks Anthem 7 running shoes squeaked on marble steps.

INT. METROPOLITAN MUSEUM – AFTERNOON

Where I come to find my marbles again.

In the vast sunlit hall, the silence was immense. Dust motes floated through the fractured beams of light like lazy angels.

He stayed near the galleries where the sunlight still reached, drifting between marble and oily shadow like a man unwilling to tempt the dark. The air felt old, preserved—heavy with the memory of thousands of footsteps that would never return. He was willing to brave the lighted sections, compelled by his need to keep feeling love for something.

He wandered between pillars and paintings, his shoes plodding softly on the polished floor. One painting, a naval battle, held his gaze: cannons firing, sailors screaming, ships torn apart by foam and fury.

"They all fought for flags," Henry explained to his imaginary tour group. "Until someone invented flag football."

He clapped a few times, just to hear the sound. The echo stretched across the room and came back to him as a kind of hollow applause. Henry bowed, deeply, to the invisible audience.

He moved among statues, fake-reading plaques aloud with mock reverence:

"Anonymous. Anon. The world traveler, Incognito."

He paused before a headless Apollo and raised an imaginary glass.

"I bet you were jogging in my neighborhood."

Sunlight shifted, pooling across the marble stairs, drawing him downward. Each step seemed to pull him further from the sea air, further from the world he remembered.

By the time he reached the bottom, the stairwell had opened into glass and light.

Through the panes he could see the city—rooftops, quiet streets, towers catching the afternoon sun. Somewhere above, faint music drifted through the air, distant and familiar.

Henry smiled. "Well, at least someone's rehearsing."

INT. LINCOLN CENTER – MORNING

He stepped through the museum doors and into sunlight that felt strangely theatrical, as if a spotlight had been waiting for him. The plaza beyond shimmered—tiles, fountains, columns—everything too clean, too silent.

Lincoln Center.

Henry's shoes made a soft rhythm as he crossed the square, each step echoing faintly between the grand facades. The fountain in the middle sputtered to life for a moment, spitting a few weak arcs of water before dying again. He gave it an approving nod.

That was me. Until I stopped drinking so much citrus juice at one time.

"Relax. Don't rush. Let it flow, fill, then flush," he said.

He climbed the steps toward Avery Fisher Hall. The great glass doors were already open, their handles smeared with dust and the faint residue of handprints long faded. Inside, the air felt preserved, heavy with the memory of applause.

He found the grand piano onstage, its lid propped open, a black whale stranded in a sea of velvet seats. Velvet and vacant, he was careful to note. No seats occupied.

Henry sat down on the bench, cracked his knuckles, and pressed a key.

The note rang out clear, lonely, echoing through the vast emptiness like a confession.

He smiled. "Well, Henry… time to play for the end of the world."

His fingers stumbled through a few bars of something that was almost music—half "Moon River," half muscle memory. Then he felt an almost-innate movement take over briefly. Fingers making chords, he was amazed to hear them start into Floyd Cramer's "Last Date."

The sound filled the hall, blooming and collapsing at once. He swayed, eyes closed, pretending he could still feel an audience breathing in the dark.

When he went as far as he could with it, he was finished, and he rose, bowed deeply, and waited for applause that would never come. Only the faint hum of the building answered.

Oh yes, there is the applause. Gradually growing. Swelling. Enormous applause! Cheers and accolades!

As he turned to leave, sunlight rippled across the stage, stretching long and golden. Each step down the aisle seemed to carry him further forward in time, as if the day itself were turning pages.

By the time he reached the doors, the sound of his own footsteps had softened into something new—something like seashells held to his ears.

Waves.

EXT. HUDSON RIVER – LATE AFTERNOON

When he stepped through the concert hall doors, the sound of waves became real. The afternoon had ripened into a heavy gold haze, and the Hudson stretched before him—wide, leaden, lazy in its coruscation.

Henry stood at the pier, sporting a weather-beaten captain's cap, a fleece, a navy blazer, white shirt and dark trousers, with slip-resistant shoes. Something borrowed, something blue. The sleeves were a little long, but he carried himself like a man who belonged to the sea.

A small rowboat bobbed at the edge, its bottom boards stained with old rainwater marks and a few brittle leaves. Henry crouched, inspected it, and tapped the wood as though it might respond.

"Structural integrity: questionable. Crew morale: low. Perfect."

He untied the stern line, then climbed in and took his seat at the oar. The boat drifted lazily from the platform, rocking with a rhythm too calm for confidence.

The skyline glimmered across the water—gray towers softened by sunlight, their reflections undulatory. He dipped his hand into the river, watched the ripples spread outward until they dissolved into the city's mirrored skin.

From his coat pocket, he pulled out a tangerine, peeled it in loose spirals, and tossed the rind into the water. It floated briefly before sinking, trailing orange oil that glowed against the murky surface.

"To the fruit gods," he said.

A faint breeze stirred, carrying the smell of the river and something faintly sweet, almost floral. He leaned back, closed his eyes, and let the boat drift a while longer.

When he opened them again, the water around him was turning shallow. The boat bumped softly into solid ground.

EXT. LIBERTY ISLAND – MORNING

He had grown a beard by the time he reached Liberty Island—a scraggly thing that looked like it had been negotiated rather than grown. The wind off the harbor whipped at his loincloth, her favorite well-worn piece of expensive costume. His sandals slapped the cracked pavement. A rifle hung from his shoulder. He walked knot-kneed and grimacing, a well-rehearsed parody of life imitating art, or maybe death imitating life imitating art—he couldn't remember which, only that there was supposed to be a line.

Before him, the Statue of Liberty loomed—still, enormous, green, overlooking the incoming fog bank. Henry gazed up, jaw tight, wincing through the mist.

"You maniacs," he croaked, voice cracking like a bad actor's first take. He dropped to his knees and raised a fist.

"You finally did it. You blew it all to hell!"

He gave the moment every ounce of melodrama he could muster. The seagulls weren't impressed. One screamed at him anyway.

The morning fog wrapped around, as Henry stood, stepped forward, and stared sadly at his beard of shaving cream in the mirror before lifting the razor blade to his cheek. "Cut and swipe."

INT. PENTHOUSE BATHROOM – NIGHT

Steam rose from the sink. Henry, now clean-shaven, turned off the tap and towel-dried his jaws. He studied himself in the mirror, robe hanging loosely around his frame. Leaned in, making a frown. Adjusted his posture, knot-kneed again. He raised one fist with Biblical intensity.

Henry (deep, theatrical): "Take your stinking paws off me, you damn dirty apocalypse!"

The guy had range. All the yelling. The teeth. That one knee always forward, like he's just now realizing he has legs.

Truth is, Charlton made it look noble. I make it look like a raccoon with arthritis.

He paused, then struck another pose. This one weirder. His jaw jutting out, he bent slightly and swung his hands over his turned patellas.

Henry (grunting): "I am become monkey."

He straightened, tightened his robe. A dab of aftershave. A practiced smile. He nodded once, satisfied.

"Well, we're still here."

He wiped the mirror again, just to be sure, and whispered, "Back to the game."

INT. PENTHOUSE DEN – CONTINUOUS

The electric football game buzzed faintly on the table. Tiny plastic players shivered and spun in erratic circles. Across from Henry sat tween brother Bart, a Coke can sweating on the coaster in front of an empty chair.

I never realized how young you were.

Henry leaned in. "You really think the Jets have a chance?"

Bart reached over and turned the speed control dial behind the goalpost. As the vibration increased, Bart let his rude belch reply. He laughed in his annoying way and shook his head to get the blond strands off his strawberry brow-patch.

"Right," Henry said, watching the plastic teams converge and spread. "Browns all day, baby. I'll be Jim Brown." He hummed the "Heavy Action" Monday Night Football theme, until his ball-carrier turned and headed to the sideline. "No, Jim, no!"

He flicked the switch, off. They began setting up for the next play. Home team Browns on the twenty-five. Jets were in a jagged formation.

"Where'd you get this?" Bart asked.

Henry started: "Mom—Dad—" Henry closed his eyes. "At a novelty shop. Yesterday."

"Yesterday? Santa Claus got me this for Christmas."

"You? Don't you mean... *us?*" Henry scoffed. "Santa Claus? Really? How old are you again?"

"You don't remember?" Bart turned down the speed control, leaning forward.

"Remember?" Henry echoed.

A pause.

"Do you remember my name?"

"What?" Henry blinked, frowned, considered. After a moment of confusion passed, his eyes lit up. "I remember your name. *Barf-bag.*"

They both laughed. The field hummed to life, vibrating violently. The players quivered, clattered, fell over. "Okay! Too much! Too much! Cut it out! Cut it—!"

EXT. METLIFE STADIUM – DAY

The hum became thunder. Henry was suddenly there—on the field itself, sprinting between fallen tackling dummies and blocking sleds. Semi-uniformed from leftovers in the locker room, Henry was the MVP. He juked left, dodged a mannequin in shoulder pads and helmet, stumbled, kept running, cleats too snug on his feet.

The empty stands stretched endlessly upward, a cathedral of silence.

Henry crossed the end zone, threw his arms high, and screamed, "Touchdown!"

The echo came back to him like a crowd's delayed memory—ghostly cheers swelling in the rafters. Henry bowed, spiked the ball, danced around it, then doubled over laughing until he nearly fell.

"Bart!" he shouted. "You see that?"

He sat down in the end zone, laughter collapsing into breathless sighs. Around him, the rapturous roar of the vast fan-filled stands emptied in a dispersing wind, and the coliseum loomed with increasing silence—row after row of empty blue seats rising into the pale daylight.

Except—one sound—

A faint but continual single clapping.

Henry was struck still. It was somewhere above him—slow, deliberate, echoing through the steel rafters.

"Bart?" he called out, eyes searching, unable to lock on location. His voice came back smaller, swallowed by distance.

The single applause continued for a few seconds more—then stopped.

Henry stood. The ball rolled away and thudded softly against the goalpost. He brushed dirt from his borrowed uniform, then jogged toward the sideline where his tote bag sat on the bench. Inside: his flashlight; also, the Glock, socks, shoes, shorts, and a folded shirt.

He changed there in the open, the way soldiers used to shave in foxholes. The uniform pants and jersey—cleats too—he folded neatly and left on the bench, as if someone might need them later. The air inside the stadium felt wrong now—too still, too hollow.

He slung the bag over his shoulder and headed for the tunnel.

The first stretch was clearly visible, scattered with old paper cups and faded end-zone confetti. The deeper he went, the more the light dimmed. He turned on the flashlight. Its beam cut through the dark, steady, white, alive.

The tunnel narrowed, bending slightly. His footsteps echoed in a long, metallic sigh. Then ahead—a faint rectangle of brightness.

He quickened his pace.

Dust swirled in the beam as he approached the exit. The sunlight grew, filling the tunnel's mouth, washing out the darkness behind him.

Henry shielded his eyes and stepped out.

EXT. NEWSSTAND OUTSIDE ABRACADABRA NYC – DAY

He winced against the brightness. The stadium was gone, far behind him now, a week or more. Before him stretched a quiet street he recognized vaguely—a place once packed with weekend crowds. A toppled lamppost leaned against a yellow cab, cemented mid-turn.

Across the sidewalk stood a newsstand, its glass cracked but intact. Behind it, the weathered facade of Abracadabra NYC—a costume and magic shop—still displayed sun-faded posters of capes, wigs, and latex masks.

Henry started across.

Inside the dim store, a mask faced the window—its rubbery grin distorted by time. For a moment Henry froze, thinking it moved. The light shifted across its glossy eyes, and he flinched, hand going instinctively to the Glock 17 in his bag.

He exhaled when it didn't move again. Just a mask. Just reflection and nerves.

At the newsstand, the magazines lay fanned out beneath a film of dust and age. *TIME, GQ, Vanity Fair*—ghosts of headlines that no longer mattered.

Then, at the edge of the counter, under a misplaced rubber Viking helmet, something glossy caught the light.

Henry picked up the helmet and stared at a magazine cover.

Après La Vérité.

A model and a male actor—Jim Caviezel—posed mid-laugh.

Nora Fullilove.

Henry stared at the page, his fingers absently twirling the helmet by one horn. For several seconds, his mind went blank. No trace of thought, no awareness of time—just the faint hum of wind and the slow drift of a man whose brain had quietly shorted out.

He inhaled, momentarily unfocused, then raised and lowered the helmet a few times, indecisively.

What was that I was doing?

He placed the helmet on his head and looked around.

"Grace," he said quietly. "Grace... I pray will fill my plate."

Where did that come from?

A grin twitched at the corner of his mouth. "Guess it's dinner time in the Twilight Zone." He shook his head, amused at himself, and his scalp tingled. He teetered, then straightened.

"I must be hungry. Yes. Food, yes."

He looked down the empty street and added quietly, "Something warm would help." He stepped off the curb and onto something squishy. The gum on his sole stuck with each step to the bus bench, peeling up in sticky ribbons with each lift of his foot.

EXT. CONEY ISLAND – MORNING

By some strange turn of hours—or maybe the city itself had spun him forward—Henry was now sitting on a bench beneath the shadow of the Wonder Wheel. The great circle loomed above him, motionless, its cars swaying faintly in the sea breeze like ornaments from a forgotten season. Motionless, but alive in his mind. Each bolt and beam sparkled in the pale sunlight, the carnival suspended, silent, awaiting the audience that would never arrive.

Henry smiled, teeth biting into the juice of the morning sunlight, and whispered, "Ahh. Here we are again."

A gull perched on one of the beams, preening, as if the whole park still belonged to it.

He pulled off his shoes, then his socks. The breeze tickled his twitching toes, and he smiled, turning his mind off to those discolored, fungal-streaked nails. The morning wind was cool and kind. He watched the gull hop from one car to another. He stretched his legs, toes brushing the air, savoring the absurdity and the small freedom of being exactly, utterly, alone.

"Still running smoother than me," a random thought shared with his ears.

He leaned back, listening to the faint groan of the abandoned ride. The air smelled of salt, oil, and old sugar—memories trapped in wind.

After a while, he murmured, "Grace... before breakfast... fill my life." *A prayer?*

Nearby, the wooden horses of the carousel glimmered in the sun, glass eyes wide in eternal surprise. He closed his and could almost hear the faint kazoo fanfare he had played, now echoing across the sand and peeling paint, a memory and a promise folded into one.

For a moment, he was both everywhere and nowhere. And somehow, that felt just right.

Henry opened his eyes and let out a quiet, satisfied sigh. The city sprawled around him, empty but full of stories. The wind tugged at his hair, carrying with it the faint smell of salted popcorn. He pulled a handful from the red bowl and filled his face, then leaned in to the telescope.

EXT. PENTHOUSE BALCONY — NIGHTFALL

Henry could not sleep. Again.

He had eaten what passed for dinner—an apple, slightly bruised, slightly shriveled, and a spoonful of peanut butter that now lived in the back of his throat. He drank two cups of black tea, first hot, second not so hot, still warmer than the night.

The night was warm, slightly humid, and the city below thrummed in that invisible way it did now, a low hum in the marrow. Forty floors up, the wind teased his thin T-shirt and brought no relief.

He sat on the balcony, an ice pack wrapped in a towel on his sore ankle, the telescope angled toward the world he no longer belonged to.

This was the hour of them.

He no longer tried to keep track of time in numbers—no clocks, no sun once it fell—but in behaviors. The scurry hour. The scatter-and-slither. The hour when the streets swelled with movement like blood behind a bruise. He touched the side of the telescope like one might pet a loyal dog.

He leaned in.

At this distance, the city became geography—an old map crawling with ink. Dark swaths pulsed through Central Park, blotting the spaces between trees. They poured through iron gates and climbed lampposts, hung from branches like vultures re-imagining evolution.

He adjusted the lens. A balcony two buildings over flashed into sharpness. A shape was crouched there, motionless—something between a man and a myth. No eyes, but it turned as though it felt the glass on it.

Henry pulled back, heart thumping. The shape remained still. Watching. Or sensing.

"Okay," he whispered, wiping sweat from his brow. "Okay, no stars tonight."

But he looked again.

Downtown, alleys became veins. Creatures moved in unnatural herky-jerk patterns, like puppets handled by the drunk. Some crawled on all fours. Others stood, turned their heads without moving their torsos, then slunk sideways as if gravity offended them.

He found a narrow rooftop behind a shattered CVS and followed the motion of something small and quick—a rat, he thought, and confirmed it seconds later, zooming in as another shape descended upon it.

This one was lean. Female, maybe—though gender had long since lost meaning in this charnel menagerie.

She crouched. Snatched the rat. Held the squirming body of scurvy fur up to her yawning grin of enormous fangs. As the rat fought back—futilely—its teeth sank into the drooling tip of her tongue.

Her jaw unhinged with a wet series of pops, and she brought those jagged pinnacles down.

Bit off the still-screeching head.

Snap—crackle—pop.

Henry blinked. Nauseated disbelief gripped him. His feeble attempt at wit died before it could reach the surface.

With two more bites, the body of the rat was devoured. Only the tail remained twitching between gray lips. Then it broke off and fell.

Henry nearly vomited, but didn't.

He finally whispered, "Bon appétit," and closed his eyes.

When he opened them, the creature was gone. He did not know if it had leapt or dissolved.

In the streets, clusters of them huddled near rusted-out food trucks, under scaffolding, and inside empty subway entrances that fumed stale breath into the air. He focused on one intersection. The wind picked up a plastic bag and carried it down the avenue like a ghost with errands. A manhole cover trembled. From it, fingers emerged. Not hands. Just fingers. First three. Then ten.

He inhaled, lids brushing lenses.

Now nothing. Just the cover, in place.

"Sure," he murmured.

He lowered the telescope. Sat back. Closed his eyes and listened.

Some nights he imagined the city whispering to itself.

Tonight it laughed.

23

I never imagined this apocalyptic life in Cinemascope would come with such a soundtrack.

You'd think if the world ended, the music would stop.

Turns out, it just keeps going.

Sometimes it's even on shuffle—one minute it's Chicago, the next it's some sax-heavy smooth-ass jazz, like the apocalypse is trying to seduce me. And I hadn't had any good sax in a long, long time.

That morning, I was out trying to clear a path down Broadway— not for any heroic reason, just because I figured if I could move a few cars, maybe I could pretend I lived in a city where people still drove somewhere. The kind of city with traffic jams and honking horns, not just empty streets and nothing but the sound of my own breathing.

First few cars were dead as a doornail. Batteries fried or keys long gone. Then I climbed into this faded Mitsubishi Montero, with a CD player installed. Above, attached to the visor, a sleeve holding several discs. I pulled a random one down, fed it to the player, hit the power button and watched it get sucked in. Upped the volume just as the music started. Then lyrics: George Benson's smooth voice sang "On Broadway." And I was sucked in.

I sat there, feeling like the universe just handed me a mixtape.

George sang to me in a way I'd never heard before.

"The lights are bright on Broadway."

That's right, that's right, by George.

I can't give up. I need to find bright lights.

I leaned back, closed my eyes, and let the song roll through the empty street. I imagined the crowds, the cars, the laughter. Not that it made me want to cry or anything. Okay, maybe just a little. But who's measuring?

When the song ended, I didn't move. Just sat there, like I'd been given a secret handshake by the city itself.

I was being talked to, and it felt incredibly phenomenal.

A new and important ingredient had been added to my existence, reminding me it's called life. And a new intel mission was assigned to me from the higher-ups: find the voice. Find the message.

The next day—or maybe it was the same day, I've lost the ability to measure time—I climbed into another dusty SUV, and Gerry Rafferty's "Baker Street" came on. That saxophone...

"Yes, yes, ... light in my head, dead on ... dead ... another crazy day ... and I'll get drunk tonight."

Raphael Ravenscroft's riff: if loneliness had lungs, that's exactly what they'd sound like.

I sat there in the driver's seat, crying into my sleeve, then laughed at myself for crying over a woodwind. The human brain is a very stupid instrument. But memories flooded my mind, and I was experiencing indescribable awe. Faces, events, adolescence, dreams— pouring through me like a fantastic parade, too powerful to grasp or hold still for even a second.

And then it passed. The parade turned the corner. I was left in the silence afterward, in the hollow where no souls lived. So there was some cost involved in this seeking endeavor.

Like my head's a crowded room and all the wants and needs are shoving each other toward the door, screaming to get out. And there's no one to hear it but me. No one to tell me to stop. So I don't. I let it happen. I keep walking, keep moving through the empty streets with this noise in my head, like maybe if I walk far enough, the crowd will thin out.

The city isn't done with me yet. Somewhere out there, another voice is waiting. Another song. Another message.

A few days later—or hours, or a lifetime—I stumble on a little blue hatchback. Pop the door, drop in, notice the CD player, crank the ignition. A quick search uncovers a few discs. I pop one in, and the speakers jolt alive with Duran Duran's "What Happens Tomorrow."

The mid-chorus hits me like a shot of sunlight through a cut-glass tumbler. My chest lifts, and for a moment, all the tangled wants and needs, the empty streets, the dead-end destinations—none of it matters. Only the music exists.

I laugh out loud. "You're a long, long time ago, boys. Tomorrow? I'll tell you what happens tomorrow: tomorrow ended. Today—the extended version. Today, the dead day, just dies on and on. Can't skip it. Can't end it. Can't end myself."

The dashboard lights flare weakly, a faint green washing over my hands. I press my palms flat, feeling nothing but pretending it's warmth. I linger there, watching the flicker, listening to the song, imagining the car itself is trying to keep me company.

Slowly, I drift. The glow swells in my mind, painting veins and shadows across my fingers, and for a moment I close my eyes and see it everywhere—traffic lights bleeding the streets awake, elevator buttons buzzing with life, neon signs flickering like distant stars. It feels holy, ridiculous as that sounds, a heartbeat of civilization in the emptiness.

And then the real world nudges me back. Sunlight—sharp, insistent—glints off the candy-apple taillight of the wrecked car ahead. The red lens pulses, alive, and my chest tightens.

"Protect me if you can, I can't show you how frightened I am."

I whisper into the empty car. "Believe, believe, believe... yeah, I've got to. Believe, believe, believe."

Another day it's "Stayin' Alive" in an old Ford Taurus, and I take it as a mandatory memo from the boss. "Thanks, Bee Gees. Message received." But that did beg the question: Am I alive?

I had R.E.M.'s "Stand" playing in the penthouse one day, through the speakers of a newly acquired boombox on the counter, as I stood out on the balcony, eyes on the heavens.

I'm standing, I'm standing. Dang, I've been standing here quite a while. Shouldn't I be doing something more besides contemplating directions?

The song floated up into the white glare, and for a second, I swore I saw something move up there—like the sky itself was shifting its weight, trying to decide where to stand.

I look down into the city...

Where to next? Talk to me.

And then there's the station wagon already parked at the curb along Fifth Avenue. I seek, it plays: Harry Nilsson's "Coconut" spills out — and suddenly I'm eight years old again, barefoot in the backyard in Cleveland, Chief Wahoo grinning over the bill shading my eyes. Dad's flipping burgers, the whole block smells like charcoal, and my biggest worry in life is whether the ice cream truck will run out of Bomb Pops.

The song ends and I don't move. Afraid if I breathe too loud, I'll scare the memory away.

Then came the real find: a hybrid SUV, its battery barely alive but enough to spin a disc. Not music this time. An audiobook. Some motivational speaker droning:

"You are the architect of your own happiness."

"Oh, really? Tell that to the horde of nocturnal freaks who think my jugular is a Capri Sun."

I start collecting these. Music CDs, audiobook CDs, portable players, batteries. Not hard to find, done smartly—the idea building momentum, like a new way to experience ecstasy. But deep within, a word is growing stronger in the mix: Perform!

Back at the penthouse, I set these players up in different corners. One looping "Baker Street," another with a man reading Moby-Dick, *and in the bathroom, a British woman calmly narrating* How to Make Quiche. *I laughed, impressed with my ingenious lunacy.*

I pour myself a glass of wine and stand in the middle of the room like I've just thrown the best party in New York. "My guests are polite," I tell the empty air. "Nobody double-dips."

I was in a midnight-blue Maserati Quattroporte when I discovered it:

The Ohio Players. "Love Rollercoaster."

Funk bassline, horns, the works.

And then — the screaming.

That horrible, discordant shriek from somewhere inside the buildings around me. The creatures—waking? Warning? Laughing? Hard to tell.

The song keeps playing. I get out, wanting to feel the certainty of my game legs ready to run. The bass thumps. The horns punch the air. The voices—human once, not anymore—rip out from the shadows, echoing down the block.

I just stand there, halfway between running and dancing, wondering if this is what partying in hell sounds like.

It's hard to take the end of mankind seriously when it's choreographed to funk, I tell myself, wanting to be convinced that my dogged humor will scat the cat, but fear is overwhelming at the moment.

22

Henry's legs still ached from the morning jog, or maybe from simply existing. Along with the tripod, he carried a battered pair of binoculars slung around his neck, scavenged from an old observatory shop uptown. He sat up before the tripod near the rail, where the wind thinned into a whisper. From here, the city stretched out in blanched colors.

The Roosevelt Island tram hung crooked between towers, cables slack and frayed, tendrils of alien growth clinging, glistening like wet vines in the pale sunlight.

Through the telescope, Henry saw something inside. An impression, almost like a person's figure. Frail, motionless, head bowed—if that was a head.

He twisted the focus ring. The image wavered, then locked.

No. That's impossible.

A woman stood at the glass, her posture patient, almost serene, as if she were waiting for the city to apologize.

Or a mannequin. A very realistic mannequin.

And who would be decorating the city with mannequins besides me?

And I'm not losing my mind today. Nope. I can't get up there.

Which means… I'm hallucinating.

The tram swayed once—barely perceptible—then steadied.

When Henry looked again, she was gone.

The eveningfall haze had a thickness to it, like the city was trying to remember how to breathe. Henry lifted the telescope's cap and leaned in, adjusting the focus until the skyline sharpened. The first shape he caught was the Empire State Building, rising solitary from the south like a survivor too proud to admit defeat.

I'd thought about it. For, like, a second. I mean, a hundred and fifty floors. Not taking those stairs. Yes, I want to stay far enough away from the hell zone below. But, so far, up here, far enough, so good.

I make the rounds. The Empire, the Chrysler, the Waldorf Astoria.

Southward, the river's a strip of foil, catching light it doesn't deserve.

Liberty's still standing, torch out, arm tired. I thought I saw her wave once.

Probably heat haze. Probably wishful absurdity posing as hope. Hopeful that I'm cracking up, and none of this is the real world.

And farther out, almost to the ocean—something turns. The Wonder Wheel, maybe. A circle of color against the blur. One of the cars is still hanging there. I could swear it moves. The city's alive in the way a photograph is alive—when you stare too long, something always seems to move. If I stare long enough at it, will I make someone else appear?

Let's try the binoculars.

Eh. Those seagulls passing by over there seem real enough.

No chance of getting committed today, doctor?

He blinked hard, lowered the binoculars. A tremor in his wrist. He told himself it was the wind. Then leaned back into the telescope, adjusted the focus, and scanned Roosevelt Island again.

There it was—like a rectangular glitch in a digital picture, suspended in the sky.

And for a moment, a fragment within the fragment, a shape within the glass. *Waving now?*

Henry scooped out the last of the peanut butter and stuck the spoon in his mouth.

He panned slowly east. The Chrysler Building appeared next, all fang and ornament, its chrome crown fractured in subdued sunlight. From this angle, it looked almost clean—untouched, impossible. Its spire flared like a lie told beautifully.

Still standing. Or, like me, pretending to.

There—just below the crown—he caught a glint, then a human outline.

He drew a breath. A woman again. *The same one? Maybe.*

She stood by the window, gazing outward as if searching for someone specific.

Henry pulled back, checked the building with the naked eye. Nothing.

He returned to the lens. The shape had reassembled—ghostly, darker than before.

He murmured, "That's impossible," and felt absurdly comforted by his own disbelief.

He wiped the hot-shower sweat from his brow, refocused the telescope, and brought the lens lower. The Waldorf Astoria filled the view now, its windows dark and regal, like rows of tired eyes watching the city fade. He traced the ledges with the telescope, cracked glass, the faint flash of light on aluminum or marble on a windowsill—maybe a frame, maybe nothing. One set of curtains slightly parted, figure-shaping the darkness beyond.

He adjusted the focus again. The shape wavered, barely visible, then gone. Henry frowned, searching for movement that might explain it. None came.

Henry's hand drifted to the camera on the side table next to him. He picked it up, turned it on, and peered through the viewfinder, aligning it roughly where the telescope had been aimed.

A message bar appeared: OUT OF MEMORY

For a second—only a second—he saw her: a silhouette of a woman in one of the high windows across the street, unmoving, almost graceful. His breath caught. He adjusted the zoom. The figure held, still as a statue, almost dissolving into shadow, like an image on wet film fading to black.

Frustrated, desperate, he tried to take a picture, anyway. The camera chirped in refusal.

I know, I know. "Read the sign, pal." No memory card.

Henry moaned, working the optics, the view blurring in and out of focus, as he tried to memorize the elusive image beyond the message.

New message flashed: BATTERIES EXHAUSTED

The screen went black.

21

The elevator hung motionless two hundred feet up the shaft. Black. Airless. A coffin of dead silence. Henry pressed himself against the mirrored wall, his breath shallow, the air inside already stuffy.

Don't panic, don't panic. And then Henry silenced his thought, his ears perking up.

Far below, faint and distant, came an indistinct hum, a creeping vibration in the vertical conduit.

14 seconds.

The backup generator coughed awake.

A louder but low mechanical hum rolled through the car. The floor lights sputtered, then held a weak amber. The elevator jerked, groaned, and began to move. Henry clutched the railing, pulling back from his reflection and the breath stamps he left on glass. He braced for the lift to continue rising.

Instead, he felt the "recall" descent.

5 seconds.

And through the ceiling speaker, tinny and unshaken, came the brassy, bouncing trumpets of Herb Alpert's "Spanish Flea".

The chipper melody chirped and swayed, as though this were any ordinary night. As though he were returning from cocktails, not from a fire alarm that had rattled him awake.

8 seconds.

Dread ratcheted through Henry's lungs. The faint hum had steadily amplified, the sound waves now surging with increasing density through the walls, pulsing against absorption. Something spine-chilling was rising all around him. Like exhalations of smoke softly over the deep, throaty crackle of fire getting louder, the one wave was becoming many.

He jabbed at the button for 39 again and again, but the car ignored him. His ears popped.

12 seconds.

Down it went, carrying him into the unearthly noise rising from below. Descending into hell.

... 4... 3...

The screams were overwhelming, the decibel level piercing his ears as he covered them futilely with his palms. His own scream was pushing through his body, rushing to the exit.

... 1

DING!

The doors slid open on the lobby. Henry stepped out before realizing what he had stepped into. Darkness, in the form of swirling black mist, moved like a spirit over the scene. A figure burst into Henry's path—a freckled, teenaged boy, screaming, his entire body crawling with strangely quivering wriggles. Henry stumbled back. The boy nearly collided with him, then fell quaking between the elevator doors.

"Spanish Flea" kept playing, jaunty and oblivious, as the lobby convulsed beneath a stuttering light-show of flickering fluorescents. Endless, ear-splitting screams—like a banshee bandsaw—ripped through the sanguinary orgy. People scattered helter-skelter in blind panic, slipping on marble, colliding with each other and walls, swallowed by shapes not human—pale, hollow-eyed, teeth wet, glistening, sharp.

A woman was dragged across the tiles, her throat torn open. From the wound poured black ichor, smoking and hissing where it met the polished stone. Her body seized violently, bent backward in an impossible arc, then snapped upright with machine-like speed. Eyes rolled back—then opened, milky white, fixed on nothing and everything at once.

A man, stripped of clothes, tripped over a fallen bag, rolled, scrambled to his feet—and froze, cringing. A figure loomed over him, skin stretched too tight, limbs jerking in staccato bursts. Teeth clacked as if tasting the air. The man screamed, a raw, ragged note. Two more figures joined in—too fast to see.

Several monstrous formations were tearing through a dark crimson trash bag, spilling debris everywhere.

Not a trash bag!

Buzzing tubes flickered a horror-house extravaganza, and shadows split and merged like living ink. The lobby had become a grotesque omnium-gatherum: polished marble bruised, shards of glass flying, bodies in motion, faces ripped, screaming, slipping in black smoke. Yet through it all, "Spanish Flea" continued, brightly upbeat, mocking the carnage as if the world had always been this cruelly musical.

Henry fled, hugging the wall, dodging an artsy ornament table, the lobby directory, a sun-shaped mirror—then stumbled hard and fell into an open elevator. He cowered inside, shock taking hold, the panel just out of reach.

The doors stayed open too long. From the threshold, he watched panic collapse into slaughter. The flickering bulbs made the scene strobe—a man falling, rising as something else; two residents slamming into the glass doors, only for them to shatter inward; a dozen writhing bodies twisting and changing, the contagion spreading in seconds.

His eyes darting everywhere—no escaping—and yet out of nowhere one horrendous figure now appeared in a most bizarre posture moving toward Henry. At first a blur. Then he saw its face.

It was female. But deeply off—in a way that mattered.

Her jaw stretched wider than it should have, as if her skull had melted and been reshaped. Her cheeks peeled outward, skin thinning, veins like spiderwebs visible beneath a translucent, yellowing membrane. Her eyes rolled up, then snapped open—pupils enflamed, burning into Henry like molten metal. Hair, once dark, seemed to liquefy; strands slipped from the scalp like black ink running down porcelain. Blood dribbled across her crown, framing the monstrous grin that stretched across her widening mouth, until her lips twitched as though they'd forgotten where to stop. Her complexion shifted through hues—pale, gray, greenish—flashing in the harsh, fractured glow above. Squiggling lines swam under her skin like worms of fire on dying ember.

He had seen enough horror movies. Now he knew, they never got it right—not like this—not the way he was seeing it, face to morphing face. This was real. The nightmare that he'd always woken up from as a child, mercifully, before its final, graphic reveal, now it was out, now it was real. And he couldn't wake up.

And she was wearing red pumps. Clumsily, unbalanced, each step sliding on the marble tiles. The *click-clack* of heels against the floor was a grotesque punctuation to the horror, a human echo in a body that was no longer human. And perhaps those heels—he would speculate on for days afterward—were what kept it from leaping straight into him with thrashing claws, tearing him apart with those evolving cuspids—chalicerae—snake fangs, whatever they were, whatever name his panicked brain couldn't reach. Not then. Not until therapy—when therapy came in writing much later.

She twisted forward in a diving torso motion, arms outstretched, wielding, one leg arched across the line that reopened the closing doors.

"Hold the elevator!"

Henry's stomach dropped.

"Fudduh-puh-gah!" came out first—instantly, weirdly—and was overtaken by an ungodly belch of fright. Of all the mind-searing, horrific moments to be overtaken by a burp, this had to be it.

The creature jerked back, nostrils flaring. The sour burst of wine on his breath seemed to burn her, the lights above sizzling her skin. Her eyes bubbled, wet and white-hot, and she shrieked, retreating but not retreating, her right heel caught, preventing her. Caught in the platform-to-hoistway clearance. While the other shoe tapped incessantly on the landing sill.

And the doors kept closing, opening.

Henry had time to assess his attacker, from which nothing helpful was gained. Beyond her, the rest of the lobby and atrium became fever-dream unreal. Victims shook violently, their faces twisting, bodies morphing in seconds. Henry caught flashes: a man's face contorting, a woman's nails splitting into claws, eyes bulging and rolling, hair dripping with crimson. Every transformation was too fast, too grotesque, too impossible—reality warped in strobe-lit fragments. Some were turning, looking in the direction of the elevator.

As this she-creature seemed to find forward motion again and leaned in to get to Henry, Henry pivoted on a cramping-leg pirouette and threw a right kick up at her, which sent his slipper flying off, over her shoulder and into the lobby.

Henry gasped, unable to scream, his right foot's sock caught on the middle fang of her lower set, wedged between his toes. Her drool, icy and thick, soaked through.

The music changed overhead. Barry White and the Love Unlimited Orchestra presented "Love's Theme."

The sweeping, sultry strings and funky wah-wah plucking filled the car, a smooth balm against the raw, strobing nightmare. But the she-creature wasn't deterred. Her arms thrashed, claws screeching across the polished walls as she fought to keep balance, jaw dropping as Henry's leg pulled. One stretched fingernail ripped into the inner thigh fabric of his khaki shorts and pricked his flesh.

Right sock remaining hopelessly hooked, Henry yelped, tried to jerk free—the sudden tug pitched him backward into the side wall near the panel. In a reflex, he banged at the buttons. Nothing lit. She tumbled in, oddly spinning, her mutated foot kicking the red pump out into the lobby. She fell against the wall opposite Henry, head down, twitching, confused by her own contortion. The elevator doors closed. A slight mechanical bounce and it started upward with a shudder.

She twisted out of her head-down position, her disjointed arm bent on her grip of the handrail beside her. Pulling herself up midway, she turned, a headlong and tilted gaze finding Henry as he backed up the wall. She staggered on her one remaining red heel, hissing a garbled code of vocal nonsense. Then, with a grotesque, head-first lunge, she collided with his stomach.

Air whooshed from Henry's lungs. As he sank into a squat, his hands scrambled against her torso to push her away. Her hot skin peeled and clung to his palms.

He struck the back of her head with his fists. She dropped to a crouching position between his knees, snarling. Her fangs glinted an inch from his thigh.

Instinct took over. Henry kneed her throat. She reeled, clawing blindly—and somehow hooked his khaki shorts at the waistband, ripping and yanking them down as she fell away. Henry tumbled forward onto his knees, then scrambled to regain footing.

She had a sudden advantage over him, rising up faster.

The elevator jerked violently, then halted. She scrambled, frantic, teetering on her single heel. The doors slid open just as her balance gave way. With a screech, she toppled out into the second-floor hallway, rolling across the carpet like a rag-doll. The red pump was off.

The doors hung open, letting Henry watch the creature untwist and turn.

BLAM! Her head burst below the scalp where the bullet hit.

Henry gasped, sliding to the floor, shorts hanging from his knees. He couldn't tell what was real anymore—but the gunshot split everything back into focus.

A large silhouette stepped between the doors, gun leveled, deep voice rolling like thunder: "You one o' dem craze maderafockuhs?!"

Henry jerked upright—yanking his shorts to the catch, hands flying up.

"Whoa!" His voice pitched soprano. "As a matter of *foct*—No!"

The shorts dropped again.

"Not yet!"

The imposing burly figure in coveralls turned to the panel and fobbed for the lowest level—P2.

"You come wit me! We get de blor-dee hair out, abeg!"

The doors closed. Henry yanked his shorts up again and realized the clasp was gone.

The music kept playing.

The elevator hummed downward. Henry's heart wouldn't slow.

When the doors opened to P2, the air exhaled heat and motor oil —the breath of a sleeping machine. The scream-filled throat of the building chased them out as the burly Nigerian led Henry through a grid of dim lights revealing a sparse scatter of parked vehicles.

"A lotta peepo out."

"I should've been out, too."

Crossing this concrete catacomb, Henry noticed the big man's shambling gait—a reflexive tilt to spare his right hip—while Henry, wearing two black socks and one left slipper, limped harder from a cramp in his foot. Imani was sweating profusely, a burdened man who wanted to run but was already spent.

"You're the maintenance man?" Henry asked.

The Nigerian glanced at Henry, then pulled his set of keys from a pocket. His dark-brown thumb found the keyless remote. A beat-up white Chevy Silverado truck, single-cab, back-parked in the corner of the turning bay, flashed headlights with a light chirp and heavy clicks in unison.

"You — you dat penthouse ma-han."

"Henry. Gorestriker."

"Hen-aree." The big man nodded, catching his breath. "Imani. Adeyemi."

They opened each side door and climbed in.

"What da hair, Hen-aree?"

"I don't know."

Imani's chest heaved as he spoke, voice low and shaken. "I come in lobby when da pahwer go out. Aw dahk, sai-lent. Den I hear dem—craze creachus—pushin' da glass, comin' inside. Eh run fuh de stair." He wiped sweat from his brow with an unsteady hand. "Two o' dem see me, fo-loh. Come in de door before it uh close. Eh reach de second floor. Den—de gen-uh-ray-tuh kick on." He snapped his fingers sharply. "Light flick, come back. I look-ted down—dey stand dere, bottom step. More o' dem, in de door open. Jus' lookin' up, ah tweested. Try figyuh how to move, like dey fuhget how leg wuck. Den dey hiss, tuhn back. Back to lobby. Skehd de sheet out o' me. Eh fuhget ad may gon. Me shoko."

"I'm glad you remembered."

Imani let out a short laugh that wasn't humor. "So skehd I swallo my a-kscent."

Henry stared through him, still half-petrified. "Maybe they can't," he said about the stairs, though the thought didn't comfort him. "I hope you're right." The gears turned slow in his head. A moment later: "A-ha! Funny."

Sitting gave each man a moment's reprieve. Imani cranked the ignition—engine roaring awake, speakers popping as cranked-up Sting crooned "Heavy Cloud No Rain."

At once, Henry felt a claustrophobic fear tightening around him—a cinching, like the seatbelt webbing had turned to muscle and coil, a boa constrictor testing for pulse.

"This—cloud?"

The truck jolted forward, gears whining.

"Hen-aree. Gore-streaker." Imani's thick fingers turned down the volume.

"Yeah." Henry sparked. The fake smile fell. "Uh-Money Ah-de-yummy."

The truck revved and started up the incline to P1.

Henry didn't notice Imani's tears until the big man blurted with laughter: "Yummy man, dat me!"

Rubber shrieked against concrete as he took the next incline hard, barely braking.

The truck's engine rattled like a dying air conditioner as it climbed the ramp toward the garage exit, slowing. Henry kept both hands gripping the dashboard, feeling every vibration through his palms. Imani's breath came loud and ragged beside him, the kind of exhausted panting that sounds half human, half mechanical. The big man's eyes were wild—glazed with panic and determination.

Ahead, the gate lifted slowly, links clattering on the spool above. Beyond it, faint mist, a blue-gray smear of citylight against the concrete mouth.

Then—a cry.

"Help! Help us!"

Both men snapped their heads.

A woman, in tattered, stained blouse and trousers, stumbled into view from the left, clutching a small boy in pajamas—three, maybe four—his blond hair matted to his forehead. Henry recognized him.

"Are we going to die?"

Her voice cracked, echoing off the walls. "Please! Please help!"

Imani's reaction was immediate—he raised the 9mm pistol.

The woman gasped, eyes locking on the gun, and her legs gave way. The child clung to her waist as she sagged backward.

"Ah, no—no, no," Imani muttered, lowering the weapon, aghast at his own action. He shoved it toward Henry. "Hold dis!"

"What?"

"Hold am, I say!"

Before Henry could respond, Imani had already flung his door open and lumbered out, boots scraping concrete. He caught the falling woman just before her head struck the floor, her son still wrapped around her.

Henry climbed out on the other side, a tight fist sustaining his britches, the other hand holding the gun by its barrel, unsure whether to point it, drop it, or pray with it.

Imani was sweating, trembling—a bull on the verge of collapse. His coveralls were soaked through the chest, his breath shallow and staccato. "Put dem—put dem inside," he rasped. "We go now!"

Henry looked at the truck's cab—the single seat, the cramped interior.

A pause. Henry and Imani locked eyes. They both knew it.

Henry pulled his socks and slipper off, set the gun down by his fallen trunks, stepped out and bent to help lift the boy. "Okay, okay. You want to wait for me?" he said, trying to sound practical, sane. "I can go get my car key and follow you out."

Imani's eyes darted toward the exit gate, then back at Henry. He was shaking his head, but not in disagreement—in disbelief, like a man underwater trying to remember which way is up.

"Okay? You'll wait?" Henry said.

"I wait," Imani said finally.

After setting the boy inside, Henry stepped back to help Imani with the unconscious woman. He noticed her pale skin was aquiver, flecks of blood caught in the curls of her sandy-blonde hair.

Henry almost forgot the penthouse keys in his crumpled shorts—a small ring of one card, one fob, and two keys he carried often, unlike the car key fob, which was more of a pet rock in Manhattan. He fished them out quickly, turned for the elevator, then hesitated. "What if I get stuck?"

"Huh? Hold your breeches." Imani fastened the mother and child in. "G-Gen-uh-ray-tuh pahwered by gas—run forev-ah. Go."

Henry nodded, hesitating just long enough to glance at the woman and boy huddled in the passenger seat—then limped into a run toward the farther express elevator, cramp loosening with each step. His feet slapped the concrete, then across one sunken drainage grate he never saw—its dipped edge catching his toe, yanking it hard, snapping his stride and almost pitching him into the shadows ahead.

The doors opened easily, the button light humming with a faint orange glow.

Welcoming his moaning return, Chuck Mangione sounded joy in performance:

"Feels So Good."

He stepped inside, scanned the key card, and waited.

The ride up felt like being held inside a giant's lung. Each breath echoed off the walls. When the doors opened at the penthouse level, he ran to his unit, keys rattling in his hand. Or was that his nerves flossing his teeth?

Inside the apartment, Henry jerked a pair of snug sweatpants on and pocketed the keys. One key teethed him through the warm fabric, and for a second he thought it might be sucking blood.

The city lay dark and distant through the windows. Beyond the balcony, a distant helicopter was spinning out of control over New York Harbor—a flicker of light, a whirling insect—until it clipped Lady Liberty's torch and burst into flames.

Refusing to believe what he'd seen, Henry shoved his cold bare feet into running shoes, grabbed the car fob off the counter, and hunted down his phone.

He took one last look at the room.

Then he bolted—back to the dreaded boxed-in descent.

No time for stairs. Gotta keep it cool.

The elevator's descent seemed slower now, as if the car resisted returning to hell.

"Let's forget this crisis, shall we, and focus on the breezy-disco optimism I'm providing for you."

Oh yes, please.

But as the descent passed the lobby, and though the human screams beyond had ceased, the strange gurgling noises still leaking through the doors nearly stopped his heart.

When the doors parted again, the point of arrival echoed emptiness.

The truck was gone.

"Eh-Money!"

Henry stepped out. The air felt heavier—disagreeable. The gate was closed.

He jogged toward it, heart drumming. Near the yellow-striped bollard before the exit ramp lay the gun—shorts, slipper, socks, right where he'd left them. He picked them up and turned a slow circle. No sign of Imani, the woman, or the child. Just echo and concrete.

Something crunched underfoot. He looked down, then stepped back quickly. Imani's master fob. He stared at it for a beat, then bent, picked it up, and shoved it into his pocket.

Wherever he was, he wasn't coming back.

Henry's car waited nearby: a silver Mazda MX-5 Miata RF, forgotten beneath hardtop dust and fluorescent haze. He unlocked it, slid behind the wheel, tossed the bundle onto the passenger seat, and started the engine. The sound was deafening in the emptiness.

As the roadster approached the ramp, Henry slowed to a crawl—didn't want to stop unless the gate was too slow lifting. The coiling grille groaned and clinked, mechanical yet panicked—a faintly absurd soundtrack to his trepidation.

And the kind of high-speed efficiency we've all come to expect.

And that was when he saw them.

Shapes spilling from the darkness beyond the gate—bent, jerking, gathering speed. Their limbs found rhythm as they converged. Eyes flashed like wet pearls in the fluorescent vapors.

Henry got snagged in the reel. Pulse detonating in his ears, courage clotted in his spine.

Instinct seized the wheel. He slammed the Miata into reverse.

The tires screamed, fishtailed—

BAM!—the rear end of the Miata shrieked against the concrete bollard, the rear of the car giving way with a metallic crunch. The impact sent a violent jolt through the car's frame, but the seatbelts instantly went taut, holding him back from the steering wheel. A moment later, they gave a little, releasing some of the pressure as his body was whipped back and forth. The horn blared under the force of his palms, and though he was still rattled and his neck was screaming, a cold certainty settled over him: the car had taken the worst of it.

A shriek tore through the dark. At first Henry thought it was his.

A tall, crooked shape stumbled forward on the ramp and landed on the hood with a thud that buckled aluminum. The windshield starred, spider-webbing under the creature's weight.

Henry screamed, in pain and fear, as if waking up mid-beheading.

He reached for the gun, came up with the shoe instead, and clutched it awkwardly while fumbling for the weapon.

He flung the door open, gun and shoe in hand, and stumbled out, running. Behind him, the thing on the hood began to crawl—its segmented, reptilian fingers pulsing as they tapped the cracked glass, like impatient knuckles on a coffin lid.

The gate chains rattled violently as the first of the others slammed against it.

Henry's next scream began low in his throat—a dry gasp—and grew, rising with each footfall pounding toward the elevator. His neck muscles inflamed, his throat burning, Henry's vision blurred with tears, and his right shoe slid on grease, nearly tripping him.

He stopped short of a brutal collision with concrete at the elevator landing. This wasn't the express elevator.

Henry hit the call button again and again, smacking it with his slipper, the gun clutched backward like a useless toy in his other hand.

The creatures were spilling through the gate now, their bodies jerking forward under the dying fluorescent light. Their slow-burning flesh became a thickening fog that crept over them and along the floor.

The elevator doors opened halfway.

Henry dove inside, hand yanking his pocket out—keys spilling, clattering over the granite tile. He bumped his head bending, roared, snatched the keys and master fob, and lunged forward with a fencer's spring, thrusting it at the reader. "See how protected I am!" Then he hit a button—or a few—anything—and fell back, just as the first few monstrous shapes reached the edge of the landing.

The doors inched inward.

A looming shadow emerged through wisps of smoke, a gnarled hand of death, jittery and deformed, zeroing in faster than seemed logical, brushing the seam as the doors closed—just as Henry's scream hit its full pitch.

Beneath his own impossibly high squawk, Henry heard it clearly—the song from the ceiling speaker, warm honey dripping through the panic. "Manhattan Serenade." Nostalgic. Elegant. Playing beautifully. The orchestra swelled; strings rippled like water on a summer night. The brass section sighed.

The elevator began to rise, smooth and slow, carrying him upward through the echo of his own terror. Outside the shaft, something pounded against the steel. Horrendous bird-calls shrieked below. Inside, the music played on—Manhattan's love song to itself.

DING!

Henry, one fistful punching his pocket, the other hand pressed to his head, blinked at the glowing public-access button he'd blindly selected, just as the doors slid open onto the darkened lobby.

The rectangular spill of light stretched open across the polished stones—and there, in its center, sat his right slipper, strangely patient.

Beside it, the red pump lay on its side, seemingly bored to death.

Carnage lay strewn beneath the steadily increasing glow of the lobby lights, as the last of the creatures escaped the building to find more darkness. One regrettable glance up was too much, and Henry dropped his focus immediately to the rectangular light.

Stay with the slipper. Don't lose it. Don't lose your mind.

Henry swallowed hard, stepped out, quickly snatched his stray slipper, and ran like an out-of-shape fullback for the express elevator.

It arrived almost instantly, which felt like forever.

Tumbling in, he scanned his key card while thumb-riveting the CLOSE button, almost breaking it.

The whisper of faraway laughter cut off in the seal, and the car began its ascent.

20

Henry crouched low beneath the broken ticket booth window and listened.

Nothing but the low thrum of distant wind and the familiar, soft ticking in his own head—the sound of not thinking too hard.

He adjusted the rubber Viking helmet clinging to his scalp, plucked a popcorn fragment from his beard, and ate it. He chewed fast, like a rat.

Leather belt snug at his waist, gun in holster pressed to his hip—he still wasn't sure if it was right, but at least it made him feel official, like a secret agent with no security clearance.

The device was an Italian-made "Backboss," a niche piece of gear he'd salvaged a few days ago.

He hoisted the small gas generator strapped to his back and, shifting the weight of the black bag in his right hand, crept inside the lobby of the Regal Olympus, once a twelve-screen multiplex and now a mausoleum of sticky carpets, collapsed posters, and things that stirred when you didn't look too closely.

The front windows let in clean sheets of daylight—sunlight strong enough to make the floor sparkle with glass dust. Henry moved through it carefully, reverently, like a man in a church he once hated but now missed. He remembered fighting with a teenager here over whether *Inception* needed a sequel. That had been... how many years ago? Or yesterday? Time was rude these days.

The manager's office sat just to the right of the main lobby, its door slightly ajar. Henry nudged it open with his foot and stepped inside.

Empty. Good.

A faded corkboard hung crooked on the far wall, plastered with outdated shift schedules and a yellowing "Employee of the Month" photo featuring a kid with braces and dead eyes. A drawer yielded a heavy key ring labeled "PROJ," its laminated tag curling at the edges. Henry smiled.

Back in the day, projectors ran on servers, computers, automation. Now? Wires, lightbulbs, gasoline—and luck.

He slipped into the hallway behind the concession stand, unlocked and opened the employees-only access, and took the stairs up to the projection level. His blue high-tops made soft chuffing noises on the rubber steps. From below, he heard something shift in one of the theaters—something soft and moist dragging across carpet. He didn't stop.

The projection hallway smelled like burnt plastic and old popcorn oil. One door was labeled THEATER 7: LOCKED. Henry knelt, found the right key, and slipped it into the lock. The click echoed like a gunshot.

He waited.

Nothing came.

Inside, the projection booth was untouched since the world had ended. A chair, some spools of sticky film, half a roll of duct tape, and the old Christie projector—more dust than machine now, but it would do.

Henry set the generator down in the hallway like a newborn and knelt beside it. He pulled the coiled orange extension cord from the black bag and plugged it into the generator. A faint smell of gasoline drifted up, sharp and acrid. He inhaled carefully—no use getting woozy now—and fed the extension cord through the open doorway.

He uncoiled the rest of the cord to the projector, mated it to the power cable, then returned to the generator. The scent of gas hung in the air, tugging slightly at the edges of his concentration. He gave the starter cord a look of uncertainty and firmly gripped the handle.

"You better not embarrass me."

He yanked.

Nothing.

He yanked again.

The machine coughed, sputtered—then caught with a low, grumbling *brrrrrrrmmmm*. It got louder at once. The smell of gasoline sharpened, but Henry pushed the discomfort aside. He went back and watched the bulb warm.

Then he waited.

He figured he could survive for probably twenty minutes, but five to ten minutes was all he needed.

From this vantage, he couldn't see the auditorium below—but he didn't need to. He knew what was down there.

They liked the dark. Loved it, even. Like rats, mold, and failed relationships.

The projector screen in Theater 7 flared to life with a sudden, brilliant blast of white.

It began almost instantly.

Below, in the auditorium, there was a wet rustling. Not one sound, but dozens. Maybe hundreds. Shifting bodies. A low, irritated hiss—*like someone waking up to find the coffin wasn't closed.*

The creatures scrambled. He could hear them clawing over seats, pushing past each other, shrieking in that bone-dry way they did when their comfort was disturbed.

He imagined them recoiling from the white heat of the screen like cockroaches when the kitchen light flips on. He imagined long limbs shielding eyeless faces, gnarled fingers pressed to skulls, whispering something that wasn't words but still somehow meant *Why?*

Henry leaned against the doorway, eyes on the glow.

A second later, a film reel spun up and began playing—*The Good, the Bad, and the Ugly*, because Henry had standards. Ennio Morricone's score leaked into the upper vent and dripped down into the room like golden acid, barely heard under the generator's rumble.

"Things couldn't get uglier. And Bad? It's never been worse." He smiled faintly. "But today—today Good is coming to town."

Henry chuckled and coughed.

"Don't like the classics, huh?"

He watched for a minute longer, letting the reel run and the smoke accumulate. It didn't matter that no one was watching the film. What mattered was the light, the rhythm of it, the disruption of their peace.

A kind of revenge.

He leaned back against the wall, listening to the chaos below, and let himself smile—a real smile, toothy and strange on his face. Then he coughed again, a flicker of dizziness catching him off guard.

"You're welcome, Clint."

They swarmed the aisles, pushing their way through the back exits, scattering to other auditoriums. Their shrieks echoed like a warped orchestra tuning up too fast.

Henry leaned against the window frame, basking in the panic like it was sunlight.

"This one's for the critics," he said.

With a sigh, he started to pull away when something down below caught his eye. Even Clint was squinting at it in disbelief.

A shape. Not moving.

Henry stared harder. One of them—impossibly still—sat alone in the middle row.

Not fleeing.

Not shrieking.

Just sitting. Watching.

Its posture was perplexing. Human. Shoulders low, arms resting at its sides like it had forgotten to be afraid.

Henry stared, eyes widening, as the image blurred.

The creature didn't move. Didn't flinch or blink. Just kept its face toward the flickering screen, eyes glinting with a quiet, terrible calm. Sizzling, smoking, disintegrating.

Henry's skin prickled.

Panicky, without a word, Henry stepped away from the window, gathered the extension cord and bag, and left the projection booth. Picking up his pace now, he reached the machine on weak knees, stumbling; he killed the generator and hoisted it up. His hand caught his throat.

He didn't remember breathing again until he stepped into the lobby's sunlight.

Outside, the heat clung to him the way the rubber Viking helmet clung to his forehead—tight, sweaty, ridiculous. His unkempt beard itched along his jaw as he shifted the generator on his back, the straps digging into his shoulders. He stared across the silent plaza, half expecting something to lunge from behind the ticket kiosks, and scratched his beard like a dog after a flea. His eyes uncrossed and he felt his body working up to deep breaths again.

Nothing else moved. Nothing else breathed.

Instead, waiting at the curb as if it had rolled out to greet him, was the old ice-cream trike—three wheels, dusty cooler compartment up front, its cartoon decals faded to ghost-pastels. One of the handlebars was wrapped in brown medical tape. The whole thing looked like the city had coughed it up for him, like a consolation prize for surviving another hour. At the moment, he couldn't remember where he'd come across it before.

"Perfect," he muttered. "My noble steed." He tried to bow but the generator threw him off balance.

He set the unit down with a heavy clunk, exhaling. The weight leaving his back made him sway for a moment. He unbuckled the gun belt next, pausing at the absurdity of the holstered revolver paired with the toy-store Viking horns.

"Alright," he said softly, "let's not scare the ice-cream crowd."

He stowed the belt and revolver inside the front cooler, beside a small stack of library books (a Shakespeare omnibus, a dictionary of slang, a poetry anthology); a bottle of sweet Moscato; a week's worth of thawed Lean Cuisine meals; and an assortment of magazines and comic books. He closed the lid and placed the small generator on top, where it always rode.

Wait, what else was there? What was the other thing I wanted to get?

Oh, yes, a laptop.

Henry took his ready-to-roll position on the seat and gripped the handlebars. The pedals resisted at first but loosened with steady pressure.

He was about to push off on the trike when he stopped.

Someone—a slender, feminine figure—stood at the far intersection. Watching him?

The perplexed king of balderdash leered, lifting a hand to shade his eyes, though the Viking helmet's horns made the gesture awkward. Heat haze distorted everything past a block, turning the figure into a wavering cutout, like a cardboard standee left out too long in the sun. She didn't move. Or maybe she was moving so slightly he couldn't be sure.

He leaned forward on the trike, his beard brushing his collar. Weeks of growth. Weeks of riding this same ice-cream trike up and down these streets, hauling home whatever scraps of civilization he could find. Weeks without seeing another person—alive or otherwise—standing still like that, head tilted, posture calm, almost… curious.

"Hey!" he called. His voice cracked. He cleared his throat and tried again. "Hey!"

The figure shifted. It wasn't a startle or a flinch—more like she simply stepped out of the line of sight, as if turning a corner on an errand she'd meant to run anyway.

Henry waited. Pedals still. Breath held.

Nothing.

"Right," he murmured, rubbing at his beard. "Okay. Not ominous at all."

He pushed down on the pedals, slow at first, letting the ice-cream trike roll forward with its familiar wobble. The generator rattled gently on the cooler. The stack of books thunked against the wine bottle. The whole contraption sounded like his life normally did—unsteady, improvised, noisy enough to make him feel like something real still existed.

His horns bobbed as he picked up speed.

He glanced once more toward the intersection.

Empty.

As he pedaled into the street, a gust of warm wind pushed dust down the empty avenue, erasing any trace that someone had been standing there at all.

Henry swallowed.

"Great," he muttered. "Now I'm seeing ghosts in broad daylight."

He didn't look back again.

CUT TO:

The echoing clatter of rubber wheels on marble.

Henry guided a battered luggage cart across the Fontaine's lobby, the sound bouncing off the dark, high-ceilinged cavern like a ghost of its former luxury. The cart was stacked with his scavenged haul: the small generator balanced on top of the cooler, the week's worth of thawed Lean Cuisines shifting in their cracked plastic trays, the wine bottle wrapped in a pair of shirts to keep it from shattering, the books and magazines layered like bricks on a wall he kept rebuilding.

He pushed the cart toward the express elevator. Its tarnished doors parted with a reluctant— Ding!

Henry rolled the cart inside, straightened the load, and scanned for the penthouse.

Without hesitation, he stepped back out.

The doors slid shut, and up and away his cargo went. Henry waited until the hum of the machinery settled back into silence. Forty floors. He'd climb them, like always. The trike was chained outside to the Fontaine's dedicated bike rack near the fountain.

The city was quiet again.

Was there something he'd forgotten?

He wiped sweat from beneath the Viking helmet, the rubber sticking to his forehead.

Only as he set his foot on the first step did the thought return—unwanted, persistent:

Who was she?

He shook his head and kept climbing.

"Jogging"

by Henry Gorestriker

Jogging in the heat, feeling beat and defeated.

A neighborhood of dead eyes passing,

On the sunny street I'm searching,

Kick— push— keeping feet behind me

Down this dislocated path.

Faster moving, sweating, gasping,

Choking as my lungs collapse,

Inhaling and exhaling,

Anxious sprinting, vision fogging,

Wrought and taut from heat, and ending,

Melting now, and slowly dying,

To this neverending jogging.

19

The afternoon sun hit the awning like a slow leak of aureate light, pooling in a soft wash over the faded red letters: THE CRACK-UP COMEDY CLUB. There was a time that red had meant neon, and the letters had buzzed like the city's heartbeat. Now the paint just flaked away under all that tender gold, like the place was trying to remember itself and couldn't quite manage it.

No wind. No traffic. Only the low hum of a generator somewhere beneath the street.

Henry approached with the mirror tucked under his arm—a bar-restroom classic, rectangular, streaked, smelling faintly of disinfectant and defeat. *Defeat and de hand-prints.* He carried it like something sacred, and maybe it was.

He opened the door, the sound of the latch echoing down the empty block. The air inside met him in a stale wave: mildew, burnt dust, old fryer grease. He bolted the door behind him, out of habit more than safety.

Down the black steps, the light thinned, replaced by that faint yellow haze leaking up from the sub-level.

The hum of the generator grew louder.

He descended slowly, Chelsea boots crunching the grit on each step. At the bottom, he stood facing the room—the same room where he had collapsed weeks earlier. Only now, he'd made small changes: cleared tables to create a single aisle; moved the stool to center stage; ran cables to an area backstage where the generator sat in a tangle of extension cords; positioned several potted plants to form a protective wall around his stage-lit circle of life.

He'd stayed this course, focused, and felt mentally stronger for it. Days of jotting down ideas, planning, studying the building, gathering supplies, slowly constructing.

The mirror went up next—against the wall, angled slightly toward the stage. He took a step back and studied it, then adjusted the stool by inches until it sat directly under the brightest of the three spotlights. He turned on the lamps, then one by one, killed the rest of the lights in the room, until only the stage glowed.

A single white orb.

His new domain.

His throne.

Of course, a king has to earn it, of course, of course.

He looked at his reflection in the mirror—face drawn, eyes rimmed red, a beard that had lost all sense of proportion. He mouthed a few words to himself, testing expressions. A grin that didn't fit. A wink that didn't land. The bearded king of balderdash. Older now, feeling tired, but not done.

He whispered, "Boundaries. Always know your boundaries."

The stool's legs squeaked as he nudged it forward. He knelt near the edge of the stage, where a thick black cable ran into a box just beneath the lip. He tested a switch with his boot—once, twice. The faint click satisfied him. He affixed the stage skirt. Neatly pressed. No wrinkles.

Then he crossed to the generator, topped it off with the last of his scavenged fuel, and pulled the cord. The engine coughed, then steadied into a low growl.

He checked the bulbs. All working.

The stage lights burned hard, pushing back the shadows.

He walked to the back of the club, where sunlight peeked faintly through a half-buried sidewalk window of frosted glass. He slid the metal cover into place, sealing off the narrow suggestion of daylight. The room settled back into half-night.

He stood there in the silence for a long moment. Then:

"Now I just need material," he said softly.

INT. PENTHOUSE – NIGHT

Henry pulled up to the table and leaned over the blank page staring back at him.

"Mind racing at the Indy 500. I need a quiet country road, away from it all."

Not a diary. Material. Just fragments of memory, nonsense, and whatever else spilled out.

The pen kept tapping on his noggin, like it knew something helpful it wanted to share.

Henry took a breath, staring at the pool of white paper, as the pen dived in.

"I'll just start writing gibberish, until my fingers hurt. Or something clicks. I want this to be good. I want to enjoy whatever happens. I want to die laughing."

I was awakened from what I might have mistakenly assumed was a nap—but, given this— what do you call it?—apocalyptic space-cloud coming down…

…Either way, I was on the fortieth floor of The Fontaine Residences, which sounds luxurious until you realize you won't be using the elevator (and I haven't done cardio since, oh, the Bush administration)…

…Bodies roam the streets at night, hunched and twitchy, like meth-addicted ballerinas in a Tim Burton fever dream. Their eyes glow faintly, their skin is—well, somewhere between "decomposed" and "enthusiastically exfoliated," and they move like they are auditioning for a horror-themed TikTok dance…

Henry removed his glasses, rubbed his eyes, and sighed resignedly. "Is this me?"

...which I later deduced with my great deducing mind must have most certainly been the critical inspiration for the phantasmagoric catastrophe of a city gone bad. Maybe I was in a coma. Or maybe a really weird acid trip—LSD-laced Redenbacher popcorn, perhaps? Or dreaming in a metaphor, the kind they use in arthouse films where the character sleeps while society collapses—meant to signify man's ignorance, or his gluten intolerance. In my case: overindulgence in unearned luxury...

Henry paused, reading back. "I sound like a Harvard professor... losing his mind."

...I'd never seen a space-cloud before. Well, Dennis Weaver, as McCloud, riding the horse through Times Square—that was... kind of out-there...

...This thing beyond my balcony, above the skyline, clawing and spreading—above and beyond the effort to find words to describe it...

Henry swirled the wine in his glass.

…This cloud—black, twisting, swirling like a salad spinner filled with alien squid ink, churning undigested macrocosm and space cheese...

…waiting for Rod Serling—black suit, tie, cigarette, creased brow, dark stress lines tight on his teeth-clenched grimace—to open the door and show me the way out of here. He probably dropped the keys in the Twilight Zone...

The pen tapped lightly against the table. Maybe staring long enough would make sense. Maybe not.

...Even in reflection, I can't quite shake the absurdity. The cloud, the screams, the creatures, the bricks, the protocol—I survived all of it.

And yet, it feels like the punchline I can't fully hear, the joke I'm too exhausted to deliver. Or maybe it's a joke only I am allowed to tell...

Henry drummed the pen on the page. The words weren't moving fast enough. The glass made a small clink as he set it down. He blew out a frustrated breath.

...and as Chief Wahoo leaned over the campfire, stars resting in his eagle eyes, about to say something profound—the alarm blasts me awake, pulling me out of it...

...I've seen a couple of them on rooftops? That isn't even possible. They don't climb...

...It was unnervingly loud, drowning out the dissonant horn effects on the TV. Even Heston concurred, screaming, "It's a madhouse!" The noise itself was impossible to ignore, but in retrospect, it was also absurdly ridiculous. A fire alarm. Forty floors up. Maybe no fire at all,

just chaos punctuated by bureaucracy. Yet it felt like an artillery strike. My pulse still remembers it...

Henry leaned back and closed his eyes, meditatively. "This might be helping."

...And I, Henry Gorestriker, the last surviving man—with questionable cardio, a crate of sodas and a basket of apples, and an unfinished screenplay about a talking cat learning the ninth meaning of life...

...But let's not rush past the real tragedy: there are no bagels left in Manhattan. None. I'd kill for a sesame. Possibly with garlic, just to be safe...

"Okay. I feel like I'm dying, but I'm not laughing."

...You don't climb! What the hell was that?...

...shouldn't be forgotten. And yet—just erased. A memory. Not helping me...

...And maybe that's enough...

...Maybe this is all a test, and the walls will open, and—and you guys can come out now! I've worked all night on this, at least give me a passing grade, I don't care how bad, just let me graduate! Please!...

Henry dropped the pen and rubbed his sore fingers.

...Now, I sit here, writing, recounting it all—piecing it together from memory, from instinct, from scarred synapses that refuse to let me forget. The fire alarm. The balcony. The elevator. The lobby. Milestones. In the narrative I keep telling myself.
I survived. I am here. Somehow...

...This is it. My moment. Humanity's final stand. A stand-up routine. Tonight, we die laughing—

INT. CRACK-UP COMEDY CLUB – NIGHT

The generator throbbed in the dark, rhythmic and almost human. The air was thick and restless.

Henry stepped through the curtain, notes trembling in one hand, Glock in the other. He placed the gun slowly in his holster and sat hesitantly upon the stool's seat, pages trembling in his fingers. He stared out into the black. Nothing.

Then—faint shifting. Wet friction on the floor. A hiss from somewhere near the back wall. The creatures had come. Darker shapes pooled at the far edges, clinging to the corners, refusing to resolve into anything distinguishable even as his eyes acclimated to the room's murk.

He cleared his throat.

"Well," he said, voice small, cracking, a man in the spotlight, awaiting execution. His eyes didn't blink; they couldn't. The light baked his face, drying sweat before it could fall.

Something in the dark shifted its weight. Tables creaked softly, wood expanding, contracting under invisible hands.

The black around him seemed to breathe back.

A guttural rasp somewhere in the dark.

Henry's laugh was nervous, high-pitched.

He saw it then: movement just beyond the light's reach. A shadow slumbering, folding in on itself, then stretching. Limbs—or what passed for them—dragged the floor. Claws traced slow circles along the boards, testing the perimeter, recoiling the instant the light brushed them.

A hiss answered from another side. Then another. A low chorus, reptilian and restless.

Henry's jaw vibrated. The paper in his hand quivered so violently that the notes made a whispering sound, like tiny flags.

He waited. They waited.

His throat made a dry, involuntary sound, halfway between a gulp and a groan.

Then, finally, his voice—small, strangled, the next word a ghost leaving his mouth:

"Ooooh."

It hung there, stupid and human, in the cavernous dark. He forgot his words.

Nothing replied.

Then, a pulse of air—warm, rancid—blew from the shadows. Something big exhaled.

Henry finally shuddered.

His lips twitched, trying to shape calm.

He whispered again, louder this time, though his voice cracked down the middle:

"Tough crowd."

The room exploded.

A roar ripped through the dark—hideous, serrated, not one throat but many layered into a single shriek.

Henry flinched, nearly losing his footing. The mic stand rattled.

He lifted his notes like a shield.

The papers shook, caught the light, flashed white—then slipped from his fingers.

A few pages fluttered down the stage steps, vanishing into the black below.

For a moment, nothing.

Then the sound—paper tearing, shredded by unseen claws.

Henry stood, the empty stool cushion squeaking, and wrapped his hand around the Glock gleaming faintly on his side. His chest hitched once.

He whispered, barely audible:

"I—uh—for me."

He fumbled through his remaining pages, eyes darting up every few seconds. "So, uh, funny thing about loneliness." He paused, sweat coming down now, running into his mouth. "You start talking to yourself, then you start answering. Then you start losing arguments."

He waited. Silence.

He smiled, desperate.

Henry dared not step back. The light was a fence. Behind him: curtain. Beyond that: nothing he could reach without turning his back.

He could feel their eyes, dozens of them, boiling faintly behind translucent lids. Watching.

He lifted a shaking hand, as if to gesture to the invisible audience. His words crawled out through a dry throat:

"I've never felt more alive."

Something shifted near the bar. A low scrape, like claws on wood. Henry clamped up, throat to spine. Then forced a shaky grin.

A nervous laugh burst out of him — the kind that isn't laughter at all but panic given sound. He tried to turn it into a line, something practiced, something normal.

"Is this… is this how lobsters feel in the tank at the restaurant?"

He swallowed.

"You don't want to eat me. I'm high in cholesterol."

The silence that followed was ocean-deep.

Then came a low rumble—not laughter, not even anger—a collective shift, like meat dragging across tile.

Henry's eyes danced, his face twitching between terror and performative grin. He tried to steady his breathing, but it came out uneven, comical in its futility.

"I used to—uh—bomb a lot onstage."

Henry started laughing, an outburst he couldn't pull back in.

I've lost my mind.

A faint chittering answered him. Henry laughed too hard, his voice echoing weirdly through the room.

Finally, finding rhythm of speech again, while continually pulling tears of laughter off his face, he tried another bit, almost pleading:

"I—I read somewhere that laughter releases tension!" Henry closed his eyes, head tilted back, throat gurgling laughter and ecstatic moaning. He picked up the Glock and pressed the barrel against his mouth, trying to stifle the overspill of laughter. "You folks seem… tense! Maybe that's just your—uh—facial situation!"

Henry felt his gut hurting. Laughing out of control. A man about to be ripped apart.

Then came the shriek.

18

Henry climbed out of the bedroom closet.

His legs tingled from crouching all night.

He kept the pistol raised, both hands trembling under its weight. The weapon was still smudged with Imani's fingerprints; Henry hadn't dared clean it yet. He had no idea if the safety was on, no idea how to tell. His brain wasn't taking questions at the moment. Still—it felt fire-ready.

He ducked into the bathroom to give the porcelain a quick powerwash. That took forever. "Now streaming." He sighed, popped two aspirins, and moved on.

The bedroom was silent except for air whispering through a cracked window. Sunlight slanted across the bed in pale streaks that looked almost holy after the chaos of the night before. He studied the corners, the doorway, the closet again—checking and rechecking. Nothing moved.

He continued through the kitchen, the balcony, the pantry, the guest bedroom, the office. He unlocked the entry door and peeked out into the vestibule. No darkness. Sunlight was on patrol.

Back in the bedroom, he limped slightly to the side of the queen mattress and plopped down on the disheveled duvet. Dropped the firearm. Dropped the shoes. Checked the lightly bruised little toe of his left foot—slightly discolored, no pain.

"No more deformed than usual."

He wiggled all his toes, then got flashed by a thought of naked Teletubbies. He chuckled, which told him he wasn't quite ready to face reality.

Madness doesn't come with a script, he realized, crawling back and bracing the sore base of his neck against a pile of pillows. Touching his crown reminded him of the head-bump. Then, with a "fuhgeddaboutit" to the CPAP, he settled in and slept.

His anxieties were too weak to carry on in the morning light. His last thought—more of an unscripted prayer—whined for her safe return by the time he woke.

Sleep folded over him like a blanket too heavy to lift.

He dreamed of cages. Metal bars, torchlight, the sound of breathing that wasn't his. Heston in rags, screaming behind straw. Then it was Henry in the cage, laughing instead of screaming, because that was somehow the rule.

You have the car keys.

The cage became an elevator. Floor numbers flickered and reversed, then vanished altogether. He was falling, maybe rising. His reflection stared back—older, bruised, missing something he couldn't name.

They're downstairs.

A horn echoed. A black limousine idled at the curb. A woman's hand pressed to the glass, her mouth moving silently through the smoke.

You know the rules.

Then stars—his telescope aimed at the night sky, only it wasn't the sky. It was a slow-turning fetus, glowing like a constellation, floating in the dark.

A heartbeat the size of the universe.

Love you.

The words repeated, over and over, soft as breath.

He reached out, fingertip to the lens—

—and woke, gasping softly.

Light rinsed the room, still and impossibly calm.

Henry edged into the great room, his shoes snuggling on thicker white socks, scuffing against the hardwood. The penthouse smelled of popcorn-and-wine memories.

"Hello?" he called softly. His voice sounded like someone else.

No answer.

He said it again, a little louder, but it vanished into the morning light.

Henry crossed to the balcony doors. His reflection wavered in the glass—a wide-eyed man with a pistol and three days of age in one night. He stepped outside, felt the morning air hit him like frigid medicine. The city was eerily still. Sunlight glinted off silent towers. No sirens, no horns, no traffic hum—just the wind combing through a ruined distance.

He pulled his phone from his pocket. The screen was black. He pressed it. Nothing. Pressed again, harder, as if stubbornness could raise a signal. No service. He held it up, half laughing, half pleading.

"Come on, bars. Just one bar. I'll take half a bar." His stomach growled. He closed his eyes. "And a couple o' protein bars. And a happy-hour bar.—Better yet," he smacked his lips, "that breakfast bar. Mucho mocha, barista."

Nothing. He slept for a second, standing there, then revived. He shook, breathed, and felt a new rush of wakefulness.

The panic came fast—animal panic. His breath quickened, legs stiffened as he stepped forward. He scanned every balcony for another human shape, but there was only glass and sunlight and the occasional drifting scrap of paper.

Henry turned back inside. The penthouse seemed larger now, emptier. He crossed to the foyer and left the door open as he moved into the vestibule, the gun still but not steady in his hand.

He paused at the elevator bay. One elevator. Half-open. A rhythmic thunk softly echoed— bumping. As his heart slowed, the music drifting out let him know "The Girl from Ipanema" had survived.

As the motor hummed, the chrome doors, trying to close, tapped repeatedly against a small silver trash can wedged between them. Henry stared, remembering the night before. He must've done that—must've thought blocking it would help.

He exhaled shakily, held the gun against his chest, and with a careful nudge of his foot pushed the can aside. The doors met with a gentle kiss, and the silence that followed felt louder than any sound.

He waited. No motion inside. No whisper of machinery. Just his own pulse in his ears. He aimed the gun again, backed away, and turned toward the stairwell.

A shiver of a laugh tickled up his back at the sight of the kitchen broomstick wedged between the push-bar and the wall. He'd leaned against it, braced like it could stop a truck, but the thin wood bent under his weight, tilting with a creak. Nothing would stop the world if it wanted in. He pulled the broomstick out and propped it on the frame.

The heavy fire door gave way with a reluctant squeal. The concrete steps fell away beneath him, echoing with the faint groan of a building that still thought it was alive. He hesitated—half expecting a shape to dart across the landing below—but nothing moved.

"Okay," he whispered to no one. "One floor at a time."

He began to descend, the gun shaking slightly in his grip, footfalls quiet as prayer.

"Hello?"

As Henry reached the first mid-landing, the stairwell door above wheezed a slow, dying breath before clicking shut. The sound made him jump. He fumbled the firearm, then strangleholding it, choking the jitters—thumb squeezed the magazine release. The extendo dropped like a hockey puck. One foot kicked it toward the dark shaft; the other stepped on it, a near-fall rescue. *Close call.* He bent quickly, snatched it with one hand, and slid it back in—correctly, somehow. *Not qualified to even be a novice.*

Silence stretched, heavy and waiting. He took a shallow breath, ears straining for the smallest echo.

Then he reached the next landing and tried a louder, trembling "Hello!"—his voice cracking between fear and disbelief. Nothing. Just shadows, just the hollow drum of his pulse.

He pulled Imani's master fob from his pocket and tapped it against the RFID reader. The door clicked open, revealing an empty, narrow corridor. He stepped in, every toe testing the floorboards before committing weight. Morning sunlight spilled through slim windows at the far end.

"Hello?"

Several apartment doors flanked the passage, each one dark, silent, and waiting. He checked the guest unit first—empty. Then the office. The pantry. Each door swung open to nothing, hinges whispering complaints.

After the first few doors, he tried different approaches. He rapped on one. "Police, ma'am. Open up." On another: "Knock, knock. Who's there?" On another, light, rapid tapping: "Deadpan delivery."

All empty apartments. No one. No sense of humor.

If you gotta laugh to keep from crying, and no one hears it... were you, and are they, thinking to keep from thinking just as crazy as you think you are?

"Hello?"

By the fifteenth floor, the repeated hellos had grown hoarse. The stairwell felt endless, alien, as if each floor were a threshold to some unknown world. He imagined Imani, the creatures at the bottom step, the stairs between them. He imagined them lurking somewhere, waiting, hesitating, testing their own limitations.

"Hello?"

Henry's voice cracked as he called again—less a greeting now than a plea, a thread thrown to the vanished world. Each floor passed slowly, measured, more haunted by emptiness. The air carried a faint tang of concrete and steel, a ghostly trace of a building that once breathed with people. Now, engineered air, trapped, with nowhere to go.

He paused, listening to his echoes—every stairwell step, every heavy sigh, every mumbled worry. Shadows pooled and shifted as he descended. A thought crept in: the building had been drained of life, and he was the last drip.

Eventually, Henry reached the door to the lobby.

"Dey stand dere, bottom step."

He considered Imani's words, while staring back up the gray chute.

"Nothing up there. No signs of anyone. Anything. Nothing."

He swallowed hard, then turned hesitantly back to the lobby door. He wasn't ready to go there yet. Last night, in one glimpse, the lobby had burned itself into his memory: a tornado-whipped slaughterhouse.

Don't lose it. Don't lose your mind.

He continued his descent to the next level.

At the bottom of the stairwell, he hesitated, heart hammering. The basement lay ahead—hidden, cold, and silent.

"Hello?"

He stepped forward, gun raised, sweat slicking his palms. And somewhere, in the depth of the building, the silence answered him with a stillness that felt almost alive.

The Equipment Room door was propped open with a rubber wedge. Fluorescents buzzed brilliance, casting harsh light over caged machinery, a soupy mop sink, with bucket and boots at its side, and radios charging on a desk. Shelves of tools, fixtures, parts, and folded gear—a gun belt and holster molded to a Glock 17—lined the walls.

No humans. No Imani.

Henry blinked until the image of the lobby's horror above dimmed in his mind. He exhaled, returned to the stairs, and made his way to the garage.

The red stairwell door labeled P1 opened out from its faintly-lit fire-resistant enclosure onto the asphalt expanse that seemed different in daylight. Henry's eyes adjusted. He spotted his Miata, wedged against the bollard near the exit ramp, damaged—plastic trim loose, windshield caved in. He walked closer but slowed down, wondering if one of those creatures might be sitting there, waiting to take him for a ride. He circled the crumpled side, inching closer on the curve, until he could see nothing was waiting. He opened the door, grabbed the keys, and slipped them into his pocket. Shattered glass everywhere. He stepped away, kicked the door closed, then started his walk up the ramp. Habit kicked in. Hand urgently diving into pocket again, he found and pressed the fob's auto-lock button. The car beeped, obedient, locks clicking. Safe and secure, he thought, then felt his humor plunger pull one struggling chuckle up his throat. As if it meant anything now.

The street outside was a cemented traffic jam: abandoned cars, doors open, blinkers still flashing, chrome pressed against chrome, the whole street locked in a silent collision. Henry edged forward, wading through currents of disbelief and acceptance, and muttering "Hello?" at shadows, at glass, at every hint of movement. No answer.

A flickering sign caught his eye: _HOLE FOODS. One burned-out tube left the name broken. "Whole… Hole… huh," he muttered, and sucked his lower lip. Hunger drove him forward.

The automatic doors stood open, stuck mid-welcome. He wondered if the produce had survived.

"Hello?"

Inside, the air circulated yesterday's fresh aromas: produce, baked breads, spilled blood and intestines. A fan clicked somewhere in the rafters, trying and failing to spin. Weak sunlight refrained from the endcaps.

"Hello?"

His voice wavered up through the aisles. A box of cereal tilted off a shelf and fell with a soft thud. He nearly fired.

"Okay," he whispered. "Too loud."

He moved carefully, past the checkouts, into the produce section. The fluorescent lights overhead were mostly dead, but a few still flared intermittently, giving the apples and oranges a funhouse shimmer.

He picked up a Gala apple, turned it in his hand. It was hard, pretty, slightly tinged, but the color comforted him. Without hesitation, he sank his teeth into it. It tasted sweet, he chewed slow and swallowed.

"Hello?" he said again, testing the air.

A sound answered.

"*Yyyuuuhhhuuuhhh.*"

Far in the back, behind the butcher counter—something like a grunt. Wet, short, and human enough to twist his stomach.

Henry jellied, the apple moist in his hand.

"Okay," he breathed, barely audible. "That's... new."

Another grunt, closer now, dragging with it a scrape, like a shoe sliding through bone dust.

Henry took a step back. His heel hit a wire basket and sent it rattling.

Then, from the dimness of the backroom, something shambled forward—gray, sinewy, and uncoordinated, its skin slick and twitching. It crawled half upright, half sideways, its eyes flinching at the spill of sunlight leaking through a cracked skylight.

And that's when my brain decided to help.

So, even zompire grocery clerks don't like customers eating the merchandise. Good to know. But what I really learned at that moment —what I want the scientists of tomorrow (if they exist) to write down— is that fruit is your best friend when you're being attacked by a monster. Fruits, plants, anything that grows in the sun? I also threw tomatoes. Are those fruits or vegetables? Never mattered in school. Now it's life-or-death produce trivia.

(Note to self: when loading a shopping cart, don't set your gun on the child seat flap.)

The thing hissed—a kind of wet gargle, like a drain choking on hair. I ducked behind the produce stand, grabbed a lemon. Ever throw a lemon in terror? It's surprisingly effective. I hit it in the chest—chest? It had several possibilities. Anyway, it flinched, staggered off-balance into a table of flowers and 'Get Well' balloons, and shrieked horribly in a scalded reaction. I took that as science.

So I kept going. Apples, oranges, one perfect avocado (tragic loss). Each one smacked and rolled, and the creature kept twitching like it had a citrus allergy. I was making progress, or at least compost.

We had some real chemistry going between us. I even started taking bites and then throwing. Discharges from open wounds put the burn on it.

Then my arm cramped. And that's when I realized—I'm in a grocery store, surrounded by sunlight, fruit, and optimism, and I have a gun. So naturally, I panicked and tripped over my own shopping basket. Fell straight on my ass, staring up at the skylight like divine intervention might send down a kitchen appliance, probably a blender, because why not. A puree was purely Grace. It'd be her weapon of choice.

I got to my feet, grabbed the gun, aimed, and three rapid shots fired, exploding watermelons on display, splattering all over this alien Mr. Whipple. Apparently, I'd squeezed the Charmin.

The creature screeched, reaching for me—I slipped and fell, jerking back—then the light shifted, a stronger beam cutting across its shoulder. Smoke. A smell like burnt pork and barbequed basement. It reeled back, screaming.

And me? I'm still lying there, banana in one hand, loaded gun in the other, praying I don't mix up the punchline.

17

The audience was silent except for the hum of the generator in the back. One spotlight hung low above Henry, who sat on the stool like a model posing in cashmere and double-pleated pants. The mic was already in his left hand, but he didn't speak. His right hand rested on the Glock 17 across his thigh, thumb brushing the grip like a comfort object.

He breathed. Rubbed his freshly-shaved jaw, already damp with sweat. Looked down at the tiles as if they're cue cards, his dark running shoes heel-hooked on the footrest, knees bouncing restlessly. He raised the mic to his parting lips.

Then—

"So… yeah, I know. I took the elevator. After the fire alarm. That's how horror movies start, right? Or end? That, and a line like, 'I'll be right back'. But I had a condition, folks. I did—I do. A doddy-doddy-dee. I have. It's… complicated. The clinical term is something like… uh… 'episodic… retro-urgent… object dislocation anxiety.' Yeah, it's a clinic no one goes to.

"Basically, if I forget where my phone is, my brain could bowl over thinking I've lost myself.

"And yes, maybe that's not a real condition. But my therapist said, 'If it gets you out of a bad dinner party, you don't argue with the diagnosis.'

"So… I took the elevator. Went alone. Because I forgot my phone. But not my fear of crowded elevators. That's the kind of guy I am. There is the deeply withdrawn claustrophobic kid in me, and I don't want to say he's 'buried deep inside' because he might try to find a hole in my head to get out. But, if I'm alone on the elevator, I'm pretty certain he won't be there."

He smiled faintly. The kind of smile that says he's still deciding whether it's funny.

"You know what happens when you take the elevator just as hell breaks loose, folks? Nothing. At first. Then everything. First, it gets very quiet. Then very loud. Then it ends."

A pause.

"No it doesn't."

He leaned forward.

"The front desk guy's name was Elvis. Not *the* Elvis. Not *cool* Elvis. Elvis with this accent and attitude. *Clipboard* Elvis. *Not-my-friend* Elvis. But he didn't deserve—I wouldn't wish what I saw on my worst enemy. Not him. Not Charles, who I always thought was a friend.

"I'm alone. I go up, alone. I guess that makes me the winner, huh.

"Sealed up like a Hot Pocket in a microwave."

A single phoney chuckle from the shadows? Maybe in the back of Henry's mind.

"Anyway, the power goes out. I'm stuck between floors. Somewhere between Heaven and—uh—Manhattan Hell.

"And then I feel it. Something awful.

"Not quite hearing it yet—but feeling the dread. Something *in-ex-plic-able*. (A word I learned from Edgar Allan Poe when I was ten, right after he ruined my sleep for life.)

"Power kicks on, and I'm going down—not slowly, but not quite able to catch up with my stomach—straight into the jaws of death and hell. Literally. Like the world was going through a blender set to 'urban renewal,' and I was the next frozen banana to drop in. And I really believed I was about to die, even before the doors opened."

He ran a hand through his hair.

"And I'm just standing there like an idiot holding the railing, listening to the end of the world through a ten-thousand-dollar Schindler lift system.

"That's a lot of peeled bananas in that blender.

"Mother of fruitcake! Why do I say these things?"

He paused again.

"By the time the elevator rescued me from becoming pulled chicken—or maybe a subway pretzel left too long under the lamp—I knew some of me was forever lost."

Real quiet. Henry's throat tightened, his emotional meltdown gag reflex kicking in.

"I think Imani might've made it. I haven't found his truck anywhere yet. I—I don't think anyone—else… survived. But that means he won, too. Right?"

Silence.

"Elvis… never left the building. I didn't even know his last name. Or maybe I did? I want to say—*Pineda?* Yeah, that's where I got 'Pinhead' from. Pretty sure.

"I've decided to let him keep the twenty. I should just let it go.

"And then Charles... Charles… my dear Charles. I don't remember. *Red?* I will try to find out. I think his name-tag is still there —somewhere."

Another pause. He swallowed. Then:

"Forgive me. Forgive myself.

"You know what the real lesson is, folks? Never leave your phone on the toilet lid, in the event of an emergency. You go to grab it and— *ploop!*"

That got a laugh. Not a big one, even though drawn from his own memory bank's laugh account.

Henry smiled—small, tilted, sad.

The spotlight tightened.

He cleared his throat, tapped the mic once, and murmured:

"I'm Henry Gorestriker. And I took the elevator."

16

Henry woke to the hum and clank of machinery. For a moment, drifting between sleep and dream, he smiled. She was back. Knocking at the door, that was the sound he was hearing.

He ran to the door. "Wait!" he shouted into his phone. He couldn't wait to tell her about his dream, while it was still fresh and vivid in his memory.

He swung the door open.

She stood before him, snake fangs drooling, hobbling on one red heel, smoke curling out of the hole in her widened forehead.

He screamed.

His eyes flew open. In his ears, his heart hammered, but over that, another sound hadn't stopped. It echoed faintly through the concrete ribs of the Fontaine, rising and falling in a steady rhythm.

The elevator.

Henry sat up too fast in bed, his temples pulsing with a dull ache. He tried to remember—had he cut the power last night? He always did.

Always. A ritual: flip the breaker, kill the hum, then climb the forty flights by foot, safe at the top. If the elevator was running now, it was because he had forgotten. Unless he hadn't.

Another groan of cables. Lower down, maybe the tenth floor. Someone—or something—was moving in his building.

Henry pressed his palms against his eyes until colors bloomed behind them. "It's nothing," he whispered. "Just the old guts of the place... heaving." But the words didn't stick.

He slid out of bed, moving barefoot across the cool floor, and pressed his ear to the nearest wall. The elevator ground again, stopping somewhere in the dark beneath him. His stomach tightened. New shivers spilled over the tremors from his nightmare.

The last few days he'd used that cage to haul treasures—a gaming system, CD players, a generator, an aluminum bat and a basket of baseballs, a parachute from a surplus store, a mini-fridge that was keeping it cool. He was excited over his findings. Did he forget, in all the excitement? Becoming more absent-minded? Leaving it on, because he had to open it at the top, to retrieve things—because, otherwise—

He needed the elevator. The elevator was his, not theirs.

He crossed the penthouse barefoot, passing the mini-fridge set near the kitchen's old one. Its little motor buzzed, bottles inside beaded with cold sweat. The hum of it usually soothed him—it meant power, control, the illusion of civilization—but now it only underscored the other hum, the one crawling up the building's spine.

The sound stopped during the time Henry was putting on clothes and shoes and locating the pistol. He knew, even as he started his floor-by-floor patrol, the Fontaine was empty of any other living being, or unliving thing.

For the next several mornings, Henry prowled the stairwells, creeping down flights with the gun on his hip, the baseball bat balanced on his shoulder, pausing at every landing to listen. Nothing. No movement. Just the hollow sighs of the Fontaine, breathing out its emptiness.

Still, the thought gnawed: if he wasn't alone anymore, who had come home with him?

Were the ghosts finally coming to haunt?

15

Okay, first of all, Pete Sampras had no right to be this smug. I mean, yes—fourteen Grand Slam titles, all-time great, devastating serve—and the hair, don't get me started. But today? On this court? No chance.

"Henry Gorestriker steps up to the line," I narrate aloud, bouncing the ball, adjusting my hold on the size 3 grip of a brand-spanking-new Wilson Hyper Hammer racket I found behind a checkout counter at Dick's Sporting Goods. "Down match point. But determined. Shorts are slightly too tight, means just right. Socks, well, slightly mismatched. His opponent? A ghost from the golden age of cable television."

Wham.

The ball rockets across the net, catches a dead spot on the cracked asphalt, and flutters off like a wounded bird. I raise one hand, victorious.

"Ace," I whisper, panting. "Still got it."

You should see the stunned look on Pete's face.

An enthralled morning crowd explodes with applause beneath the clear blue sky. Okay, there is no crowd, but don't ruin it for them. Just the rustle of dry leaves in the chain-link fence and a single shoe abandoned near the baseline.

I imagine John McEnroe shaking his head. "You cannot be serious," he says from the shadows. "That was out."

I smile. "You're out," I tell him.

Another toss. Another ace.

Another. And another.

Sweat holds like hair gel above the black headband I decided to wear today. It smells faintly of heat, overexertion, and whatever passes for confidence these days.

"Advantage: Me."

I toss the ball one last time. My vision splits briefly. Two nets. Two suns. Two of me?

No time.

Serve!

The ball blurs across the net.

And comes back.

Just a soft, lazy pop. Barely over. But returned.

My muscles weaken.

The racket drops from my hand.

It lands with a dull thwack.

The ball rolls to my feet, innocent.

"No... way."

Then the knees go. The elbows. The long fall of a middle-aged man with low blood sugar and possible post-apocalyptic brain damage. Or something else going on. I feel the heat of the court rush up to greet me, and the sky tilts, dissolves.

Darkness.

Twilight. Not quite night. That violet hour. The between-times. A soft, stubborn ringing hangs in my ears. My mouth tastes like old dust and nerves, as if I've been chewing on cardboard too hard.

The Viking helmet is gone. Right, I didn't wear it today.

But I've got my racket, me old battle-axe. And I've got me balls. In a big bag. At least what's left that I haven't sent over the fence. Sorry, boys, but if you rolled down into a gutter... sayonara.

I sit up slowly. The court is empty. But not silent. There's a hum, deep down in the concrete. Or maybe in me.

My hands search my pockets. The wrinkled map is there. My "vehicle chain." I trace the ink with trembling fingers. "Vanilla Swirl" (the ice cream truck). "Reliable Dave" (the beat-up sedan with a Spider-Man air freshener). "The Tank" (postal jeep, no brakes). I marked them with stars. I don't remember when. I don't remember why "Reliable Dave" smells like vinegar.

I press the map to my chest.

I stand, and wipe a bug off my nose.

And sway.

There's something wrong with gravity. It's leaning.

I step forward. The fence creaks behind me.

I stop.

No footsteps. No breath. No wind.

Just the fence… breathing?

I walk faster. I reach the gate, which is now closed.

It wasn't closed before.

I open it slowly.

It creaks like it knows a secret.

The city looks familiar. But too big. Too far apart. Streets that should connect don't. Alleyways tilt. A manhole steams with the scent of burnt vanilla. The light is fading, but it's not fading right.

I follow a path I think I recognize, past a newsstand, and zigzag through what looks to me like a matchbox-playset intersection packed with crashed vehicles, left destroyed by a giant toddler who had a real bad temper tantrum.

A shape moves past the window of an old diner. I freeze. But it's only me. I think.

I duck behind an overturned mailbox and breathe.

Was that ball really returned?

Maybe a bounce. Maybe a trick of spin. Maybe Pete Sampras is still alive and playing low-level ghost matches in Central Park to stay sharp.

I try to laugh.

Nothing comes out.

Shadows are closing in, deepening.

Eventually—minutes, hours, years—I spot this cab. My cab. The one I named "The Believer." A yellow Crown Vic I've never started, but trust implicitly.

I slide into the back seat. Why the back seat? Why, indeed. Was I expecting Travis Bickle to be at the wheel, ready to get me out of here?

The smell of sun-baked leather and faded air freshener hits me like a childhood memory. There's a blanket. A banana peel. A chess piece on the floor. Knight.

I close the door. Lock it.

I rest my head against the plexiglass partition.

"Pete," I whisper, "if you're still out there... nice return."

My vision blurs.

The hum in my skull rises again.

A woman's voice, gentle, from nowhere:

"You never learned how to fall properly."

A hand on my cheek. A giggle. Ski slopes. The color red. A drink with an umbrella in it. A hotel room with sunburned feet sticking out of a bed sheet.

I blink.

Alone.

I check the time on my broken watch.

Not time yet.

Because the sound of something large is scratching past the cab outside, slow and careful, like it's looking for change in the asphalt pock-marks.

And please, Henry, tell me, why the back seat? Was there something I was thinking was here?

Ah, maybe this wad of old gum stuck under the seat. In the event of an emergency, where I might need to ingest something that will kill me instantly.

The sound outside the cab is gone. But I keep my eyes jumping from window to window, until, finally, the strain is felt and I bring them in, close the lids quickly, and now I look inside me.

What happened to me at the court?

At that moment, I'm suddenly remembering my teenage years of epilepsy. Did I—? Did I have a seizure? No meds for decades, no problems. And then, one well-thrown brick clips my head?

Eyes open again. Wake up, idiot! It's not getting lighter! Let's get out of here!

I slide out of the cab and crouch low. My legs are knotted ropes. The air tastes like copper—creatures are near.

Shadows flicker between wrecked cars. Two shapes. Maybe three. Their movement is unnatural, like film running backward.

These avenues have somewhat-cleared, doable paths to drive through. Which means, I'm close to home. (I'm glad I kept my day job.)

I need wheels.

Henry crouched low as he moved through the wreckage, breath hissing between his teeth. The city was a Rubik's Cube rearranged and unaligned tonight—too many angles and mismatched colors. And too much silence. Only the sound of his glow-in-the-dark Nikes crunching grit, squeaking, and that faint hum, like a live wire vibrating inside his skull.

Something—*a rat?*—scurried through nearby trash, playing kick the can.

He spotted movement ahead. Two of the creatures slid between the frames of burned-out cars, their limbs jerking in strange, puppet-like rhythms. A third one moved farther back, hunched low and sniffing the air. They hadn't noticed him yet.

Henry scanned the street. No ice cream truck. No postal jeep. No "Reliable Dave." Just a single vehicle that looked, for all the world, like a bright, high-gloss, Pure White miracle: a Volkswagen Beetle at the curb, under a flickering streetlight, with some clearance ahead of it. Clearance for take-off.

Let there be keys.

Henry crept forward. Every motion was slow, deliberate. He pressed a finger to his lips, shushing his own breath. He wasn't certain, but he felt some distance—maybe thirty yards all around—working to his advantage. He pressed against the coldness of the car and raised his head to window-level. Inside, there were keys, dangling from the ignition like an invitation.

The driver's side door gave a treacherous creak when he opened it. Henry flinched, trying to still his nerves, and waited.

Nothing moved. Good.

He carefully placed the sports bag on the back seat, the passenger seat layered in dried fluid and decay, something skeletal and unmoving watching him through a hollowed eye socket.

He slid into the driver's seat, knees smashing against the steering column. Pain flared, sharp and brief. He grunted. Then, a finger to his lips, he hushed the hardened sketch of broken human remains with its jaw-dropped silent scream turned on him, refusing to shut.

Too close. He groped for the seat lever and yanked.

The seat shot back with a brassy clank.

Henry winced.

"Shhh," he whispered again, trying to realign the back support, and then, once settled, a quick securing of the seat belt.

Ahead of him, the creatures twitched but didn't turn. He exhaled and reached for the key.

Click.

Nothing.

Click-click.

Then the car's CD player exploded to life.

Frank Sinatra's voice filled the night:

"You're driving me craaaazy! What did I do?—"

Henry jolted like he'd been tasered. His hand flew to the radio, stabbing at buttons, but all he did was crank the volume louder.

"What did I dooooo—to you?!"

The creatures stiffened. Their heads snapped toward the sound.

Glass shattered. A pale, rubbery arm burst through the rear window—followed by a throat and jaw that rammed into the jagged frame. A long, knifed shard of glass caught deep under the creature's neck, snagging it in place. Claws tangled with the headrest, then grisly fingers scratched Henry's hair, found the headband and curled over it in a tight grip that yanked Henry's head back.

"You know I'm so in love—with you!"

Henry screamed—a thin, high-pitched whistle of air. He opened the driver's side door, and the dome light flickered on, causing the creature to wince and recoil—but the shard in its throat held it anchored, jerking its head back as if hooked.

He twisted the key again—*VRRRM!* The Beetle roared to life. Henry slammed the shifter into Drive and floored the accelerator. The car pitched violently as it surged ahead, dragging the creature with it as it thrashed and shrieked.

The seat lever, knocked loose earlier, chose this moment to malfunction. The driver's seat reclined with a violent thunk, almost onto the back seat. Henry's leg stiffened to keep his foot on the pedal.

Before Henry could sit up, the creature's face lunged down into the car, the shard digging into its jugular and forcing its head in at a sick downward angle. Its teeth snapped for his throat.

Frantically, his hands exchanged the grip on the Wilson racket, and with what little strength he had left, Henry managed to shield his face. The grid of natural gut strings caught the monster's fangs; its jaws clamped and twisted. The creature, held by the glass in its neck, struggled forward but couldn't reach its screaming meal.

Groping blindly, Henry's right hand sought the sports bag— flashlight, gun, anything. His fingers found the half-zipped opening and dug inside.

The creature's jaws worked fiercely, beginning to chew through the strings with wet snaps and tearing fibers. Desperate, Henry's hand yanked out and shoved a tennis ball into its closing gnashers, wedging solid Wilson rubber between the teeth.

Sinatra crooned, oblivious:

"You're driving me craaaazy!—"

The VW hit the curb, bounced—and then the street erupted. A storm-drain grate shoved itself upward as a tangle of creatures clawed their way out from underground. Mud, trash, and bits of broken pavement flew in every direction.

The Beetle's front wheels slammed onto the tilting grate like a springboard. It launched into the air, Henry screaming as the creature's head twitched just inches away—still hooked, its neck grinding on the glass; and the momentary angled view beyond the windshield was skyward on a blur of dark towers. Then, downward into shifting shadows.

CRASH!

The car plowed through the plate-glass window of a costume shop. The force finally tore the creature free of the window shard, its torso whipping under the flipping Beetle. The car came down on the side of its dangling ruined legs.

CRUNCH!

The smashed VW continued to roll to an upside-down ending among a rain of broken glass and wigs and assorted outfits. Motion detector lights flicked on—miraculously. An alarm went off somewhere.

Henry dangled in his seat belt, stunned, blood trickling past his eyes. Sinatra's voice warbled faintly from the mangled speakers:

"You—know I'm so in love—with you!"

The dying hiss nearby drew Henry's attention to the trapped figure writhing weakly, half-buried in costumes. Its head lifted one last time, sporting a pink troll wig, which seemed to swallow the dissolving tissue.

As quickly as possible, Henry, in supercharged panic mode, struggled and freed himself from the vehicle and crawled until he could stand in the lighted area. Through the VW-sized hole in the wall he could see menacing figures growing in numbers on the boulevard, slowly creeping his way.

Henry crouched and went in search of a back exit.

The streets stretched out before him in a tilted blur. Fog clung low to the ground, an eerie, bluish soup that made the shapes of stalled cars and broken signage look melted. Henry staggered through the haze, clutching his ribs, trying to focus.

He didn't know how long he'd been sprawled out on the blue acrylic that afternoon. The route he'd planned—his sequence of stashed vehicles, safe paths, fallback points—had unraveled with his mind in the chaos of that damned tennis court. His head was thick, mouth cotton-dry, and his legs wouldn't cooperate with anything resembling rhythm.

And now—they were coming.

From behind. From alleys. From beneath shattered storefronts. That unmistakable sound: the dry rasp of flesh on asphalt, the chittering whine, the rhythmic shuffle of too many limbs, the sloshing wave of weighted veins. Hungry.

Henry broke into a limp-run. The sports bag of balls, batteries, bullets and blaster thumped against his back. His flashlight bounced with each step, cutting shaky cones through the mist. The creatures were close—closer than he'd thought—and gaining.

Then he saw it.

A fire truck.

It sat at a crooked angle in the middle of a four-lane intersection, hemmed in by husks of abandoned taxis and sedans, its red paint dulled to rust-orange. The windshield was cracked, but the cab looked intact. Most importantly, the aerial ladder hung suspended—an elbow set in a bicep flex—reaching skyward, but low enough at the rear to climb.

Henry didn't think. He scrambled up the side, shoes slipping on soot-streaked chrome. The moment his hand touched the door handle, a chorus of screeches erupted behind him.

He flung himself into the cab.

Keys in the ignition.

Please, please...

He twisted.

The engine groaned. Once. Twice. Then: ignition. A deep diesel roar shook the cab to life.

The dashboard lit up. Henry hit every switch he could find—sirens, strobes, spotlights. A klaxon wail tore through the city canyons as blue and red pulses lit up the fog. He slammed the doors shut as the first creature clawed at the side mirror.

They weren't stopping.

He leapt from the cab into the narrow steel trough behind it, then clambered up to the aerial platform's bucket. The ladder creaked beneath his weight. The controls—familiar enough. A joystick, toggle switches, safety interlock disengaged.

"Up. Up. Up—"

The hydraulic system groaned and lifted the bucket into the air. Ten feet... Twenty... Forty...

The creatures swarmed the truck below, crawling over its tires and bumpers—a black tide of limbs, mouths, and convulsive rage. He could smell them now: damp fur on dead fish, sealed in a box of sewage, threaded with a mold that shouldn't exist, and rot.

Higher.

When he was high enough that their reaching claws looked like twitching shadows, he let go of the controls. The ladder locked into place. The sirens below wailed on.

He hovered above them, half in fog, half in starlight, clinging to the safety rail and panting like a man who'd just escaped hell.

Minutes in slow-turning wind became hours.

The advection fog thickened, swallowing edges, softening the night until everything blurred. His vision dipped, then steadied, darkness pressing in the mix. The shrill cries became a hypnotic annoyance under the blue mist.

Morning.

The sun crept through the smoke.

Below him, the street was still. Empty again. The creatures had fled with the dawn, back to their burrows or nests or wherever it was nightmares went to sulk.

The fire truck was silent now. Its engine had given up sometime in the night.

Henry tried the ladder controls. Nothing. Without power, the hydraulics were dead.

He looked down.

Far below, the rungs of the aerial boom stretched in a narrow ladder-bone spine. Not exactly OSHA-certified, but enough to climb.

He muttered to himself as he swung one leg over the railing.

"I swear, if I survive this… if I… If I did, or did I?"

The first rung was greasy. The second, sticky with soot. The ladder creaked as he descended, slowly, arms trembling. He didn't dare look down again.

When his shoes hit the top of the truck, he let himself rest, forehead against the cold metal.

A wild, boyish joy lit him up. "I got down it! Got down! Yeah!" he sang.

"Beginner's slope," another voice whispered. "Beginner's slope."

I didn't go straight home.

Not because I had a better idea, but because I couldn't remember where home was. Not at first. Everything looked the same down there. Same burnt-out signs. Same broken glass. Same crushed dreams. A boutique storefront had a mannequin in a wedding dress slumped against the window. I saluted her. We were both overdressed for the end of the world.

At some point I found one of my old route markers—an arrow chalked on a light post, pointing uptown. Had to have been mine. I even signed it "H."

The sun was bright and mean when I got back to the Fontaine. My thighs were shaking from the climb, and the headband—it was definitely squeezing my brain now. Probably cutting off blood to the part that once had common sense.

Back in the penthouse, I collapsed onto the couch with the grace of a tranquilized buffalo.

My face hurt.

I realized I was smiling.

Hadn't meant to.

"That was so stupid," I said aloud.

And then, quieter:

"How did I let you talk me into that?"

A woman's hand brushed my cheek.

"I told you," she said, "you should've prepped with the ski instructor. You seriously should've stayed on the beginner's slope."

I chuckled. Or sobbed. Hard to tell anymore.

Then I opened my eyes.

I was alone.

"...Huh?"

14

Henry turned the corner at a half-jog, chasing a silhouette that had flitted into a side street like smoke. He wasn't even sure why he was running. Maybe because this feminine figure had moved like a person —upright, quick, purposeful—something the world didn't offer him anymore. That was rare. That was hope. But this was also the fourth— or maybe the tenth—time he'd chased the ever-elusive distant figure in dark clothing. The number never held.

He skidded to a stop.

There, in the middle of the alley, stood a man.

Older. Barefoot. Wrapped in layers of coats, his beard tangled like Spanish moss on a rusted pole. He was muttering into a cracked flip phone—no battery, no service, no world left worth dialing.

"I told you, Janine," the man barked into it, "if the birds start chirping Morse again, we initiate Protocol Tangerine. That's national. That's not negotiable."

Henry gasped.

With a slight paranoid twitch, the bearded man glanced over his shoulder, swiveling on his heel, eyes wide on Henry now, head tilting back.

Henry blinked. His breath came fast. This wasn't the silhouette he'd chased. This man hadn't been running. But he was speaking—actual words. Not a moan, not a hiss, not a snarl. A voice.

"Uh… hey," dropped from Henry's open mouth.

The bearded man hushed the phone with a curled hand. "Notify HQ. They sent the wrong emoji."

"Uh," Henry stammered, "I think—I thought—didn't see—you—see—someone else?"

He turned to Henry, eyes sharp but unfocused. "Someone else… *here?*"

"*No?*" Henry was ebbing from shock to apprehension.

A brief interlude of awkward silence.

"That's a lovely tie. Or was that your own idea?"

"What? Who—where did—whuh—how—?"

The bearded man spoke to the phone: "Hold on, sweetheart. A scratch in the record."

"How are you… *here?*" Henry's detectives couldn't agree.

"I'm a slight shade of blue today, thank you. Third one from the left."

Batman leaned in to Henry's ear, voice gravel and shadow:

"Brainpan's gone sideways."

Henry flinched and pushed his whisper through a fist: "*Holy— Froot Loops.*"

Poirot stepped forward delicately, moustache twitching:

"Hmph. Sideways would be an improvement."

Henry raised an eyebrow and puckered his lips.

Holmes expounded with careful diction:

"Even chaos would seek distance."

Henry nodded in agreement to the smoke ring drifting over his shoulder.

Marlowe dragged his heavy eyes up from the cigarette floating in his stein:

"Sideways? Pal, that guy's doing somersaults through a marble maze in street chalk nobody bothered to draw."

Henry took the laugh-punch to the nose—and caught a snort in his sinus cavity.

The bearded man looked at something invisible at his side, then returned to Henry.

"My friend asked you a question... *Identification code?*"

Henry hesitated. "I... left it... in my... other... apocalypse?"

The man shot a grin, snapped the phone shut with a confident click, and announced: "Irwin Platt. Category Seven. Cart certified. Nightwatch. Exempt. And you?"

"Um... Henry. Sears Catalogue. I mostly tell jokes. For no laughing... matter. Doesn't."

Henry shook his head, springs and cogs tinkling in the machine between his ears.

"A clown! Excellent." Irwin nodded, delighted. "They don't eat clowns. Too much irony. Makes 'em bloat."

"Good one. Maybe clowns... taste funny?"

Henry offered a half-laugh, not sure if Irwin was dangerous or just alone too long. He glanced down at the man's shopping cart, a cluttered shrine to nonsense: VHS tapes, mannequin arms, a sun-faded gnome, mustard bottles, a radio duct-taped to a flashlight.

And bricks. Six of them, stacked neatly.

Atop the pile: a Cleveland Indians cap. Familiar. Faded.

Henry's blood congealed.

"That hat," he whispered.

Irwin turned a full circle. Just hummed to himself, tuneless and eerie.

"Where'd you get that hat?"

Irwin plucked the NY cap up gently, brushed it off. Inside—*yes*. A bloodstain. Dried in the shape of a moment he couldn't remember.

"Shhh," Irwin said. "Sure. Found it. Raining bricks that day. Good bricks. City bricks. The real kind."

Henry stared. "You throw bricks?"

A pause. Irwin tilted his head. "I throw lots of things."

"At people?"

Irwin raised the phone again. "Of course I remember the activation codes, Janine! I'm not the one who nuked Philadelphia!"

Henry stepped closer. "You hit me."

Irwin snapped the phone shut again and sighed. "You think they let me keep real supplies? I only have what's authorized for a Category Seven Resurgence. That's not you, is it?"

Henry couldn't help it—he smirked. "I'm more of a… Category Four. On a good hair day."

Irwin twitched, sniffing. "You smell like a Six. At least a Six-point-three. Have we met?"

He leaned closer. "Are you broadcasting?"

"Only the reruns," Henry managed, his voice feeling duller.

Irwin's fingers entwined in matted hair as he scratched scalp, then looked up—and in his eyes, something flickered. Recognition. Maybe guilt. "We saved each other," Irwin said quietly. "At Krikenheimer." He studied him harder. "*Oogie?*"

Henry said nothing. The name rattled in his chest like a marble.

Irwin held the cap out. "You want it?"

Henry took it, slow and careful. It felt like reclaiming something stolen from his own memorial service. Chief Wahoo was a ray of sunshine, and the child in Henry was rescued.

"This shouldn't be forgotten." He paused as it blurred in one eye. "And yet—"

"And now here we are," Irwin said. "You got a plan, Oogie?"

"Just the usual," Henry replied. "Survive. Laugh. Rinse. Repeat."

Irwin lit up. "Recursive salvation! Yes! Exactly!"

Irwin leaned in, his voice dropping. "They'll all come tonight. I hear them practicing. Laughter's sharpening its teeth."

Before Henry could ask, Irwin flipped his phone open again and wheeled the cart down the street, talking to no one.

"Janine," he said urgently, "put me through to the pigeons. Code red. 'Fourteenth and Delusion.'"

The cart's wheels squeaked in rhythm. Henry watched him vanish into the heat haze.

He stood in the silence, the hat in his hand, the blood stain dry against his thumb.

Madness used to be a warning sign. Now I wonder if it's the only way left to stay sane.

13

Sun-bleached posters of grinning cartoon faces lined the walls, their cracked smiles mocking him from every angle. A stuffed Pikachu sat in the display window with one ear chewed off and a plastic eye missing—like a war veteran who'd seen better days.

Well, if this isn't a metaphor for my head right now, I don't know what is.

Henry stepped through the shattered front of the toy store, staying within the stretch of sunlight. Beyond its reach, the shadows hissed— thin, reptilian warnings. He didn't linger. At the checkout lane, a few toys and games sat stacked and waiting, as if someone had carefully arranged them for him. He grabbed Battleship and exited fast.

If I took you home with me, then I'd have no reason to get out. And I have to get out.

"Henry, who are you talking to?"

He stopped. The voice—her voice—cut through the air, light and amused. But there was nothing behind him except broken shelves and dust. He adjusted the box under his arm and left without looking back again.

In Central Park, Henry parked the Huffy mountain bike next to a concession stand. (He'd lifted the bike off the back of a Jeep Cherokee on Forty-third—*you know, a gentleman's five-finger discount.*) He wheeled it toward a bench he half-remembered. He thought he'd once had a picnic there with someone, but the memory felt like a photograph left out in the rain.

He set up the game. The open area was bright—green grass, blue sky, bathed in afternoon sun.

"No hot dogs today," she said.

Henry's hand paused over the game pieces. The voice was close, soft, teasing. He looked at the empty bench across from him and then back down at the grid.

He lined up his ships: a destroyer, a cruiser, two submarines. No aircraft carrier.

Of course. Apocalypse or not, I still get the defective box. Story of my life.

"Okay, Henry. A-4. No, wait. B-7."

Henry got up and switched seats. *Battleship: The Monodrama.*

"Boom! You sunk my battleship!"

"Congratulations," he muttered. "You are now officially insane."

He laughed—the kind of laugh that starts too high and ends the same way, like a bad jazz note.

"Are we really doing this?" she asked, as if the idea of playing a board game in the middle of the park was too absurd even for her.

"Doing what?" he asked, keeping his eyes on the board.

"Playing Battleship. Alone. In a park. Talking to a box like it's your therapist."

"It's not therapy," he said. "My friend, Dr. Grimby, assures me I'm already making real progress. Gained some real insight."

"Have you considered this is the apocalypse? You're alone? In Central Park?"

"What are you, my mother now? Because if you are, I'm putting you in the fruit cellar."

"Are you seeing this?"

"Seeing what?"

"Some wildlife at nine o'clock. Coming this way."

Henry looked across the field. A tiny rusty-brown shape raced toward him, yapping.

Henry's face lit up. "Lenny!"

The Chihuahua wagged its tail vehemently.

"Lenny! How in the world did you find me?" Henry burst with tears and laughter. He picked the dog up and cradled him.

"I told you about Lenny, didn't I? He was our first dog."

She didn't answer. The silence stretched, filled with sunlight and a breeze that might have been her breath.

"It's your turn," he said finally. "Go ahead... C-5... Oh wow, another miss. You're terrible at this game, you know that?"

"I let you win," she murmured.

Henry smiled faintly. "Yeah," he whispered. "I know you did."

For a while, he just sat there, letting Lenny lick his chin, staring at the board, pretending the warmth of the sun was her hand on his shoulder. Pretending the faint hiss of the wind was her laugh.

"I'm glad you're here, too."

An epiphany. And where's the symphony?

I remembered something. Something I knew I should never forget. So I'm writing it down.

The test. Faint pink. Faintly positive. The test.

It was in the medicine cabinet. I remembered. Not there now, but I remembered.

I didn't remember where I'd put it, but I remembered it.

Here's the interesting thing: I remembered this happening before —when I remembered this before. Déjà vu. It went away. I'm writing this down. I didn't before. But I remembered, and now my mind wants to rest.

But not yet. Not yet. That test is here; it didn't walk off by itself.

I didn't walk off with it. No. Why would I do that?

My heart did that thing—thump-thump, like it was trying to escape my chest. Panic, quick, sharp, hot, crawling up my spine. Where was it? I needed to know. I had to know.

I ran my hands over the bathroom counter, drawers, shelves. Empty. Empty. Empty. Bristles from the toothbrush, like little soldiers standing at attention. Bristling. They knew more than me. A single cough drop fused to its wrapper stared back. I muttered something to my reflection about memories and ghosts. I looked like a ghost. Then. But I remembered me.

I tore through the penthouse like a man possessed—under papers, in boxes, behind things I'd meant to organize... weeks ago? My brain kept looping. I knew it was here. I just knew it was here.

Then I spotted it—a box, tucked up high on the guest bedroom closet shelf. Memorabilia. Dusty envelopes. Old photographs. The test pressed flat, protected, guarded. Relief? Maybe. Shouldn't I take it down and check? But the shelf was too high. Step stool in the laundry room? Kitchen? I couldn't remember.

Walls closing in. Air getting thinner. Chest tight. Hands trembling. I gave up. I had to get out. Anxiety attack. Not since years ago. I'd forgotten.

Down the stairwell, the smells enveloped me. I had to breathe. Step by step, deep inhale, deep exhale. Concrete, dust, something else in the air. Or maybe—

Hands swinging, long strides. Apartment, cabinet, top-shelf box— distant now, like a dream slipping through fog. I didn't remember the test anymore. Didn't need to. Rhythm of walking, pulse in ears, inhale, exhale, and that tiny, fading sense of a secret somewhere up high, patiently waiting.

A few blocks away, the memory faded. Pink line. Soft click of the cabinet. My vow to guard it. Gone. Just a shadow of panic lingering in my chest. I shook my head. I could feel the secret somewhere. I was still guarding it, even if my mind had let go.

Something in the air? Pigeons fall.

Something inside me? Maybe I'll fly.

12

Henry stepped up to the mic like it might bite him if he didn't approach slowly enough. The stage lights were hot, harsh, a white glare that made the shadows beyond them seem thicker, alive. Somewhere out there, past the tables and chairs, past the glow's protective ring, something scraped softly against the building.

"So… uh," he said, adjusting the cord, "first show in a while. Not since—"

He stopped. Not because he didn't remember, but because something in the dark made a sound like teeth shifting over concrete.

"—never mind."

A cough rasped in the emptiness. Could've been the generator. Could've been something else.

Maybe a rat's head went down the wrong way.

Henry tugged the flashlight from its belt slot and cast a sweeping beam into the darkness. The briefly lit encounters—recoiling, hissing, alien flesh searing in its sweep—shook ice cubes in his blood.

"Good evening, ladies, gentlemen… assorted crawling nightmares.

"Glad to see so many of you made it through the meat grinder.—I mean that in the best way. You look… partially digested—which, believe me, I say with admiration.

"You—sir—yes, you with the gaping chest wound and thousand-yard stare. You give the term *lounge lizard* a whole new meaning."

Henry lit up, hearing faint laughter.

"Ma'am, you'll have to put some clothes on and stop making those cringy sucking sounds. We're not auditioning for *Deep Croak*." A beat. "Unless you brought a demo reel. Then, by all means—go for it."

He shook his head. "I'm not really a dirty-joke kind of comedian. I once tried to write one about a pimp, long ago. Don't know where it is."

Henry locked up, mind going blank. "What was it?… Oh, yeah. This pimp… rides a motorcycle for the California Highway Patrol… didn't have enough gas. But hey… I think I might've stumbled on the first TV sitcom for the porn industry. It'd be called *Chimps… Chips —Pimp?*"

He cleared his throat, leaned in, voice dropping into character, auditioning:

"'Excuse me, baby, I got you ladies on the turn out. So don't be gettin' out o' pocket. You on my road now… and dat's a big exit fee.'"

A pause. Henry exhaled, awkward smile, shoulders shrugging: "No? Yeah… I… uh, if I find it again… scratch that one off the list."

Somewhere in the *Bahahas*, a pipe burst with enigmatic guffaws.

"What a grisly-looking group tonight. I've seen fresher faces on a taxidermist's wall. Even the barflies... have *bar-flies*. A lot of walk-ups tonight. A lot of groaners, too, huh?"

Henry leaned in to the mic.

"Maybe—just maybe—if you hadn't *eaten* your funny bone, a good belly laugh could've helped your digestion. You'd be tickled... and surrender your life of death." Another beat. "Oh? You were laughing? My bad. I thought that was your spleen leaking.

"You—you look like you've been on a date recently. With a shovel. And a priest.

"Am I right?"

More laughter evolved from nothingness, and the comic bare witness.

Henry bravely pulled a folded paper from his cargo pants' pocket and unraveled it. Right fingers moved the note like the slide of a trombone while left fingers briefly shifted his glasses to find the best focus. Then he read:

"Popular saying in the Mumbai Mafia: *Buddha*-bing... *Buddha*-bang... *Buddha*-boom... Probably why they meditate before a hit."

Henry let a goofy mouth-rimshot spill out. "*P'tch-tchh!* My *Bri-tish* sense of humor. I apologize in advance.

"If not for *Libra–Aries* compatibility, we wouldn't have *libraries*… I thank you. Gemini thank you."

Rimshot. "My *Bri-tish* sense of humor. It's a condition.

"I held an AA meeting for all my burned-out flashlight batteries. Alkaline Anonymous. Support group's really growing—No charge to join."

Rimshot: "*Bri-tish!* Bob's your uncle!

"I jog now. Not because I enjoy it. Not that I know of. I mean, do I? I jog to… jog the memories. To… joggle my neurons? Because I can't Google.

"Thanks for the memories? Lighting the corners of my mind?—Bulb's burnt.

"There is something on my mind… I wonder what it is. Still waiting for the results."

Henry pulled the stool in and sat down. His head tilted, face softened, and shoulders slumped briefly. "Old material. Comedy disasters. Pre-apocalypse.

"If I keep living in yesterday, I'll… shorten my days—and that's a good thing now. But if I can't remember yesterday, I'll forget how to live… and never know I forgot.

"So I think I'll finish that thought tomorrow.

"I keep forgetting to take my Prevagen.

"You know, the older you get, the more thoughts you get. You got a problem—overpopulation. The new ones haven't even registered. The old ones are leaving—tired of the slow traffic. Housing problems.

Just not the place it used to be. Honestly, if it were me, I'd leave my head, too."

Henry squeezed out a puckered face, like he'd just sipped sour wine.

"Keeping your nose to the grindstone—is certainly nothing to sneeze at.

"I found out, when the shoe was on the other foot, I didn't have a leg to stand on. *P'tch-tch!*

"I had a friend… born with a silver spoon in his mouth. Still managed to speak with a forked tongue... Real cut-up. Ironically, not the sharpest knife in the drawer."

A drop of sweat hit and smeared the next cue.

"So, I'm kind of a late bloomer. Put off marriage for many years... or maybe the other way around. Finally, got hitched. Listen, you think comedy's about timing? When her biological clock is ticking—no beating around the bush. *P'tch-tch!*"

Henry froze for a split second, caught off-guard by his own snicker-snort escape. Then he pulled the reins and continued the ride.

"I used to go on first dates like I was interviewing someone for a position I didn't actually want to fill. 'Where do you see yourself in five years?'

"She'd say, 'Married, active husband, two kids.'

"And I'd say—'Wow, the CEO. So, if I hire you now, can I get early retirement?'"

His voice carried well in the room, even without laughter to bounce off. The joke landed anyway—on himself, like always.

"When I turned fifty, *Lord* appeared to me in a dream—standing on a balcony. Drew me in. Sculpted wave of hair, one arched eyebrow surfing it.

"'Call me Jack,' he said. 'And welcome to the big Five-Oh.'

"Woke up today. No one on the balcony. No theme music. Danno never booked me. Lord left. I ain't got *Jack*.

"Remember coffee shops?" He went on. "Ordered a latte with almond milk, and the barista asked, 'Lactose-intolerant?'

"And I said—'No, no—me and Dairy go way back. I loved her. She was a good cow. I just don't want to end up tied to a stall... Been through it once already. Got real ugly. Things didn't go down well. And there was a lot of nasty paperwork at the end.'"

A scrape again. Higher this time, maybe from the ceiling. Henry tilted his head toward it, eyes patrolling, then pressed on:

"Any movie buffs here? Ever see *Deliverance*?... Betcha didn't know... Ned Beatty's first *part*."

Rimshot.

"I went to the dentist once, before all this. He tells me I grind my teeth at night. I told him, 'No, my teeth grind my teeth, all day. My teeth never sleep.' He says, 'That sounds like anxiety.' I said, 'No—um —this is the sound of my anxiety.'" Henry opened his mouth wide and made a loud vibrating *"eeeyy-yey-yey-yey"* sound from deep in his throat. "Which won't let me grind my teeth—which increases my anxiety. (Actually, that's my Zuni fetish doll impression. I think I met its mother recently.)"

Several wet, dragging hisses from the shifting darkness.

He gave a short, mock-serious nod.

"So, he suggested I gargle raspberry juice. Which isn't that easy. Have you ever tried blowing raspberries in reverse?"

Henry blinked twice, slow, and reached for the mic stand with his free hand—just a fingertip's worth of contact at first, as if it anchored him. He pulled the mic from the stand and amplified his breath with it.

"Grocery stores," he said. "Used to play soft jazz—I love jazz—and I'd forget what I came in for. I'd go to check out, and I'm buying green onions... salted peanuts... some Jazz Apples." He leaned in, voice dropping almost conspiratorially. "And what I actually came in for was… red hot chili peppers, cranberries, black-eyed peas... and meatloaf.

"Seems like there's something I'm forgetting... but I can't remember what it was.

"I haven't had any memory… for as long as I can remember.

"I stopped by the old McDonald's on Eighth… you know, just to see if the milkshake machine finally healed." Henry switched into a goofy, high-pitched hillbilly voice: "My milkshake don't work. I *cain't* get a good suck through. Maybe my straw's upside-down."

The audience was roaring with laughter in Henry's head. Henry chuckled.

The lights hummed, as if trying to out-buzz whatever was in the walls.

Henry smirked faintly. "I once had an idea for a movie about a guy who survives the end of the world. Finally, wrote a spec script. Got produced before it got accepted, and I'm the star." A pause, longer this time. "But, as qualified as I am, I really want someone else to play me."

Some sudden feedback, and Henry jumped from the nearest floor speaker. "Jimmy Caviezel!" He smiled nervously and stared cross-eyed at the mic.

He reset his eyes on the darkness and chuckled lightly.

"Is there an exorcist in the house? I look around, and, yeah—feels like a field trip to the Pazuzu Zoo. Two-for-one possessions on Tuesdays. Threesome Thursdays. Tried 'em. But I still feel empty inside."

He wiped the mic, leaned in.

"Thirsty crowd. Listen, if you're waiting in the comedy club punch-line..." A beat. Deadpan. "...the juice is spiked tonight."

He turned halfway, the mic cord snaking across his path, prompting a quick but clumsy dance shuffle: a half moonwalk, a half stumble, then caught his balance with a squeaky-shoe lean on the black curtain behind him. His fingers caught hold. He checked, and, yes, still well-lit in the circle of life.

"Of course, things are not okay. But hasn't that always been the case? Things have always been not okay. Prehistoric times—things were *not okay*."

Henry shrugged. "Things were just… *Ooooooooook!*"

The reactive laughter from the lit audience beyond gave Henry's straight face a struggle.

"I try to stay positive. I'm not having a break*down*, I'm just cracking *up*."

Henry smiled. "And this is the Crack-Up Comedy Club. Where I can't club you to death, but I can drop some bombs.

"You've been a terrifying audience. Thank you, for not eating me."

Sunlight poured through the wall-sized windows of the penthouse, slanting across the dusty floor like liquid gold. It made the debris in the corner sparkle—the overturned chair, the cracked blinds, the open notebook with scribbled jokes scattered like confetti.

Henry's eyes watered, squinting against the brightness, as if the day had snuck in while he slept only half-awake.

The city below was quiet. Silent, really, except for the occasional scrape or distant thump that carried faintly up the forty flights of stairs he hadn't yet descended. Light had a way of making things look normal, even when nothing was.

Henry stretched, feeling every knot and ache from last night's performance—the tension in his jaw, the phantom hum of the stage lights still buzzing behind his eyes. The notebook lay open on the kitchen counter, coffee-stained pages fluttering gently in the warm breeze from the open patio door.

He picked it up, leafed through the sketches and jokes he'd performed, laughing softly at the absurdity of some of them. The raspberry juice gargle, the Jazz Apples, the CEO joke—they felt like relics of another life. A life that, in sunlight, seemed almost imaginary.

11

The sun glanced through the high branches along Bennett Park, the early-afternoon light soft enough that Henry dared a longer walk than usual. The slope on Fort Washington Avenue had been a minefield of stalled sedans and abandoned SUVs for weeks, but today he had a mission: clear the incline so the next time he needed to escape, he wouldn't go flying down it like a grocery cart on a hill.

He reached the crest, hands on his hips, surveying his crooked kingdom of metal.

"All right," he muttered. "Let's play traffic cop."

Most of the cars he pushed or rolled aside were standard, boring, city-life husks—Honda CR-Vs, Toyota Camrys, that one Subaru with eight different bumper stickers about national parks. But then—half-buried under blown leaves and a city's worth of silence—he saw it.

A red 2001 Plymouth Prowler.

It looked like a cartoon hot rod that had aged into a mid-life crisis. The kind of car someone bought after a bitter divorce but before therapy. Henry grinned.

"Well, don't you look spicy."

He tugged the door. Unlocked. Inside: leather seats, a faint smell of coconut air freshener, and—miracle of miracles—a 6-CD changer, the first one since the world ended.

He slid behind the wheel, feeling absurdly cool for someone in a world without witnesses.

The ignition turned.

The Prowler coughed, then roared to life, loud enough to startle the pigeons on the nearest lamppost.

Henry flinched.

"Shh, shh, don't do that," he whispered, patting the dash. "Think stealth. Ninja car. Quiet car."

He hit the "CD" button.

Disc 3 loaded.

Dave Matthews.

Henry sighed. "Of course. Of course you'd be that guy."

He pulled away from the curb anyway.

He drove slowly up the incline toward the northern tip of the island, weaving between the vehicles he had already nudged aside days earlier. The Prowler handled better than anything he'd driven since the collapse—responsive, eager, as if it remembered how to be a car.

Halfway up the slope, he saw it.

A Peterbilt 579 tanker, gleaming silver, hulking across both lanes like an old giant taking a nap.

What? What are you doing there? I don't remember you.

"Come on." He slapped the wheel. "Come on, you fathead, get your fatass truck outta my waaaaay!" Then he laughed.

The truck did not move. Trucks never did. Trucks had no manners.

He stopped a good thirty yards behind it. Grumbling, he reached to switch CDs—anything less self-important than Dave—

And the next track began.

"Oh."

Henry's hand hovered over the center console.

The opening chords trickled out like soft light through cracked blinds.

Then the voice. That voice. He remembered why he liked Dave Matthews.

His breath caught.

"Oh," he whispered.

Her favorite song? Something about this song? Their favorite? An engagement ring?

His chest tightened—not painfully, but sweetly, like someone tugging a ribbon tied around his ribs. She rose to the surface of his thoughts so suddenly it knocked the air out of him.

Her laugh—light, musical, effortless.

Her fingers—warm against his.

The rooftop dance—sun catching the multi-tinted layers of her auburn hair.

Her voice whispering something he couldn't quite hear but could feel in his bones.

He closed his eyes.

The music filled the Prowler completely, drowning out the world, replacing it with something soft and golden.

A montage unspooled inside him: summer sidewalks, her hair brushing his cheek, a late-night walk where she slipped her arm around him and said—

He couldn't hear the words.

He tried.

He pressed harder into the memory as if force alone would sharpen it.

The sound of the tanker did not exist to him.

Not the soft grind.

Not the vibration in the pavement.

Not the slow backward roll.

The world narrowed to a single, trembling note in the song—and her face half-turning toward him in the haze of memory—

Until something cold touched his spine.

A shift.

A shadow.

A shudder.

Henry's eyes snapped open.

The truck was coming toward him, rolling downhill with deliberate weight, the tanker's bulk blotting out the sun. Closing sixty feet... forty-five... twenty... ten... until unlit tail lights and mud flaps filled his vision—

"Shhhhiiiiiffffttt!"

He slammed the gear into reverse and floored the accelerator. The Prowler reeled, tires squealing as Henry jerked the wheel hard left. The car fishtailed, skidding sideways. The tanker thundered past on his left, missing the Prowler's front end by inches.

Metal roared.

Air shook.

The Prowler spun to a breathless stop.

Henry's heart hammered like it was trying to escape his ribs.

He stared as the tanker coasted down the incline, gathering speed, veering off, unstoppable.

As it passed, something made him look up—just briefly. The cab. There was no one inside. No hands on the wheel. No body behind the glass. But the driver's door—

It swung slightly open.

Not fully, not wildly.

Just… ajar.

As if someone had stepped out a moment before.

As if someone had left it open on purpose.

Henry sat rigid in the Prowler, every muscle held, the music still playing softly behind him.

And for a moment—just a moment—he wasn't sure which was more frightening:

The empty truck rolling backward on its own…

…Or, her memory, feeling more real than anything else left in the world, almost lost.

Before Henry turned the lobby lights off, he stepped out onto the sidewalk in front of the club and marked the time: sunlight had dipped below the skyline. The buildings overlooking him all bled red through their windows. Layer upon layer, transparent sheets of descending shades, each a darker hue of night, fell through the atmosphere and deepened while expanding, merging shadows. The bright lights favoring the comedy club's entrance were extinguished.

Back inside, he stood in the wings, adjusting his collar, staring at the generator's indicator light. Still green. Still humming. The club had no audience anymore—not the kind with beating hearts, anyway—but he performed all the same.

The creatures filled the auditorium. Shadow forms. Rows of silhouettes, unmoving except for the occasional twitch. Their eyes glowed faintly in the dark, dull yellow like cheap candles. They didn't laugh, didn't breathe, didn't blink. But they came.

And as long as the stage lights were on, they stayed in their assigned area.

Henry stepped onto the stage, struggling to keep muscles from locking up. He found the stool and the mic and squinted into the brightness.

"So, a guy walks into a bar filled with vampires. The bartender asks what he can get for him. Guy says, 'You serve Bloody Marys?' Bartender says, 'Sure, but around here they're just called Marys. The bloody part usually screams and runs.'"

Pause.

"'And if it doesn't run—congratulations, you're the garnish.'"

Silence.

He smiled anyway. A little performance for the void.

He shuffled note cards. Most of them were blank.

"Honestly," he said, "tell me, how many of you were vampires before all this went down?"

The spotlight buzzed above him. Something in the crowd moved —just one figure—but enough for his throat to catch.

"Maybe I should've tried mime," he muttered.

Then: a pop. A sharp sound, like a bulb bursting.

The stage lights flickered. The generator in the back coughed once. Then the room went black.

No lights. No buzz. Just silence and heat.

Henry was a frozen daiquiri once again.

"Um—"

A low hiss rolled through the crowd, like wind through dry leaves. Somewhere, something shifted. Feet—dozens of them—scraping lightly across the floor.

His mouth opened, but no sound came.

Then—

A narrow beam of light cut through the dark. A flashlight. Steady. Searching. Widening.

It moved down the aisle, illuminating nothing and everything at once. The figures backed away from it, shrinking into corners, hissing softly but never touching it.

Henry stared, breath caught in his chest.

A woman emerged, faintly glowing behind the light, staring up at Henry.

She wore a dark coat, boots scuffed from travel. Her face was… he couldn't describe it. Familiar and impossible. Hair pulled back. Eyes focused like headlights. She moved forward with complete calm.

The crowd of surrounding dark forms moaned in unison, a choir.

She climbed the steps to the stage. Henry hadn't moved. His legs didn't respond. His hands trembled. His eyes followed her. The light swung, cutting back the monsters like a machete.

She raised the flashlight slightly, shining it on Henry. Her expression softened—a small, impossible smile, ghostly behind the light.

She stepped through the darkness like the angel of debt collections. I wanted to say something smooth. Something memorable. But my mouth...

My mouth chose a new evolutionary path.

"Ghhhhhuh—"

Henry crossed his eyes. And fainted.

And awoke face-down on his mattress. The room smelled like perfume and sweat. The CPAP was humming softly, the mask and tube laying on the floor, the black sleep mask twisted over his sweaty forehead. The sun lit the walls now—clean, dry light.

He sat up.

The comedy club was gone. The woman—gone. The flashlight. The hiss of the crowd. All gone.

"No," he whispered. "Imp—Impossible."

10

He left the toy store when the day's color began to tilt—later than he preferred, but still within the margin of "probably safe". The ice cream trike felt lighter and easier to push, even with the bat and basket of baseballs, the holster and gun, and a newly-acquired dartboard with darts, at times rattling softly in the cooler.

He had gone far, bike-riding, with an early-morning start. No jogging today.

Starting at Hudson River Park, he knocked some balls over the trees. Of the few shorter flights launched, he went and retrieved the balls, where the grass lay open and flat. If he knocked one through a window or sank one in between the architectural shadows, he considered it gone. He'd ride the trike in the general vicinity, giving the area a quick scan. Of the four he successfully recovered, he batted one again from the spot and watched it soar over the avenue and disappear.

And this was his unmapped back-to-the-base biking-and-batting play of the day.

He parked the trike at an intersection and stretched and walked, bat swinging at his side like he was stepping up to the plate. His interest shifted to the vehicles surrounding him.

As a moment of dizziness touched his scalp like a soft breeze, Henry sat on a bus bench and noticed a brown satchel propped on the armrest. He picked it up and looked inside. Empty. It might be usable for carrying something. Notebook? Small items? No bloodstains on it. *Nice.*

Put this on my tab.

Henry tested the strap; it felt durable. *Yeah.* He hung it over his shoulder. Patted it against his side.

He closed his eyes for a moment, light-headed. Removed his glasses, gently rubbed his lids. Tried to remember how long he'd slept last night.

He stood, rolled his neck to chase the stiffness from his spine, and staggered. Then, letting the wind lick his moist scalp-line, he squinted at rows of sunlit chrome and shuffled over to inspect a few.

A few too many.

Absentmindedly, he shopped—killing the clock—as the satchel filled with pocket-sized loot of no immediate value. Perhaps things he would stare at later: a glow stick; a lighter and some matches; an Asian man's passport *(secret Asian man Wang Zhang)*; a keychain flashlight with a dead AAA battery; a compass; some Post-It notes and a pen; a tire pressure gauge.

The street had gone soft and hazy, the sunlight thinning like a transparent curtain being slowly pulled.

At Ninth and Forty-fifth, he passed the same gray sedan he always did—battered, its nose jammed into a fire hydrant, not crashed so much as surrendered.

With his usual careful prowess, he approached, keeping a clear view of the front and back interior, everything well-lit.

Something caught his eye.

The keys.

Still in the ignition. Caked in dried blood.

Henry considered. He stepped closer, peering through the glass. No one inside—only a crusted smear on the steering wheel and some sun-faded fast food wrappers on the passenger seat. He opened the door. It creaked like a coffin hinge.

A claustrophobic dread slid into the driver's seat with Henry, as if he were being forced into this coffin, to be buried alive. He choked on a panicky gasp, but it slipped away quickly and left him smiling. The vinyl was hot enough to burn, but he didn't care. The bat landed and dropped down between the passenger door and the seat. His hand reached out on its own and turned the key.

Nothing.

No cough, no churn. A dead hum.

Henry dropped his head to the steering wheel.

"I've tried you before," he whispered. "Damn."

He smacked his lips, sniffed, and winced. "Whew."

He swiped a hand to shoo off a buzzing (fly?) that was circling to land.

"How could I forget you?"

The words were quiet, almost affectionate. He wasn't sure if he was talking to the car—or to himself. Weak laughter followed.

He lingered too long. The air inside swelled with heat, an oven closing in. His eyelids drooped. Sleep reached for him with warm, persuasive fingers, coaxing him toward something waiting beneath.

Henry stirred, his forehead throbbing where it seemed stuck to the steering wheel. With some effort, he lifted his head and felt it tilting off-balance. He reached up slowly to stabilize it and felt the skin above his eyes puffed and tender, leaking a warm smear of blood that had traced its way down toward the bridge of his nose. The smell of old vinyl and dust filled his nostrils now with burnt rubber and toast. A clot of spit and copper mingled on his chin, and a metallic taste of torn, spinachy flesh clung stubbornly to his sore tongue.

His twitching eyelid pulled back slightly from his right eye, then blinked once, then closed, and the left eye winked and went back in. Then both opened, slightly cross-eyed at first.

Through the windshield, the city was unstable, shimmering not with heat but with the strange tremor of his bloodshot vision. Towers bent fractionally at their tops. The sky bent as though seen through warped glass. He felt nausea gather deep inside him, swell up the length of his chest, and he fumbled for the latch. The door groaned open, and he pitched forward, retching onto the curb. The sound was violent, echoing against the concrete like a wound torn open.

For a moment afterward, he sat doubled in the cab, gasping, eyes wet. The tears came unbidden, not from sadness exactly, but from the body's exhaustion—he wept without knowing why. A trembling hand rubbed across his cheek, and still bent over the pavement, he let a small and almost absurd smile touch his lips. The sickness gone, however briefly, left him feeling lighter, emptied.

He pulled himself from the seat, knees shaking, one hand braced against the roof of the car. The late afternoon air wrapped around him —cooler than the inside of the vehicle, carrying the distant musty scent of the river, the acrid bite of garbage long since uncollected. His legs wavered beneath him as though the ground were shifting. He stood there for a while, disoriented, staring down the boulevard, which seemed to ripple and recede like a mirage.

The car door hung open behind him, and he steadied himself against it while the dizziness ebbed. The bruise on his forehead pulsed with each heartbeat. He touched it gingerly, then pulled his hand back at the sight of red. Dark-red. The smear on his fingertips looked almost black in the dimming light.

That's... fine. Little paint job. Little touch-up. Head's leaking... that's normal.

He lifted his eyes again, trying to focus on the street. A row of storefronts faced him across the avenue—shuttered grates, papered glass, one tilted awning still clinging to its frame. Above them, the high-rises loomed, facades mottled by lengthening shadows as the sun crawled downward. Every edge seemed wrong to him, every corner blurred or doubled. He strained, but the harder he tried to sharpen his vision, the more the buildings tremulated like a faulty projection on a fraying screen.

Where was he?

His throat was raw, his mouth bitter. He swallowed against it and turned his head slowly, eyes swimming weakly back and forth, things bobbing in the ripples.

A dented green rectangle with peeling white letters. They swam for a second before settling, forming: W 45 ST. The first word tumbled from his lips, a reflexive slip, and the sound of it startled him—dropping too loud in the empty street, warped with slur and soreness, twisted by a haunting lisp. It echoed down the canyon of the avenue and came back, distorted, someone else mimicking him.

Henry's lips snapped shut, a weak defense against the thought trying to punch through the fog—the sudden, sickening awareness of his condition. His knees buckled. His legs quivered with a small, rhythmic tremor, as if the asphalt itself were holding its breath, waiting to drop him when it felt like it.

Still, he willed his mind forward, leaned on the hood for balance, and forced the questions: Where was he? Who could help him leave this place?

The questions didn't wait for answers. They just kept coming, pushing, until his brain—under pressure—sent in the bodyguards. Nothing to see here. Move along. Interrogation over.

He could picture a tall, familiar building, but it wasn't here. Its glass face rose cleanly against the sky, yet the image wouldn't attach itself to the ground beneath his feet. Jarred—no, worse than jarred—he tried to haul in the missing details. Finger on the corner of a blurred memory flapping wildly in the hurricane of his mind.

Letting... Pot-Pock... Fox-ting.

Names he must have said a thousand times. The first keys he managed to grab. The ones that should have opened something important. But not yet.

Pop-Tart?

What else?

Images without words sparked and burned out like falling stars: creamy peach trees; plaza steps between them, their treads bronzed by sun and time. Branches. Steps. Climb. The lines crossed the moment he followed them. Every direction pointed somewhere wrong.

The green street sign quivered in his sightline, as if caught in a breeze he couldn't feel. He tried again to lock it into place, but his eyes watered, letters melting into pale streaks against the aluminum. He stared beyond, wiped his face with the back of his hand, and suddenly couldn't remember whether he'd said the word aloud already—or only imagined doing so.

"Weth-th… Fow-ty… fifth."

West.

No—north?

East. East, right.

Right was… not west.

Rest. Light.

Should have.

The sun—up.

One way… meant time.

Which… way?

East—east, though… why east?

He pressed both palms flat against the hood of the car, bowing his head. The steel still held the day's warmth, and for a moment, he felt a comfort there, a reminder of the sun, which was vanishing behind the towers. He breathed shallowly, listening for the familiar background noise of the city—traffic, voices, the endless throb of life. Nothing came. The quiet was so complete, his own uneven breaths sounded intrusive.

A flicker of movement caught his eye: a reflection high in a window, nothing more than the last red wedge of sunlight catching glass. Yet he startled, jerking upright, scanning the roadway as if someone had been standing there. No one. Only shadows layered across one another, window frames like sockets of blind eyes.

He touched his forehead again, half afraid the swelling had worsened, and felt the sticky trace of blood still there. He looked down at the sidewalk by his shoes, the dark splatter of vomit drying into the cracks. The sight of it sent a tremor through him. Proof he'd been here. Proof of his weakness.

Classy. Five stars. Would puke again.

He told himself to breathe—slow, steady—but the air came ragged. The avenue stretched away in both directions, straight as a ruler, yet he could not decide which end held the way home.

Home.

He closed his eyes to see it again. But the more he squeezed mind-muscle for tears of recognition, the more the image dissolved, becoming less a building than a trick of the mind, a hollow tower shifting every time he tried to step toward it.

His knees bent, and he let himself slide down the side of the car until he was seated on the curb. The frame pressed into his spine, as a moan spewed out in a spray of air; the concrete was cold beneath him. He folded his arms across his chest and tried to make himself small, a boy waiting to be collected. A low hum built behind his ears, a pressure not of sound but sensation, like a tuning fork set loose in his skull. He let his head tip back and stared upward.

The sky was a fading bruise. Violet bled into orange, then into a pallid yellow already paling toward gray. High above, the glass towers caught those colors and broke them into shivers, throwing twisted, kaleidoscopic reflections down onto the street. For a moment, Henry thought he saw the whole avenue undulating, as though water moved across it, bending lampposts and scaffolds into fluid shapes. He blinked, and the illusion stilled, but the unease stayed with him.

He raised a hand, shading his eyes, and tried to trace the sun's descent. The glare stung. It was lower than he expected, much lower, and with the realization came a coil of panic: night was closer than he had thought. He whispered a word under his breath—home—but it felt distant, foreign on his tongue. He whispered it again, softer, as though repeating it might draw the building toward him.

The silence pressed harder. Somewhere in the distance, a pane of glass creaked in its frame, or maybe it was only the blood in his ears. His legs shifted restlessly, wanting to rise, to run, but the rest of him refused. Every direction felt off course. If he stood and chose one, he feared walking himself further from where he belonged, deeper into a city that no longer had its lines or logic. So, he stayed on the curb, paralyzed, the shadows lengthening all around him, waiting for some sign to break the stalemate.

Bent forward, knuckles white on knees, his breath rasped, hot against the raw air. A sour trace of vomit clung to the corners of his mouth. He wiped at it without much conviction, his sleeve smearing rather than clearing.

For a few seconds—minutes, maybe—he listened. The silence pressed. Every throb of his pulse seemed like a trespass.

From somewhere far, far away, an alien shriek echoed. Maybe a pigeon. Then silence again.

His thoughts tried to line up for the headroom roll call, but some weren't in attendance, and some scattered before they could form any sense. Still, something inside him said he had to move.

Sitting here felt like sinking—deeper into something he couldn't climb out of. A head-locked feeling: if he didn't move now, he would never move again. He glanced left down the boulevard, then right. In both directions—everywhere—the energetic illusion of day was seeping into the earth, pulling him down with it.

The dizziness ebbed and swelled, and with it came a strange panic —not sharp but thick and patient, like a rising tide. His hands trembled, fear almost absurd in its plainness. He had to stand. He had to move.

He crawled back up the side of the car to find his feet again.

He pressed a palm against his temple, as though he could squeeze clarity back in, and whispered to no one in a drooling slur, "Juth... Wauk."

The car ticked—a change of temperature—a few faint dry clicks, like a clock marking the seconds he didn't have. Henry leaned against the frame, cheek pressed to the roof, eyes closed. His hand groped for the door again, as if maybe he'd climb back inside, pull it shut, let his forehead find the steering wheel again, and let the night and the city roll over him while he slept.

His legs twitched restlessly, betraying him. Even in this postictal state, his body understood the somewhat redacted orders from above, and the car was no haven.

I don't even know... You're not the same car. Where'd you go— come from?

He straightened. One hand steadied him on the door, the other caught his bruised forehead on trembling fingertips and lightly massaged. He stepped forward, shoes scraping glass, body jerking at inner electrical prods—an ill-assembled machine barely obeying its own levers. He swayed. Paused. Took another step. The pavement seemed uncertain under him, as if he'd forgotten the rhythm of walking, each step like a thought he had to push through fog to remember.

The quietness in the thoroughfare became unbearable—too wide, too loud, an empty stage waiting for a line. A tremor crawled down his arms, and he realized he was pressing both palms against the edge of the hood, fingers curling, stretching. He whispered, "Hukay," though he didn't believe it, and peeled himself free from the car's magnetism.

This step was awkward, his leg leaden, as though the pavement might tilt or give way. The next step was worse—his knee collapsed, and for a moment, he thought gravity was only a drumbeat in his head. He staggered, lurched, breath catching, then forced another step, then a fourth, counting now, each one carrying him farther from the car and deeper into the vast, disjointed quiet. Each step was an argument with his nerves.

Left foot, right foot. Three times a lady. In a row. Fast. Standing ovation.

All this time, his arms trembled as if they carried a ghost-weight. A slow throb worked its way through the base of his neck. His throat felt dry and empty, as if lined with paper.

The sunlight stung his temples, and the world tilted to one side. The wavy paving sent him wobbling. He had moved forward, and now he steadied himself on the edge of the hood again, then let go, forcing his legs into something like a stride. They responded, halting and clumsy.

A few paces on, he slowed, eyes caught by another vehicle across the street. An old Porsche, its windows dusted white with ash, its hood collapsed as if struck from above. He swayed where he stood, palms damp, unsure if he had the strength to keep going. His gaze drifted to the next indistinct shape: a blue minivan angled on the curb ahead, tires turned in.

That's a five-yard penalty. Infracshment. Infracture. Fraction. Fiction.

A faint sourness in the air. Ozone? Exhaust? The smells tangled and broke apart before he could name them.

Eyes refusing to focus for long, he had yet to notice his missing glasses.

The car door in front of him seemed too close, then too far, its handle glinting and slipping away like a fish in water.

Something tugged at him. Another shape nearby, lower, heavier, with its nose pointed toward the street. A van, or a truck. His mind swayed toward it, then back to the Porsche, the way a body drifts between shallow sleep and waking. He couldn't decide, couldn't trust the thought to stay still.

The curb pressed into his hip. He shifted, winced, and realized he had lowered himself to the sidewalk. Sat down, lay down. When did this happen? Muscles ached in odd places—as if he'd been thrown, bent, shaken. He told himself not to move yet. Not too much. Not until the dizziness let go.

This curb came out of nowhere… I am very, very uninsured.

And then the fear stirred: not of the street, not of the darkened windows around him, but of his own body—of it betraying him again, seizing up without warning. He drew a breath, held it, as if listening to the engine of his own chest, waiting for the next misfire.

He pressed his palms to the rough concrete, trying to lift himself. Muscles screamed. His knees and buttocks lifted in slow increments, arms stiffening like fold-out table legs, heels scuffing and pressing for a stance. He rose, squatted, thrust again—his effort to stand resembling the stuttering rhythm of a prisiadki dance exercise. An out-of-body moment might have lent a flicker of levity to the lucid mind he had lost.

Finally, limbs shifted properly, his body instinctively adjusting, turning over, pushing up, operating on innate programming. He found his feet again and a brief, fragile sense of balance.

His nerves jittered, his thoughts floundered, and his heart seemed out of rhythm. He gripped his knees and waited, afraid of slipping sideways onto the pavement and into some irreversible break.

Then he straightened. One leg went forward, testing the weight of the world beneath it; the other followed, slow, deliberate. Each step felt as if the pavement might tip, might crumble, might decide he had no right to stand.

A pull drew his gaze again to the street, to vehicular shapes smeared with dust and shadow. His eyes could not focus, drifting between them, lingering on one, then the other, then back, as though the vehicles were shifting when he wasn't looking. His arms swung slightly to keep his balance. His stomach churned.

Everything's turning up downside… down up… side… down. Daisies.

He stopped after a few paces. One hand touched the hood of the nearest car, cold, solid, reassuring. For a long moment, he held it, listening to the angry ape-man beating a bongo in his chest. Then, as if summoned by some invisible cue, he straightened and moved again, one faltering step, then another, zig-zagging slightly, eyes bouncing from the curb to the cracked asphalt to the blurred forms of vehicles, poles, a bike dock, a barrier—each step an act of tiny courage.

A sudden jolt shot through his head, a sharp flare: vertigo and nausea tangled together, rising from his gut to his skull, a sharp spin of balance and weightlessness making him doubt his own body. He tried to breathe through it, but the air caught in his chest. He stumbled forward, one foot dragging, then the other. The sidewalk tilted beneath him. The street seesawed, like wings trembling in the grip of turbulence. Lights swirled as shadows splashed. Cold nerves sucking on his spine, his arms lifted instinctively, seeking something to steady against.

And then—

His left palm pressed against a wall and pulled his balance. Cool brick. He pressed harder. Stock-still brick. Still cool. It didn't collapse or tip over. It caught his fall and kept him up.

His lungs were searching for a gear, shifting between faint wheezes and heavy, shuddering draws.

His head lolled forward, caught on his chest, and he had to make a deliberate decision—neck up, Henry, neck up—to bring it back upright.

For a while—was it a while?—he did nothing but stare at the shadow his hand made. It looked larger than it should. It looked like somebody else's hand. He waited to see if it would move without him. It didn't.

He blinked, trying to align his vision with the swaying world. He paused, his back against the brick wall, heart hammering. Then, with effort, he forced himself another step, then another, until he reached the curb again. He turned slowly, glanced back at the stretch of brick wall, the cool shade of tinted bluish mortar veins lacing the bruised rectangular muscles of hardened clay. He blinked for focus to decipher it.

Shadows warped and stretched at the corners of his vision. Each footfall felt uncertain, like stepping onto a gelatin surface slowly being drawn into a monster's mouth. He blinked faster, trying to pin the world in place—but it swirled instead, freezing him mid-step.

Steady... steady... or don't. Pick one.

Then, with a slow, hesitant momentum, he forced one foot forward, then another, trying to carve a path through the wavering air.

He started to follow the line of vehicles.

His journey began.

"Thix-'een."

Pavement seemed to tilt beneath him, rising at odd angles and shifting, alive and unsteady. His eyes flicked from one vehicle to another—first the white Audi, then the silver Lexus angled onto a crushed bush, then a shadowed brown Chevy truck across the intersection—unable to settle, unable to trust anything more than the scrape of his shoes against concrete.

Henry suddenly hunched forward, hit by an overwhelming wave of emotion. He cried for a moment, until blubbering sounds became chewed-up words: "Don' eeh meh! Uh-n' ee uh!"

A breeze picked up, smelling faintly of oil and something dead, and it made him stagger. He flinched, arms reaching out for imaginary supports, fingertips brushing the canvas wind. The nausea flared again, a hot pulse from his stomach up through his throat, and he hunched slightly, pressing his hand to a streetlight post to secure himself. He sighed, head tilting gently, and saw the streetlight flickering. He sniffed, wiped his face, and took a short breath.

If... if... could... just one... minute... just stop... one... spinning... minute...

Each motion felt exaggerated, like moving underwater. He stepped, then paused. Stepped, then froze. The street's shapes crossed in his vision—curbs tilting, shadows stretching, broken glass catching the dying light—and he found himself wondering, fleetingly, if he'd ever been here before, if the city had always looked this wrong. His mind tugged at the edges of recognition but dissolved into fog before it could grasp anything.

He forced a step forward, then another. His arms swung like a pendulum for balance. His chest still felt tight. Another step. Another. He drifted past the Porsche again—had it crossed the avenue? Had he? —Ignoring it now, drawn instead to the open stretch ahead, toward a block which might hold some sense of familiarity, though his mind could not remember its shape, Henry felt the deep, stormy rumblings in his head begin to dissipate.

Block ahead—square peg, round hole—ooh, I'm the blockhead? We... we square, Peg?

A tentative calm settled through him, but it was brittle, like ice forming over tumultuous water. His legs still trembled, each step uncertain, each exhalation measured, as though his body and mind were clinching the fragile truce between motion and collapse. The city around him remained an alien landscape, its lines wavering, colors shifting, edges bending beyond comprehension.

The faintest murmur gathered, voices braided into breath—strangers, parents, angels—one word: *"Try."*

He lifted his chin, felt the ache in his jaw and temple, and let his gaze wander. The roadway stretched on, a glimmering ribbon of gray and shadow. One leg trembled as he tested it, then the other, his muscles stiff and uncooperative.

A slight inhale, a shaky exhale. He shifted weight from heel to toe, each step a question: could he trust the ground beneath him? Could he trust himself? The faint whisper pulsed again in his memory—one word, one push: *"Try."*

He edged forward, hand brushing the hood of the nearest car for reassurance. Footfall. He dropped to one knee, hands reaching down to brace him again. Concrete pressed cold against his palms. Up again. Step. *"Try."* Another step. The sidewalk tilted, shadows bending, and he staggered, arms outstretched, brushing the empty air for props that weren't there.

A gust of wind rattled a loose shutter above, and Henry flinched, knees wobbling. The street seemed longer now, the avenue stretching farther than before. Yet he continued, slow and zigzagging, eyes flicking from vehicle to vehicle, curb to curb, searching for something familiar, anything stable. Footstep. Pause. Brain—body bruised.

Step again.

The world swirled in fragments—windows bending, brickwork wobbling, colors smeared at the edges. His head throbbed, a dull, receding echo beneath the pulse of the whisper: *"Try."*

Step. Another. One movement at a time, Henry began to carve a path forward, however uncertain, however small.

Henry moved faster, then slower, then stopped altogether. His brain spun after itself—like a tetherball whirling loose from the pole, every swing of his legs sending it farther out of reach.

Faster, then slower, then stopped. The landscape was a mirror image. Storefronts leaned with broken signs he should've known, but his mind wouldn't match them to memory. The block he had started on didn't fit the spinning void encircling him. He doubled back, only to find the same corner, the same shattered mailbox, the same obscene graffiti bleeding through the brick. He was there and turned and here now—the same place in another time, yet another place all the same.

Same... same damn joke... Punchline... just a circle... Follow... hollow...

Another pole leaned in and caught him. He pushed away, insistent.

Faster, then slower, then stopping. Spinning loose from the pole, then gripping it again, a tetherball volley gone wrong—his feet kicking in one direction, his brain swinging back, both chasing the other and missing, motion spiraling, until, for an instant, something landed the right punch and returned him. But holding it together too long seemed to be a violation.

Gotta keep my head... His thought, unfinished, only repeated.

Playing, but not in the game yet.

He slow-danced awkwardly, arrhythmically, around a garbage can, the garbage can leading with perfect poise. He twirled free, stumbled, and his legs crossed in protest—unsure which way to skirt the empty bike-dock. It was a moment best forgotten—and it would be. Henry struggled to untangle the mixed signals to his legs and feet, each step a stubborn argument with the ground. The street felt like shifting platforms in the bowels of an unfunhouse beneath him, pulling him into the wrong rhythm until he willed himself upright and forced the next step.

He turned again. Wrong.

Turned again. Wrong again.

The light was lowering, the world losing definition. Shadows stretched like spilled ink, slipping into cracks and alleys, growing teeth. He felt them on his neck before they were even near.

"Noth here. Noth nowuh." His own voice shook, small and swallowed by the empty rows, tongue thick and clumsy between his teeth.

His chest rose and fell too fast. Each breath snagged, like his lungs were catching on barbed wire. His vision swam. The horizon tilted. His hands clawed at the air as though the city had turned to water and he was submerged, being pulled down into the black.

He stumbled against a car door, left a sweaty handprint, and kept going. The crescent bent where it shouldn't. A building leaned where it hadn't before. His mind failed him, rewrote the geography, mocked him with familiar shapes gone crooked.

The sky deepened. Shadows overlapped. The first hints of night cracked open around him.

Panic set its claws deeper. His pulse was in his throat, in his ears, in his teeth. He staggered forward, then back, eyes darting, hunting for the light, for the line, for anything resembling safe passage.

"*Pleathe,*" he whispered, though to whom he didn't know.

He was drowning on dry land.

A gust tugged at his jacket, snapping him upright from a hesitant crouch. His fingers brushed against the metal of a nearby car, cold and solid. It grounded him, a small confirmation that something real still existed beneath the shifting world. Step. He forced his weight onto one foot, then the other. Not smooth, not confident, but deliberate.

The avenue stretched ahead, fractured in the half-light, but he caught a gleam—a reflective panel on a building, a shard of window glass angled precisely. His eyes fixed on it, and for a heartbeat, the city seemed less fluid, less bent. Step. Another. He staggered, wobbling, but the motion carried him forward.

A distant clatter echoed from an alley, sharp against the evening hush. Henry flinched, instinct pressing him sideways, but he forced himself past it. Footstep. Stomp. His lungs pulled air with a little more rhythm, his chest easing into the mechanics of breathing. He wasn't safe yet, not close, but he was moving.

Something leapt from a shadowed corner—faces appearing, a memory catching him off-guard, mugging his mind, stealing his breath. He staggered, gripping a car door for balance.

Paramedics—bright uniforms, sharp angles of light—flooded the edges of his vision.

Voices:

"His eyes are open."

"You are okay. You are being transported in an ambulance."

The words echoed strangely, as they belonged somewhere else, somewhere he wasn't, yet they carried a fragment of stability. Stomp. Scrape. His body remembered movement, remembered that it could obey.

Step again.

Each footfall felt assisted by a presence outside of himself, holding his hand, guiding, then letting go. The flickering world of bending streets and leaning buildings held still for an instant. He blinked, and the memory softened, dissolving into the background, but its effect lingered: he could move, he could breathe, he could survive.

Scrape. Stomp. The pavement felt more certain beneath him, though not entirely. Each movement, each cautious footfall, reminded him that he was not fully lost—yet. Shadows still twisted at the edges of his vision, teasing corners, elongating alleyways, turning familiar streets into strange, alien corridors.

He blinked, forcing his eyes to settle on something—anything—solid. A fire hydrant, chipped and orange, caught his gaze. He held it for a breath, letting the rhythm of his heart sync, however briefly, with the pulse of the city. He tried to remember which way he had come, which way he needed to go. The lines tangled again, but he forced himself forward, dragging one foot in front of the other like a tentative promise.

The air carried the fading scent of day-warmed asphalt, laced with something coppery. He shivered, arms twitching, rubbed his shoulders, hugged his torso briefly, as though the hug might keep the city's twisting streets from pulling him apart. Stamp. Clap. Scrape.

He pushed a finger up the bridge of his nose, instinctively.

"Crap!" he blurted, in a panicked burst—a safer stand-in for the word his tongue couldn't yet twist around—and with the lisp still tangled, it would have likely launched him straight into a ridiculous, anger-fueled fit of laughter and tears.

The word replayed in his mind, and his head wobbled on a jerky swivel, as if the spirit of a demonic Ed Sullivan had briefly possessed him. His shoulders shrugged involuntarily. He laughed and cried, anyway. He fell against the telephone pole.

And then—

It hit from behind, a bullet through the brain, rattling the edges of his mind. A warp-speed descent to the darkest depths. In a flash—

He was five again, legs crossed on the carpet, staring at the analog glow of the color television—the Tonight Show. Johnny leaned over with a cockeyed smile. "That is… really wild."

Behind him, his father glitched, stuck in a looping, warped impression of Sullivan: "We have a really big show." Lips puckered, shoulders hunched, movement blurred. His mother's voice drifted from the kitchen, sharp but softened by the distance, singing some jingle.

On the screen, Carson leaned forward in his chair, eyebrow arched, smile twitching, hands darting in rapid, buoyant rhythm. A monkey-sized, fish-headed Sullivan clambered up his shoulder, wobbling on invisible springs, eyes bulging, grin wiggling like it had a mind of its own. The live studio laughter roared, pulsing straight into Henry's chest, vibrating him like a drum. His mother's voice continued singing, voice breaking. His father's laugh—light, quick—mingled with that of the unseen audience, their applause swelling for the keyed-up, comically defensive host. Johnny Carson turned a deadpan stare on Henry. Ed Sullivan's grin split, fangs flashing.

Henry slumped, his knees giving again. An involuntary spasm—neck caught rigid, forehead tapped aluminum with a whip-crack pop—clunk!—and a spark spun behind his eyes. Shock shivered through him. Fear ignited. Pain ricocheted as he jerked away from the pole, twisting his left ankle on the turn.

Legs now pumping faster than comprehension, he surged forward, carried by a blind, panicked rhythm. The street bent and twisted under his mind's eye. Pavement rippled under flickering streetlights. Each misstep sapped a little more strength, and his left ankle shot a flare up his leg with every click and fire of the heel. Chest tightening, knees wobbling, arms waving, he tumbled with awkward balance, until the city seemed to clutch him, dragging him to a halt, left foot hopelessly caught beneath him.

He paused to regain himself, the fear still alive but beaten down to raspy exhaustion. More of him was catching up to where he was.

The city was still a shifting puzzle, but with each faltering step, Henry began to remember how to inhabit it—how to place himself in its crooked, unkind geometry. The whispers of *"Try"* echoed faintly, almost forgotten, but the meaning was clear: he could move. He must move.

A sudden awareness struck him: the satchel—his new companion—gone. Not in front, not at his side. Panic lanced through, sharper than vertigo. His hands clawed at the space across his torso, trembling fingertips brushing air. He spun, trying to orient himself—where had he set it down?

Every street looked alien. Every curb was a trap. The city seemed to mock him.

Then—fingers grazed a twisted strap. Relief surged in a breathless shudder. He yanked the satchel around, weight grounding him, reminding him that, despite the spinning streets, blurred buildings, and tilting horizon, he still had purchase on something real.

He held it up, opened it, pulled out the lighter—thumb-flicked a flame. Returned it. Retrieved the compass. Hard to read in the failing light, the dimming sky reflected faintly in its glass cover, the needle a sliver of polished iron, its dark tip shuddering between the cardinal points etched N and E.

For a heartbeat, he leaned against the satchel, chest heaving. The world was still out of orbit, still a haze—but he was moving again.

Step. Step. One foot in front of the other.

He limped on, one arm dragging along a brick wall as if its texture could keep him upright. The block stretched ahead, warped by distance, buildings leaning like spectators craning their necks to watch him falter. Streetlamps hummed and flickered, each one sputtering in turn, as though they whispered a warning he couldn't quite translate.

A gust pushed loose papers past his ankles—receipts, menus, a child's spelling test with a red F in the corner—ghosts of other lives, flittering away before he could bend to catch them.

Chasing the debris across the concrete, his gaze caught on a lightly bruised baseball resting on a cracked, weed-infested slab, like a bird's egg in a nest.

Were those weeds—moving? Flexing like fingers?

Then came the sound.

Not close, not yet, but threaded through the silence as a nail dragged across glass. A shuffle, uneven. A scrape. Then stillness again.

Henry's ribs ached. The city held its breath with him.

The scrape didn't return. No echo, no shuffle. Nothing but the faint tremor in his ears, the pressure of blood thumping against the drum. He told himself it was nothing. He wanted it to be nothing.

But the silence was worse. Too clean, too polished, as if the whole block had been scrubbed free of sound. Even his own breath came quieter than it should, sucked thin and stolen away.

He leaned forward, testing a step. The heel clicked. A pause. Nothing followed. Another step, this one quicker, his eyes darting toward the corners where the dark had pooled, slick and heavy, ready to spill.

The scrape came again, softer now—further off—or closer, disguised in its distance.

Henry's throat bobbed. He swallowed air, dry and bitter. One hand rose half-defensively, fingers trembling, as if he might push the silence back into place if it broke again.

Henry stood rooted, pulse tick-ticking up his neck. The silence pressed, thick as wool stuffed in his ears, until every faint creak of tendon, every micro-shift of his shoes on the pavement felt broadcast across the block. The air seemed tighter—sour with dust and the coppery bite of pennies ground between the teeth.

A shiver crawled up his forearms, traced the back of his neck. Night was brushing him, fingers slow and cold.

The scrape returned—long, drawn—then cut off.

Henry exhaled, shaking. He had been holding his breath. Jaw aching, ribs tight. His tongue patted dry lips.

"Wathuz. Big wathuz. Thubway thpethial. Pwobabwy thewing thwough…ah…aluminum thiding. You know how they awe." A painful laugh bubbled out, drool spilling as the tip of his tongue slipped free and smeared his chin in clumsy strokes.

The words sounded like they belonged to some old fisherman with a hook-in-the-tongue impediment—a stranger just over his shoulder. Not Henry Gorestriker at all.

Henry pushed onward, each step contested by pain, but steadier now, his balance no longer betraying him. The city's silence was deceptive—underneath it, he could almost feel a low thrum, as if the streets themselves were trembling awake. Shadows lengthened, curling at the edges of buildings. The sky above bled from pale chestnut to bruised violet, twilight settling in with the weight of inevitability.

A street sign loomed into view, warped at its base, the letters smeared in rust. He squinted hard, trying to place himself, trying to map a route back home. Nothing aligned. The names might as well have been rearranged puzzle pieces, familiar but wrong.

His chest pinched tight again. Instinct pushed him forward. His walk became a clumsy jog, a rhythm of half-trust in his own legs. But the unfamiliar blocks closed in on him, narrower, darker, and his breath came shorter. Henry's jog picked up into a ragged run, fear snapping at his heels. He pressed on, panic pounding with every footfall. He swung around a corner—too fast, too blind—and slammed shin-first into something low and solid.

It toppled beneath him, clattering sideways as he pitched forward, sprawling over its frame. Metal and bone struck pavement in a chorus of scrapes and clunks. The handlebars jabbed his ribs, the mirror cracked with a pop under his shoulder. Pain shot everywhere at once, a fresh chorus to join the old.

For a long moment, he lay tangled in it, wheezing, cheek pressed to cold concrete, half-expecting paramedics to appear, to cart him off with flashing lights and oxygen masks.

That would be heavenly.

But the sirens never came. The absurdity of the thing, lying in wait like some booby trap, struck him dimly through the haze of pain. The impact had flipped him forward. His cry strangled in his throat, pain radiating outward in cruel ripples.

When he finally dared to move, every inch felt like climbing a mountain. He clawed his way upright, back bent, breath ragged. His eyes focused at last on the obstacle.

A rusted, dust-filmed moped.

He studied the machine as if it were some strange animal he'd brought down in the hunt. Blue paint scratched, chrome dulled, one wheel still spinning with a lazy whine. The smell of rubber and gasoline leaked sharply into his nose.

His mind began to move again—slow, mechanical gears turning, studying, calculating.

Henry paused over the toppled moped, hands gripping its cold contours like a lifeline thrown too late.

The street's dimming light stretched long shadows, pooling into cracks and alleyways. From the darkened windows above, faint creaks and whispers threaded down, distant yet unnervingly deliberate. His ears twitched. Was it wind, or something else stirring in the abandoned apartments?

He forced himself to breathe, counting each shaky inhale, letting his fingers trace the moped's frame. The machine was small, light enough to lift, surely, but the thought of getting it upright felt like a climb up a jagged cliff. Every second, the city seemed to hum a low vibration through the soles of his shoes, following his movements and waiting to pounce.

Henry braced himself, nudging the moped upright. A faint rusty groan answered him. The weight surprised him—real, insistent, stubborn. Then, inch by inch, he maneuvered it to a more stable position, muscles trembling, mind clawing back toward focus. After hauling it upright, he steadied it with his knee, and for a moment the world narrowed to a single problem: balance. Two wheels. Gravity.

Keep it up, Henry. Don't drop it again.

The distant, uncanny sounds from above persisted, but for now, he had the moped, and he had a semblance of control.

The stain of dusk was thickening, approaching the descent into the lightless unknowns.

"Okay," he said, carefully. The word came out cleaner this time—still soft, still testing itself.

His head still swam, but the motion slowed, like water settling after a stone stops the flow.

Key.

There was a key.

His fingers found it without thinking.

We're way ahead of ya, buddy.

That felt important. He liked that. He liked not having to ask his brain for permission.

The engine coughed—once—then again. A brittle, rattling complaint that startled him enough to almost make him let go. Henry shuddered, waiting for it to die.

It didn't.

The vibration crept up through his hands, into his arms. Something solid. Alive.

He swung a leg over, awkward and ungraceful, feet scraping the pavement until balance arrived—not elegantly, but enough. The throttle went too far; the moped tipped, then corrected and steadied.

Henry exhaled a laugh that nearly became a sob and didn't.

"Good boy. Good… *Mopey. Mopey and Dopey.*

"I hope you can leave bigguh thkidmarkth than mine."

The seat was cold. The handlebars trembled beneath his palms, the vibration working its way into his chest.

The city shifted.

Not visually—something deeper. A sense of things waking in the erroneous way.

From the darkened windows came movement. Not rushing. Not yet. Shapes pulling themselves free of stillness. A scrape of nails. A wet, impatient sound. The night inhaling.

Henry didn't look too long.

Forward was better.

He eased the throttle. The moped rolled, then carried him into the street. The pavement dipped, sloping downward, and he let gravity take him. Wind cut across his face, sharp enough to feel earned. His thoughts began lining up behind it—not neatly, but in agreement.

Go.

Stay upright.

Don't stop.

Streetlights passed like blinking eyes. Windows slid by, dark and broken, some still faintly glowing, as if the day hadn't quite decided to leave yet.

He didn't know where he was.

But he knew where he wasn't going to stop.

A shape moved on an upper floor. He didn't look long enough to see what it was. He twisted the grip, fear translating itself cleanly into speed.

Home was up.

He didn't know how he knew that either, only that it settled something in him. Up meant light. Up meant air. Up meant away from whatever was beginning to crawl out of the city as the sky bruised darker toward evening.

Then a sound—thin, furious, flawed. It didn't echo the way it should have. It came from behind, and from somewhere above, and maybe from inside his own skull, which was becoming more and more like an old transistor radio picking up static between stations.

Henry leaned low over the handlebars and gave the moped more gas.

The street opened up ahead of him.

This section of roadway was too wide, too strangely empty. The kind of home stretch meant for the traffic that would never come home. The moped's headlamp skimmed the pavement, caught bits of paper, a crushed cup, something reflective that might have been an eye until it wasn't. Or was it?

He kept going, swerving occasionally between accident and intent.

Henry felt it before he heard it.

The shift.

A sound behind him—not a shriek, not yet—more like a decision being made all at once.

He glanced back.

Figures peeled away from doorways and recesses, unfolding themselves from the architecture. They didn't sprint. They poured, spilling into the street with a coordination that made his stomach drop.

Now something shrieked—like it was shoved to the back of the lunch line.

"Oh, thit," Henry said, frightened teeth hiding on his tongue.

He twisted the throttle.

The moped surged forward, rattling in protest. The wind sharpened, tearing at his eyes. Streetlights flicked past in uneven intervals, some dead, some buzzing faintly, as if uncertain they still had a job to do.

Behind him, the sound multiplied—feet slapping pavement, claws striking concrete, the wet scrape of bodies not built for grace but eager to try.

They weren't gaining on him; he was gaining more of them.

Converging from the sidelines. Not fast. Worse than that.

Steady.

Henry leaned low, instinct more than choice, urging the moped into a speed it did not want to give. The avenue stretched on, empty and merciless. No corners. No hiding. Distance—like a worm in converging dirt—became a squirming path through moving shadows.

A strange, ghostly shape rolled through the storefront reflections, moving inside the glass, vanishing, reappearing as brick and darkness and other shapes fractured the warped windows. Too brief, too irregular to track, it blurred the line between what was real and what was only moving—chasing, fleeing. *Mirror Henry*, stitched together from fragments, always slightly out of sync.

A shape lunged from the sidewalk, mistimed, crashing and tumbling—but another replaced it immediately, then another. They learned as they ran.

So did he. Though he wasn't sure it was true, his focus pressed down hard on that side of the seesaw.

Up ahead, the street narrowed. Not a turn—something tighter, a funnel. Scaffolding wrapped the sidewalk.

Henry didn't pause. He didn't calculate. He pressed on.

He cut for it, plunging into the scaffolding corridor. Poles nearly scraped his arms; half-lowered gates loomed at his sides like jagged teeth. Shadows pooled above and beside him, every echo magnifying the roar of the motorbike.

The moped clipped the curb, jolting his spine, but he held on. Sound ricocheted in the narrow tube, engine growl turned weapon, bouncing back at him.

The creatures shrieked with alien messaging. They surged into the street, bodies smashing gates and poles, ringing metal like twisted chimes. One vaulted, landing too close—its burning skin sizzling where a final flare of sunlight hit.

Henry swerved hard. The bike skidded, corrected, screamed.

Glass shattered somewhere to his left. A shape dropped from above, missing the scaffolding by inches, hitting the pavement and rolling, shrieking in fury and pain.

Henry laughed once—wild, broken.

"Thath wight!" he spat. "Physicth! *Dumb—ath!*"

He burst out of the far end of the corridor into another open stretch, heart slamming, lungs burning, the night still chasing—but now louder, angrier.

He didn't slow.

He didn't look back.

And somewhere, beneath the panic, a thin, dangerous thought surfaced:

I can do this again.

He cut the corner too hard.

The moped bucked, tires skipping, and for a split second Henry thought he'd lost it entirely—but instead the wheels rolled over something soft.

Not soft like freshly-paved tar.

Soft like *alive*. Soft and reactive.

The headlamp flashed over a low, pale ridge snaking across the pavement, translucent and slick, pulsing faintly as if embarrassed to be seen. It compressed under the tire, then sprang back—

—and something caught.

A wet tug at his heel.

The handlebars wrenched. His foot slid. For half a second he thought he was going down.

Henry squealed, high and involuntary, as the vine looped around his ankle, clinging with sudden intent. Heat flared through his shoe. Not pain exactly—*attention*.

The vine stretched, resisted, then tore free with a sound like peeling tape from skin.

The moped fishtailed, engine howling.

Henry kicked hard, wildly, heel scraping once, knees jerking up as the rolling muscle of the vine reached again. The moped tottered, nearly throwing him off, but he stayed upright, chest heaving, knees bowed, ankles held high to avoid being grabbed again.

Henry didn't slow.

He didn't look down.

The thought hit him anyway, sharp and unstoppable:

Did it get me?

His ankle burned. Or maybe it didn't. Maybe that was just his brain improvising.

He rode faster, the night chasing close behind—but now something else rode with him, quieter and worse.

The question.

Nightmare images shot off in his brain like fireworks: the faces screaming, the wriggles under the skin, the black mist moving, bodies convulsing—

The moped rattled beneath him as Henry shot out of the side street and into something wider—but not safer. The road sloped gently, funneling him forward, buildings rising closer on either side, their windows stacked like watching faces.

A sound lifted behind him.

Not footsteps. Not quite.

A layered scrape—too many limbs negotiating hard ground, badly.

Henry leaned into the throttle. The engine screamed, thin and strained, like it knew it was being asked for more than it had.

Shapes peeled away from doorways. From stoops. From the shallow black mouths of alleyways that had been empty a moment ago. They didn't rush him all at once. They *paced* him, testing angles, spilling into the street in uneven bursts.

He swerved.

A parked delivery truck loomed ahead, its rear doors yawning open. Henry threaded past it with inches to spare, the moped's already-broken mirror clipping metal with a shriek. The sound echoed—too loud—and the creatures answered, their cries pitching higher, sharper, energized.

The street narrowed again. Construction fencing filtered him into a single usable lane. Orange mesh snapped in his wake as something slammed into it from the side, rebounded, kept coming.

Henry ducked instinctively as something sailed overhead—glass? a sign?—and shattered behind him. He felt the impact in his spine more than heard it.

The moped bucked over broken pavement. He stood slightly on the pegs, absorbing the blows, vision tunneling. The world reduced to what mattered: light, shadow, the line ahead.

A turn came up fast. Too fast.

Henry took it anyway.

The moped skidded, tires shrieking, back end fishtailing before catching. He shot down a narrow stretch where the buildings leaned inward, fire escapes sagging low like rib cages. The streetlights here were dimmer, farther apart, and between them the dark felt thicker, alive with movement.

Something dropped from above.

It missed him by a foot, struck the pavement, rolled—and was up again instantly, limbs unfolding fallaciously, head snapping toward him with a sound like wet cloth tearing.

Henry screamed—not words, utterly sound—and twisted the throttle hard.

The moped surged. The creature lunged, fingers grazing air where his satchel had been.

Ahead, the street opened suddenly onto a long straightaway, the last of the light draining from the sky at the far end. Twilight bleeding out. Night clocking in.

Henry didn't slow.

The engine wailed. The city howled back.

And the chase tightened, clean and merciless, pulling him forward into whatever came next.

And then—

The moped coughed once, then caught.

The sound startled him—too loud, too alive in a street that had learned to stay quiet—but it held. A thin, buzzing vibration climbed up through the handlebars and into his wrists. Real. Mechanical. Something obeying him.

Henry kicked his left leg out on a sharp turn, wincing as the tingling ankle protested, then twisted the throttle before he could think better of it.

The moped nearly bucked him clear, tires squealing.

Wind slapped his face. Cold air burned his eyes, whipped tears out whether he wanted them or not. The street rushed at him in a narrowing tunnel—brick and glass and metal folding inward, as if the city were leaning in to see if he'd make it.

He didn't look back.

Storefronts streaked past: roll-down gates half-collapsed, display windows punched inward, mannequins lying in poses that suggested flight or prayer. A bus shelter loomed and vanished. A newsstand lay gutted, its papers plastered to the sidewalk like shed skin.

Seconds sucking away the light of day.

Long shadows stretched across the street, tangling together, refusing to stay still.

He twisted the throttle harder.

The moped screamed its complaint and surged. Tires rattled over cracked asphalt. He cut left, then right, following instinct more than logic, skimming past parked cars nosed into one another like casualties. Somewhere above him, glass tinkled—a small, careful sound.

Don't look, don't—

A shape moved at the edge of his vision. Then another.

He heard the scrapes. the wet, dragging shuffles, louder, congregating. Breaths replacing breeze. Hissing—clicking—*leaking.*

"Oh no," Henry gasped.

The street narrowed. Delivery trucks boxed him in, their backs yawning open, dark as slit throats. He shot through the gap between them, shoulder missing metal by inches, mirror clipping something hard with a crack that sent a jolt up his arm.

Behind him—

A shriek split the air.

High. Ragged. Furious.

Henry yelped, the sound thin and defective in his own ears, and the moped bucked as he hit a patch of uneven pavement. He fishtailed, corrected, nearly lost it—then burst out onto a wider avenue where the buildings stepped back enough to let the sky show.

Too much sky.

Another creature dropped from above.

It hit the pavement behind him with a slap and a howl, limbs splayed, skin already smoking faintly where the last of the light touched it. Henry didn't wait to see more. He tore forward, heart hammering so hard it blurred his vision.

He shot through an intersection blind, blowing past a dead traffic light as shadows spilled out from doorways and stoops. More sounds now. Too many. He dodged a few crawlers emerging from underneath vehicles, barely, as the moped's light seemed to be skipping questions on the navigation test. The dark city had finished pretending to sleep.

And still he rode.

Not home. Not even close.

But moving.

Alive.

The night was coming fast now, and the streets ahead twisted away from him, offering no answers—only options.

And he chose one.

Hard right.

Gone.

The street didn't explode this time.

It *emptied*.

Henry tore down a long, straight run where the buildings thinned enough to feel exposed. Fewer cars. Fewer obstacles. Too clean. The motorbike's engine buzzed high, strained, and the sound seemed to travel farther than it should—echoing off brick, slipping into side streets, announcing him.

Then the shrieking stopped.

Not because there was nothing there.

Because they didn't need to scream anymore.

He risked a glance back.

They were spread out now.

Not chasing—*placing*. Figures peeled from alleys, from recessed doorways, from gaps between buildings. Some moved quickly, some slowly, but all of them angled inward, drifting toward his path like debris drawn into a current. Their heads tilted as one, tracking the sound of the engine.

Henry swallowed, whispered a bruised, incoherent thought.

He cut left, hard. The moped hopped the curb, rattled across a sidewalk littered with glass and dead leaves, then dropped back into the street with a jolt that shot pain through his ankle. The grabbed one.

It flared hot, then oddly distant, like the signal had to travel farther to reach him.

Not now. Please not now.

The street ahead narrowed into a corridor—brick pressed close, fire escapes stacked like ribs. He twisted the throttle again.

The engine coughed.

Once.

Twice.

"Oh no no no—come on—"

It didn't die. Not yet. But the pitch dropped, roughened, like a throat filling with grit. The moped shuddered beneath him, every vibration suddenly loud, suddenly broadcast.

And the creatures responded.

Not with noise.

With movement.

They flowed.

One dropped from a low roof and landed in a slow-motion manner of running. Another vaulted a trash pile without breaking stride. A third didn't hurry at all—simply adjusted course, certain Henry would come to it eventually.

Predatory. Patient.

Henry's breath came too fast now. He tried to slow it, failed. Each inhale rasped, each exhale whistled through clenched teeth. The street ahead dipped under a skeletal overpass, its shadow thick and absolute.

Silence pooled there.

He crossed into it—and felt the rules change.

The engine sound flattened, swallowed by the dark. His own breathing boomed in his skull. Tires whispered over pavement. Every small noise—fabric shifting, a chain rattling, the faint tick of cooling machine—felt obscene.

Behind him, something scraped.

Not loud. Careful.

Henry eased off the throttle without meaning to, heart hammering. The moped rolled, coasting, the quiet stretching until it hurt. He could hear them now—not footsteps, not exactly. More like the suggestion of motion. Weight redistributing. Limbs brushing brick.

Sound was a beacon.

He held his breath.

The moped chose that moment to die.

The engine gave a final, traitorous *pop*—sharp as a cough in church—and went still.

Henry coasted three more feet.

Stopped.

He didn't move.

Didn't breathe.

The silence pressed in, vast and listening.

Then—

A click.

Somewhere close.

Henry swung off the moped and ran.

His foot hit off base immediately. The ankle buckled, half-numb, half-on fire, a delayed scream shooting up his leg. He bit down hard, tasted blood, and kept moving, limping fast, shoes slapping too loud against concrete.

"Shh—shh—shh," he begged himself, as if the city might listen.

A tall, gangly, masculine-wired shape, with long extensions of bushy black hair flaming over its bluish gray scalp like the wind was electric, lunged from a doorway. Henry veered, shoulder clipping brick, sparks bursting in his vision, a warmth spreading on his crotch. Another dwarfish form moved above—fire escape rattling, metal trembling.

Henry pivoted, dodging the spilling shadows that pooled at his heels.

Too many. Too close.

He spotted it then: a narrow, vertical slice of darkness between brick walls—an exterior stairwell, open to the sky, switchbacking upward.

Henry didn't hesitate. Couldn't.

He hit the first step at a run and nearly fell, ankle screaming in protest, leg lagging behind him like it didn't quite belong anymore. He hauled himself upward, hands on rusted rail, breath tearing out of him in ragged bursts he couldn't control.

Below, something hissed. Darkness surging, stalking his trail.

Not angry.

Anticipatory.

Metal rang as claws—or something like them—found the first step.

Henry climbed, not looking down.

They don't climb! They don't climb!

The thought battered him forward, a chant more than a belief.

The stairwell's iron landings, bolted into masonry, still shuddered with every impact of his feet. Paint flakes burst loose beneath his palms. Rust bit.

Halfway up, his ankle made a fist.

White heat shot through it, sharp enough to blur the world sideways. He caught himself against the wall, cheek scraping brick, the blow punching out of him in a wet, helpless sound.

Below, the hiss changed.

Not closer.

Interested.

Metal rang again—higher this time. Not climbing. Testing. Something dragged against the railing, slow and deliberate, as if learning the shape of the thing.

"No," Henry whispered, the word barely there, head throbbing, vision shivering.

He reached a landing and didn't stop. He turned, grabbed the railing, hauled himself up the next flight. Light seeped from above—not bright, but present. A window, cracked open, glowing faintly.

He staggered upward again, favoring the bad leg, hauling himself by his arms now. Each landing felt farther apart than the last. The night sky deepened as he rose.

At the lighted landing—a door.

Not locked—jammed.

Henry slammed into it shoulder-first. Once. Twice. Pain bloomed and scattered his thoughts like a microburst scattering straight-line winds.

Behind him, something leapt.

It didn't climb. It landed amiss.

The stairwell screamed with the sound of it—something burning, something furious and alive in the narrowing gap below. Henry roared back at it, animal, blind, and hit the door again.

The frame cracked.

He spilled through into a small apartment and kept moving, crawling until the wall stopped him. He clutched it, chest heaving, vision tunneling. His ankle throbbed, a pulse that didn't quite match his heartbeat.

He waited, staring sideways at the two hundred watts of glowing bulbs in the light fixture above.

Nothing came over the threshold.

Minutes—or seconds—passed. Time had lost its leash.

Finally, when his breathing slowed enough to let his lungs relax, Henry laughed.

Once.

It cracked apart halfway through and turned into something wetter.

A dresser stood against the opposite wall with a family portrait framed and propped on its top. Young, Hispanic. Family of four. Man and wife, early thirties, posing behind a boy and girl, very young. Next to the dresser—a crib, constructed but empty.

Henry lay there longer than he realized, staring at the ceiling, the light, the faces, the crib. Letting the quiet hold.

When morning came, he stirred, eyes red, muscles sore, but his thoughts clearer now, his sense of directions beginning to return. He pushed himself upright, tested his legs, and crossed the room.

Light-headed but not stumbling, he inhaled the fresh but funky city air, readied for the descent, and pushed through the broken door into the exterior stairwell.

9

The stairwell reeked of dust and rusted metal. Henry's steps echoed—slow, careful. Bat on his shoulder. Listening. Always listening for the midnight ghosts of the Fontaine. He descended several floors, not keeping count anymore.

Then—he stopped.

POP!

Then, *sssssssshhh.*

The inrush of air, the tinkling drift of falling glass.

Henry leaned over the railing, timidly. Dark shadows flickering and darting far below. The lone fluorescent tube above him hummed weakly, struggling against the dark. Beneath that feeble glow, the stairwell dissolved into spiraling blackness.

His sweaty fists tightened on the bat.

Something made him pause—faint scuffing thuds across concrete. He blinked, shook his head.

Must be imagining it.

But no—closer now. Scraping. Plodding upward. Slow. Heavy. Climbing into view.

A shadow turning the bend.

Hints of a husky figure. Shoulders seesawing. Torso bent. Low grunts. A lumbering silhouette—a monster marionette jerked upward by invisible strings.

Then a cracked, casual voice:

"Jeanine, have the mail forwarded to my new address."

Henry's laugh tore out of him—sharp, jagged, too loud. It ricocheted off the concrete walls.

Something metallic tapped against the wall.

The figure halted for a beat, listening to the dead phone at his ear —taking a briefing from the silence—then lowered it and slipped it away, climbing on with misplaced authority.

Irwin Platt.

Pale. Gaunt. Clothes tattered. Frowning, eyes narrow. He approached step by step. And then, as his face grew and clarified in the dim light, something shifted: that strange, calm plasticity spreading across his expression. Compassion. Warmth. The quiet, measured look of a psychotherapist easing into a delicate session.

It was enough to make the hair rise on Henry's arms.

"You," Henry stammered, teeth chattering, laughter leaking through the cracks. "It's you. Ha—ha! You—ahahaha!—followed me?"

Irwin climbed until only a few steps separated them, his earlier softness fading into a troubled frown.

"*Oogie?* You live here?" he asked.

"Yeah—uh—yes?"

Henry's weak laughter grew, shifting from dissipating fear into renewed relief.

"You," Irwin hissed, slightly winded, "you're the me I wish I could be… if I were you."

Henry's laughter snapped into sobs. He swayed, the aluminum barrel bouncing off his collarbone, fingers strangling the grip. Shadows carved jagged stripes across his face. His eyes darted, as if seeking the exit. He nodded—almost as if choosing the moment to faint—and his voice dragged out on ragged breaths.

"Y-yes. My home… *My* home!"

"Is that a—?"

Henry swung the bat.

Bone cracked.

Irwin's eyes widened, face contorted in shock as he toppled backward, flipping over the rail and striking the steps below—joints popping in the dark like cracking eggshells. He tumbled to the next landing, limbs bent wrong, blood streaking his temple.

Groaning, whining, panting, Irwin dragged himself up with one ruined limb, the other leg barely responding.

"Abort! Abort!" he barked, voice strangled with panic. "Save my turtle!"

Stumbling, cursing with every breath, he crumbled into the dark, finally swallowed by the stairwell's black throat.

"Genuine Louisville Slugger! Signed by—*Oogie!*"

Henry clung to the railing, laughter and tears spilling unchecked. His voice echoed wild and raw through the empty tower, as he waved his weapon:

"Oogie find! *Boogie Oogie Oogie!*

"*My* bat!—*My* home!"

As the echo died, Irwin's footsteps faded into the dark below—the scrape of rubber soles dissolving into silence. The stairwell shifted back into stillness.

Too still.

The darkness felt wrong—thicker than it should have been, as though it swallowed whatever light touched it. Henry wiped his face with his sleeve, realizing only then how wet his cheeks were. Guilt pressed against him, heavier than the suede leather tool belt on his hips.

"My… home." He sniffed. "Run."

He yanked the flashlight from the side pouch and snapped it on. The beam flickered across the landing: dust, grime, and something else —a long, thin metal pipe leaning in the corner like a discarded spear.

Glass crackled underfoot. Henry angled the flashlight downward.

Shards everywhere. The fractured remains of fluorescent tubes smashed on every landing below.

Henry stopped breathing.

So that's what Irwin had been doing—methodically knocking out the lights, floor by floor. Sabotaging the last fragile scraps of safety.

From the black gulf far below, a scream rose.

Not a call for help.

A horrible, wet, broken sound—the kind of cry made when help is no longer possible.

It went on too long.

It climbed the stairwell like a living thing, echoing upward until Henry pressed a shaking palm over his mouth to keep from answering. Or vomiting.

The light trembled in his hand.

He stumbled back up the steps, the flashlight beam jerking wildly with each stride, until he reached the lit landing. He dropped onto the cold concrete, his suede belt creaking softly as he wrapped his arms around himself, shuddering.

"They don't climb stairs," he whispered. "Remember, they're weak. They don't climb stairs. They don't climb stairs."

The words sounded insubstantial, falling to pieces the moment they left his lips. Each time he repeated them he tried to pack them tighter with certainty, but they scattered like dust.

Everything in him was falling to pieces.

And then—memory pressed in. From the telescope. Across the street.

Windows with jagged holes punched out.

Shapes moving in the shadows.

Not climbing—no—but crouching. Watching.

Sometimes leaning too far out over the sill… testing the air.

"They don't climb," he whispered again.

But another voice inside him—cold, rational—answered:

You've seen them higher than they should be.

You've seen them come up from the subway level.

You've seen them feed. On pigeons.

A second voice jeered—high, mocking:

Weak, Henry?

They're patient. Not weak.

He pressed both palms against his temples and rocked forward. The stairwell carried Irwin's scream on an endless loop, as if the building itself had learned how to grieve. It crawled across his spine. It stayed.

He whispered louder, forcing it like a prayer:

"They don't climb stairs. They don't climb stairs."

But the interruptions kept coming—every remembered window, every flicker of movement, every set of teeth waiting just out of sight.

His voice thinned, frayed:

"They don't climb stairs.

They don't climb stairs…"

In the back of his mind, the question gnawed:

What if they're waiting?

Waiting ... waiting ... waiting ...

Echoes prevailed in the dark stairwell—

a chant… a warning… a promise.

Sorrow and remorse and guilt and fear weighed in.

His own response regrettably was devoured by the dark:

"I'm sorry!"

8

Perched on the outstretched arm of a stone angel, the pigeon watched the stillness of the courtyard and cooed at the silence. Its feathers ruffled lightly in the morning sun, wind calm, sky clear, a vast blue above a hollowed world.

It pushed off, wings slicing the air, and the streets fell away. From below, a neighborhood in disarray, intersections glinting, the ghosts of massacred morning traffic mourning. The bird climbed slowly, a wide spiral around the Fontaine. The tower rose from its stone base like a relic of two centuries colliding: lower floors adorned with carved cornices and arches, sandstone shoulders bearing the weight of higher glass. The glass itself—pane after pane—was tinted faintly green, polished once, now dulled by weeks of dust. At each angle of ascent, it mirrored the pigeon's wings, shadows of flight flashing and vanishing, a thousand brief doubles accompanying the climb.

Balconies jutted here and there like forgotten gestures, iron railings casting symmetrical shadows that leaned across the facade in the early light. The surfaces shifted with altitude—smooth glass, jagged ledges, streaks of rain hardened into vertical stains. To a man, the heights would seem vertiginous; to the pigeon, they meant nothing.

At first, only the wind's hush filled its ears, then—faint, so faint— a thread of music. A guitar's drone, stretched thin, almost imagined. With each circuit higher, the sound thickened: a voice, low and faraway, descending, drifting, rising; notes floating upward as though the building itself breathed them; the music clinging to its feathers.

Up, up the piloted plumage spiraled, circling the Fontaine closely. The air thinned just enough to cool the feathers against the sun's warmth. The city widened, avenues stretching and curving, rooftops lined in quiet order, windows staring blankly as though their occupants had stepped away mid-breath. Shadows lengthened, twisted by the morning light, and the pigeon's shadow traced them in counterpoint across the jagged steel.

Nearing the top, the spirals tightened. The wind whispered along the tarps, gently and meditatively. Below, the city's silence had weight; above, the horizon arched like a promise, vast and unmoving.

At last, the rooftop appeared: a flat plateau of gravel and tar, with tarps stretched taut. Wings cupped, the pigeon settled on the edge of a tarp, its claws gripping the fabric.

The bird picked its way across the blue tarp, its head-forward carriage deliberate, methodical. Each step was a ratcheting motion: the opaline neck thrust forward, paused, then the body followed. Claw by careful claw, *scritch-scratch*, click by click, it kept its own time. The sun had warmed the plastic, and the faint clicks echoed.

As the bird reached the edge of the tarp, the terrain changed. It met the mountain of the folded parachute—a chaotic topography of olive-drab nylon and tangled shroud lines.

The bird paused at the border, its apricot eye swiveling to calculate the soft, shifting horizon. It lifted a clawed foot and pressed down; the nylon exhaled a soft hiss as the air trapped between the silk-thin layers escaped. The surface was treacherous and slick, lacking the firm resistance of the tarp.

Now, the pigeon's walk transformed into a delicate mountaineering feat. With each step, the fabric bunched and dipped, creating miniature valleys that swallowed its ankles. Its head bobbed faster now, a frantic gyroscopic stabilizer keeping its vision level while its feet danced across the unstable dunes of synthetic fabric. It spread its wings just a fraction, a sliver of gray feathers catching, brushing the air for balance. Step by step, it climbed the miniature peaks, precise, measured, as if counting the tempo on strings.

Music now filled the air, whole and present: the nearby boombox pulsing with Radiohead's "How to Disappear Completely," the song no longer a rumor but a tangible presence.

Several yards away, a lawn chair sagged beneath a bearded figure in shades, surrounded by a tableau of posing mannequins. A cooler lay cracked open, a bottle of wine inside catching the light, within arm's reach. Beyond the figure's swaying sandaled feet, the tripod stood guard over the sun-bathing pistol, and the fastened telescope held its lens on the edge of the outer boroughs.

The pigeon cocked its head, sunlight glinting off its dark eye, wings half-raised, as if it, too, listened.

Henry sniffed, rubbed at his nose, muttered something, lips shaping a soundless phrase—half a joke, half nonsense—under his breath. They pursed askew in the faintest ghost of a grin. Then, as he lifted his head toward the bird, it vanished.

He saw it—the pigeon. Living, breathing, cooing softly at the edge of the tarp. For a moment, his lips wouldn't form a word, stunned that this ethereal life had chosen his rooftop. A single tear slid beneath the rim of his shades. Then another. His breath hitched. He pressed a hand to his face, as though laughter and grief were tangled and could not be separated.

Behind the mirrored shades, tears filled his eyes and spilled freely now, streaking down into his beard. His shoulders shook once, twice, a sob breaking loose before he pressed his lips tight to hold the rest in.

The mannequins did not stir. The music carried, filling the rooftop, the city, and the fragile man all at once—wrapping him in its ephemeral embrace, the impossible persistence of life and sound in a world otherwise dead.

Henry watched, slowly sitting up, rising out of his dark cloud to observe.

"Hello," he whispered weakly. "Easy there, my little friend. My cousin from out of town?

"Do you have a message for me?" Henry sniffed lightly, blinked off a tear.

The pigeon took several quick steps backward, head bobbing—nodding yes?

"Yes?"

The pigeon lifted its tail feathers significantly. A pasty squirt emitted from its cloaca, spattering drops on the fabric rapidly. Seconds later, head bobbing, the pigeon took flight.

Henry waved. "I get it! Thank you!" Henry laughed. "Tell Chief Wahoo I said 'Thank you!'"

There it is.

Message received.

7

The penthouse was silent but for the whisper of pencil on paper. Henry sat hunched at the desk, his shoulders crooked forward like quotation marks, his left hand holding steady the edge of a yellow legal pad, his right scribbling steadily, occasionally pausing to tap the eraser against his temple. He wore a winter ski sweater with the sleeves rolled to the elbows. A single candle burned beside him in a squat glass jar, throwing long shadows that jittered across the room like stagehands. He liked the effect.

He leaned back slightly and mouthed what he had written. The words barely escaped his lips, faint and incomplete, syllables halved by thought. His eyes scanned the lines, and then he snorted—a dry little bark of breath. He reached for the stemless glass of red wine at his side, swirled it with two fingers like he remembered seeing someone do in a movie, then sipped. His tongue lingered on the taste, less for flavor than for the familiarity of ritual.

The smile came gradually. It started as a twitch at the right corner of his mouth, a confused push of pleasure, like he'd startled himself.

Then both corners lifted, tentatively, almost guiltily, as if the muscles had forgotten how. And then a sound—a genuine chuckle, warm and human—rose out of him like something not entirely voluntary.

He put the pencil down.

The chuckle repeated. It built. Something in it unlatched.

Henry threw back his head and laughed.

It echoed through the high ceiling of the penthouse, around the dormant bookshelves and the blank television, over the scarred armchair and the cold fireplace. The laugh cracked through the dusk like glass underfoot. It was wild, delighted, reckless—a bark, a bellow, then a kind of howl. He laughed with his whole body now, shaking in his seat, the wine sloshing dangerously on the desk.

Out on the balcony rail, a Serbian Highflyer—fat with feathers, puffed from the wind—had been resting. The bird tilted its head toward the sound. The wild laughter seemed to unnerve it, or perhaps offend it. It flapped its wings once, then again, launching into the open dark, gliding off over the hollowed city.

Inside, Henry wiped his eyes and leaned forward, breathless, smiling like a man who'd heard a punchline only he could understand.

He picked up the pencil, turned to a new page, and began to write again.

The candle guttered slightly in a gust from the open balcony door.

Henry gripped the mic and almost kissed the windscreen, a deep, contemplative frown forming, the heat of the stagelight summoning sweat droplets along his hairline. His upper lip snarled, and he confessed, in a whispered undertone, "I used to be bigger than this."

He heard himself emit a light snort and wondered at it. "I think I pulled too hard, and the cord snapped back too fast on the recoil. I guess it still works, just no viable outlets to test it on."

The joke fell flat—of course it did. There were no outlets, no sockets, no crowd to plug into. Just him, sweating in the lone spotlight while the dark corners of the club twitched and sighed with things that might be listening.

Henry tapped the mic. Thump. Thump. "See? Still on. Still me. Broadcasting to the void. Somewhere out there, somebody's gotta be laughing. Right? Please tell me somebody's laughing. Even you—

whatever you are. I'll take a hiss. A grunt. Reviews are overrated anyway."

He let the silence settle, pacing across the warped floorboards, following the spotlight. His shadow lunged and shrank with every step.

"I used to have ambition," he said, drawing out the word like it tasted bad. "I was gonna be a screenwriter. Write something big. Y'know, a movie people actually paid to watch, not one of those straight-to-streaming dumpster fires. Something with—what's the word?—oh yeah, *heart*."

He stopped center stage, staring into the dark, sweat dripping down his jawline.

"Then, one day, the lights went out. And the world ended. And guess who's left to pick up the mic? Not the movie stars. Not the politicians. Nope. Just me. Good ole Henry, trying to be funny so the monsters don't crawl in here and tear me apart like last week's garbage."

He adjusted the mic stand, dragging it a few inches closer, the base scraping loudly.

"You wanna know how this all started? Yeah, I cracked the case. It wasn't war, it wasn't politics, it wasn't climate change. No, no, no." He wagged a finger. "It was Doctor Finkelstein's laboratory sneeze."

Henry leaned forward like a late-night prophet.

"Picture it: Finkelstein in his lab, testing… I don't know, something dangerous. Molecules. Radioactive… breadsticks? Whatever. He leans over the microscope, and—Ack-ack-ack-ACHOO!" He threw his whole body into the sneeze, bending at the waist, then straightened as if he'd pulled a muscle. "And that's it! Civilization down the drain faster than a goldfish funeral."

He squinted, eyes glinting with mischief.

"You think I'm joking? No way. I read an article once that said sneezes travel at over a hundred miles per hour. Hundred! That's almost as fast as my self-esteem dropping when I look in the mirror."

He chuckled at his own joke—too long, too loud—then cut it off with a sharp inhale. His laughter echoed strangely, bouncing back at him like an accusation.

"Yeah, this is me… starting the dumpster fire.

"You know what's weird?" Henry said, voice soft now, intimate, posture relaxing. "I liked people. I liked them even when I pretended I didn't. Their noise. The lines at the coffee shops. The random conversations about nothing. I'd give anything to stand in a subway car again, jammed against a stranger's armpit, because at least I'd know I wasn't alone."

He turned his back to the hidden house, stared up at the stagelights, then at the black curtain.

"Now it's just me. And you," he said to the dark, raising a hand in mock salute as he turned to face his audience. "The great and terrible you. You creatures out there, whatever you are. I don't even hate you. I just wish you had cell phones so you wouldn't keep staring at me. Because staring and not laughing is just rude."

Henry wiped his face with his sleeve, streaking sweat and dust across his cheek. He walked back to the mic, cradled it like it was a living thing.

"You know what I miss most?" he asked, dropping to a whisper again. "Bombing. Bombing on stage. Hearing the silence of a hundred people not laughing at your joke. Because at least then—then you knew there were people. That they could laugh. Now I tell a joke and —" He gestured to the shadows. "What's my score with you guys? One fang out of five?"

The corner of his mouth curled in a bitter smile.

He took a long pause, letting the weight of the quiet settle. His shoulders sank. The mic, suddenly, felt heavier than it should.

"I used to be bigger than this," Henry murmured again, but it sounded different this time. Not a joke. Not even a complaint. Just a fact, hollow and unsteady.

He closed his eyes and imagined the applause, the warmth of it, the way it once filled a room like sunlight. For a second, he almost believed he could hear it. That line certainly deserved it.

Then the silence roared back in, and Henry blinked wide-eyed again,

"Have a fang-tastic night. Really try to live it up. I know you can't. I'm Henry Gorestriker. Don't forget to tip your waiters. There may still be some blood in them.

"Hey, before I let you go," Henry added, fitting on his mask again, "I remember a punchline. Here it is." He cleared his throat, smirked brightly. "Why did the chicken cross the road?"

He waved at the faces of smiling patrons, as the lights slowly came up. A lovely audience. Human and kind, smiling, appreciative.

A young Hispanic family of four waved back.

There, at the next table—

Mom.

Dad.

Jane.

Bart.

"Hey, guys!"

Back to the joke.

"No—seriously. Worst possible time of day. You're trusting your life to a moped. Something grabs your heel. Alien rabies—alien babies —who knows.

"Why did the chicken cross the road?

"Because the punchline lives on the other side."

6

The tech store had once been pristine—glass walls, white counters, brushed steel accents. Now, everything was covered in a fine layer of ash and mildew, like the inside of a tomb for gadgets. The sunlight slanted in through a high, broken window, giving the space an underwater quality. Henry stepped cautiously between the upturned chairs and cracked display tablets.

He found the laptop on a waist-high display table near the center. It was sleek. Lightweight. Mostly intact. He flipped open the lid and blew the dust off the keyboard. The screen stayed dark.

No cord. No juice.

"Come on, baby," he muttered, crouching low to check underneath the table. Nothing. Strictly display. "Just one cable. One little A/C adapter. I'll name you Lucy. You'll be my Lucy…"

A soft moan broke the silence.

Fear set Henry where he crouched.

It hadn't come from his own lips. This one had depth—like it came from a throat with meat still on it. Behind the counter? The dark hallway to the employee breakroom?

Another low moan, closer now.

Henry moved slowly. His hand found a thrown camera gimbal on the floor, and he gripped it like the baseball bat he was wishing he had again.

The least-prepared man strikes out again. Gun and bat in the cooler. Yeah.

Gotta keep it cool.

Stealthily he stood, his throat tightened, his instincts screaming for him to run—but his legs stayed bolted in place, as if caught between his past and present selves: the man who fled, and the one who cracked jokes to death itself.

He took a cautious step back.

A sound from deeper inside the store. Not loud. Not dramatic. Just a soft scrape, followed by a wet, patient inhale.

Then the laptop behind him shifted.

He spun—and saw only shadows.

Something in the hallway moved.

A flicker of motion. Long fingers? Jointed all wrong.

Henry ran, the display laptop tucked in both arms, the gimbal dropped.

Shoes slipping on cracked linoleum, backpack slapping against his side, he careened through the ruined store and burst out through the front door. Sunlight hit him in the face like a stage light and he didn't stop until he was halfway across the street.

He turned back, panting, eyes wild, and pointed toward the store's dark interior.

"I'll be back, you dusty creep!" he shouted, voice bouncing off the hollow buildings. "I'll bring a battery, and a flamethrower, and a bag of oranges!"

A pause.

"And when I do, you better have that store cleaned up and things where I can find them! I'm the customer, jack!"

Silence.

Somewhere, a pigeon flew past, confused and alone.

Henry adjusted his money belt and muttered, "That's right. Walk away."

He sat in the shadow of the awning, third table from the left. Set the laptop gently on the chair beside him. Only then did the thought recur.

No cord.

Of course.

He laughed once, quietly. Ordered an orange soda from the empty counter out of habit, then got up and grabbed one from inside, from the box stacked on a pallet. He took his usual seat again—the one that caught the afternoon sun but stayed just cool enough in the shade of the awning.

He drank.

Across the street, at the far end of the block, a figure stood motionless.

Her.

He noticed her the way you notice a word you almost remember —without urgency at first. She wore a dark jacket, her hair pulled back. She wasn't hiding. She wasn't waving. Just… standing there.

Then she started walking toward him.

Henry sat up straighter.

Okay. Fine. People walk. Women walk. This is a city. Or was. Used to be. Still technically is.

As she crossed the street, the light shifted. Her face came into focus.

Henry's breath caught.

"No," he said softly. "No, no, no."

She looked like the woman from the magazine. The French one. The one smiling beside Jim Caviezel like the world hadn't ended and wouldn't. The one whose face he had cut out so she could be with him more easily. A face he needed to look at often.

The resemblance wasn't perfect—but it was close enough to hurt.

She stopped a few feet from the table.

"Hi," she said.

Her voice wasn't dramatic. It wasn't echoing. It didn't arrive on a breeze or through a speaker. It was just… a voice.

Normal. Human.

Henry stood too fast, knocking his chair back.

"You're—that model," he said, pointing, immediately regretting the pointing. "From the magazine. The French one. You were wearing—no, wait, that was a scarf. Or maybe the scarf was implied. I don't know. The lighting was very flattering."

She smiled. "I always thought so."

He stared at her.

"You're not supposed to move," he said. "You're supposed to stay… over there. Distant. Symbolic. Is this allowed?"

"Maybe," she said coolly, with a smiling wink, "you've really flipped for me."

He swallowed a smile. "What's your name?"

She hesitated just long enough for him to realize it's his guess.

She said, "It was on the magazine. Remember?"

"Nuh—Nuh—No—Nova," he tried.

He squinted at her, searching his head like a cluttered drawer.

"Nova… No…?"

"Not Nova. That was Heston's girlfriend."

"What?"

"Have you forgotten your favorite movie, too?"

"How—did you know that?"

The model turned in her seat and pointed to a distant shape posing at the intersection a block down.

Henry followed her finger.

At the far crossing, framed perfectly between two gutted storefronts, Taylor sat tall in the saddle, sunburned and defiant, rifle slung over his bare shoulder as if Manhattan were just another forbidden zone. Nova, his quiet companion, clung to him, barefoot, dark hair loose, her face calm in that permanent, wordless way. The horse stamped and tossed its head.

Heston broke character, lifting a hand.

He waved.

Not cheerfully. Not urgently. The wave of a man who knew there was no one else left to explain things to.

Henry raised his fingers in return before he could stop himself.

"Wow," Henry said, watching the horse already turning, hooves clopping softly as they headed down the avenue, shrinking into heat shimmer and dust and memory. "You must know I'm losing my mind."

Then—motion again.

Another rider burst into the intersection at a hard gallop, coat flaring, hat low, jaw set. Dennis Weaver. Older, leaner. A lawman late to the end of the world, but still a stride ahead of Chester. McCloud leaned forward in the saddle, eyes locked on the disappearing pair, and thundered after them without a glance toward Henry or the café.

The street went still.

Henry exhaled slowly.

"I just want to be clear," he said, turning back to her. "You *saw* that too, right?"

She studied his face, amused, unafraid. "I saw you wave back."

"That's… not the confirmation I was hoping for."

She smiled again—warm this time, human. Present. Very much here.

"So," she said, "what were you asking me?"

Henry blinked, shook his head once, and focused on her like a man gripping a lifeline.

"Nora," he said. "Your name. Nora."

"Not Nova," she emphasized.

He studied her face: soft contours, delicate symmetry, a strong jawline, playful eyebrows arcing under sideswept, sun-kissed bangs. Those unyielding hazel eyes drew him in, tender and alive, pulling his thoughts from their hiding places and leaving him raw with attention.

He snapped his fingers. "Nora. Fullilove."

"You remembered—"

"Nora Grace Fullilove."

"—the whole thing. I'm impressed."

"I remembered something," he said carefully. "I don't know if it's accurate. Or legal."

She laughed—a small, genuine laugh that loosened something in his chest.

"You used to say I should go by Grace," she said. "Professionally."

"I did?" Henry said. "Well... okay. That tracks. Nora's nice, but Grace—Grace sounds like someone who survives an apocalypse. Nora... maybe, or... someone who dies in the first fifteen minutes."

"What? No. Really? You said it sounded timeless."

"I was trying to impress you," he said. "I do that." Henry retrieved his chair and plopped down.

"Mm-hmm."

She pulled out the chair across from him and sat.

For a moment, neither of them spoke. The city hummed faintly, wings flapping and birds crying somewhere far off, but Henry barely noticed. All he felt was her—the gentle, electric pull of her presence, the quiet stretching between them—and his pulse skipped in time with it.

"You're married," she said finally.

Henry blinked. "I am?"

Then elevator doors parted to a brief glimpse of nightmare in Henry's memory: a hellish creature ramming into his gut. "I was married—"

"To me," she added.

"Ah." Henry sat, rigid, color slowly coming back into his face. "Right."

"Right."

He blinked, feeling relief. "Good. Because otherwise this would be *very* awkward."

Nora smiled, too, but there was something in her eyes now—concern, maybe. Or recognition.

"Now, you must know—I love you. I do. All of you. Even your name. But *Grace*... to me it was like a meaningful lyric. Something that stayed. I didn't deserve you. And I still can't understand how I could forget you. Ever."

"You're remembering more," she said.

"I remember pieces," he said, choosing his words. "Out of order, though. Like a trailer for a movie I never saw.

"This one poem came to mind recently. I was looking at your picture."

"Wow me." She said it lightly, but her eyes stayed on his—steady. Not teasing. An invitation.

Henry considered this, lips pressed together. "Okay. Fair warning—I might oversell it."

She tilted her head. "You always did."

He winced faintly. "I—this is where it gets embarrassing."

Nora smiled despite herself.

"The petals of a rose may fade away..." He faltered, then shrugged. "I don't even know if that's right."

Nora laughed, blushing, ducking her chin.

Henry smiled back, steadied, and continued, softer now: "...but your smile—your heart—" he searched, then landed it, "—stays forever in mine."

She looked at him for a long moment.

"For, as minutes become hours—"

"Okay," she cut in, laughing.

"You're the only one for me," he finished.

"I love you, too, Henry. My poet."

The words hit him harder than he expected.

He exhaled, then spoke more carefully, as if reading from something fragile inside himself. "I remember thinking your smile wasn't for me. That it was… surplus. Like it existed before I got there —and would keep going after I left."

Nora didn't interrupt.

"And that made it safer," he went on. "Like loving a sunrise. You don't own it. You just—" He shrugged. "You just stand there and try not to screw it up."

Her smile softened. Not bigger. Truer.

"That's pretty close," she said.

"Really?" He blinked. "Because I was worried I'd veered into Hallmark."

"You never did," she said. "You always stopped just short of comfort."

He nodded, relieved. "Good. Comfort is too easy."

They sat with that, the café's low hum filling the edges.

After a moment, Henry frowned. "You once said my name meant something to you?"

She studied him. "It meant you were trying. Even when you didn't think you were enough."

"That sounds exhausting," he offered apologetically.

"It was," she agreed. Then, gently: "But it was also you."

Henry swallowed. "Do you ever get the sense," he said, "that remembering you is changing the shape of things? Like if I pull too hard, something important snaps?"

Nora's gaze didn't waver. "Yes."

"That doesn't bother you?"

"It does," she said. "But not as much as you disappearing again."

He nodded, accepting that with a seriousness that surprised him.

"Okay," he said quietly. "Then I'll try not to yank."

She reached across the table—not touching him, not quite—and smiled.

"That," she said, "is exactly how you used to love me."

A gentle breeze threaded through the café, lifting a napkin—then letting it fall again.

"Look at us, Henry. Here, together again. You helped bring me back."

"You were always here, just waiting for me to remember."

"Keep building your memories, Henry. What else comes to mind?"

"Hmm." Henry smiled, looked up at the sky, but quickly returned to her face, to make sure she didn't vanish. "Nora Fullilove. Actress and model. Married, then divorced… Dimitri Georgiou. Son, Marcus. Kept your maiden name as a celebrity. Then, we got married."

"And you thought I should have used the name Grace, instead of Nora."

"Grace Gorestriker?" Henry chuckled. "You didn't like Gorestriker."

"I liked it better than Georgiou." Nora laughed, her face glowing.

"I remember that." Henry married her laughter. "I remember all of this."

She glanced at the laptop beside him. "You brought it."

"Impulse grab," he said. "I don't have the cord."

"I know."

"You always knew things before I told you," he said. "It was unsettling. In a sexy way."

She reached out, touched the laptop lid with two fingers. Didn't open it.

"You always did that," she said. "You took the thing you needed and forgot the part that made it work."

Henry laughed, then stopped. "That feels… personal."

"It is."

He took a long drink of orange soda.

"So," he said. "Are you real?"

She tilted her head. "What does Batman think?—Does it matter?"

He considered this. "I'd like you to come see me perform."

She smiled again. This time, it felt like a goodbye she hadn't said yet.

"Onstage?" she asked.

"Front row," he said. "Or backstage. Or inside my head. Apparently seating is flexible."

She stood.

"I'll see you," she said.

"Can you tell me something, before you go?"

"Yes?"

"If you're not real, or real but in my head... how come I don't want you to go, but I feel like you are—leaving?"

"I'll try to come back with an answer to that."

He watched her walk away—this time not distant, not symbolic, but solid, casting a shadow that moved with her.

Henry sat back down slowly.

He looked at the empty chair.

Then at the laptop.

Then out at the sunlit street.

For the first time in a long while, he didn't feel entirely alone.

5

Henry emerged onto the stage swaddled in a moth-eaten doublet and ruffled collar he'd scavenged from the gutted costume shop on Forty-third. The tights sagged at the knees, and the codpiece looked like a balloon animal rearing up to break wind. The spotlight burned upon him, and he bowed in the hams deeply, one arm sweeping the air as though addressing a packed Globe Theatre rather than shadows with teeth. His other hand waved the fan-shaped pages of script.

"My curtsy, last my speech.

"Good morrow, fair citizens of Nosferatu-opolis! A fair crowd indeed. Glowing orbs for eyes, foreheads that put the Tower of London to shame, and teeth so sharp, they maketh daggers look like butter knives." His voice rang with forced grandeur, summoning Richard Burton. "How now, dost thou not applaud? A plague upon this stingy crowd!"

He slapped his chest, shook his fist at the dark, then belched. A low scraping came from the back of the club—the sound of chairs being nudged by something with claws.

He leaned toward the mic.

"Perchance you creatures crave blood—yet behold, I serve thee jokes instead! Verily, the punchline doth bite sharper than thy fang." He paused, tilting his head as if listening to a heckler.

"What sayest thou? That mine hose be most unbecoming? Sirrah, I'll have thee know these breeches once embraced the noble thighs of King Norman Lear himself!—or, at least, the understudy for Lear's understudy, who tragically died of boredom in his Fruit of the Looms."

He spun once, the cape-like tails of his jacket sparkly in the spotlight. and stumbled, then straightened back into Shakespearean posture.

"Yon world hath ended, aye, yet laughter endures. To jest, or not to jest—that is the question. To bite or not to bite—that is the other question. Whether 'tis nobler in the mind to be out of the mind or to suffer the hellacious grins of outrageous monsters, with their piercing prongs and devilish eyes; or to take arms against this excremental confluence, and by opposing... thwart these ambitious appetites with double-edged entendres and sharpened wit, and, with duller wit, some knock-knock jokes." He pointed accusingly into the abyss. "Thou wouldst have my blood! But hark—the fool hath tricks. A jest to stay the grave, a pun to parry doom! What sayest thou, O audience invisible? Knock-knock—And who's there?" He waited, cocking his ear as though the void itself might answer.

Then, in booming voice, he replied: "—'Tis I, the last man! By my troth, in good sooth, I shit you not, I swear 'tis truth. And who's there to knock but Death himself? Enter, sir, but wipe thy feet and drop thy scythe and wash thy hands before thou eat! My soul is not a Twinkie treat!"

Henry recoiled slightly, one hand over his heart, then flung his arms wide as though daring the darkness to respond. The scraping paused. He held the pose, chest heaving, tights sagging, codpiece wobbling, waiting for the void's applause. Until, at length, satisfied, he stepped back through the black curtains.

Henry stepped into the spotlight, chest puffed, his adult-sized battered, plastic green army helmet perched unevenly on his head, bugle dangling at his side, polished pistol in his holster. A window decal reading "U.S. Air Force MOM" clung to his chest like a medal. A bumper sticker reading "HOOAH!" dangled from a strap, flapping as he moved.

A dark greenish-brown waist-length jacket bore gold pins and insignia denoting rank; a fake-bullet army belt was slung over his shoulder. His waist belt held black plastic toy daggers. Four metallic brooch pins glittered faintly against the jacket.

Khaki riding breeches were tucked into tall black leather boots that thudded and jingled with every exaggerated stomp. A sticker reading "We Never Surrender!" clung to the sleeve, flapping like a tiny battle flag.

White eyebrow pencil caked his face: his left brow arched high— on fleek for a lay-up against his forehead—while the right tuft burrowed into a worried thought-stitch sewing itself across the bridge of his nose.

He raised the worn bugle and blew—a high-pitched squeal ricocheting off the walls, bouncing against the shadows in the back. He grimaced, dropped the instrument, planted his oversized boots firmly and thrust his fists onto his hips.

"Men—and monsters!" he boomed, baritone voice cracking, "I want you to remember: no bastard ever survived by cowering in a corner! He survived by making the other poor dumb bastard wish he'd stayed dead!"

He spun on one foot, stumbled into a bow, nearly toppling over. Straightening, he stomped the floor so hard the oversized boots clanged against the stage, jingling his scavenged medals.

He pointed a finger at the void, then flung it toward the tattered American flag behind him.

"All this talk of the end of the world being a tragedy is horse dung! Real survivors love the sting of battle, the thrill of the hunt, and the sweet taste of... well, whatever's left!"

Henry's arm took aim, finger jabbing the air, the oversized medals jingling.

"No monsters—no real bonified monsters—ever got a bite to eat by being courteous!"

Henry was in character, eyebrows rising and twitching, a caterpillar cabaret.

"We advance constantly! We kick the hell out of—!" He stumbled, then straightened, chest puffed, glaring at the shadows. "Everything!—And when you are asked thirty years from now, 'What did you do in the apocalypse?'—you won't have to say, 'I hid under a pile of cadavers!'"

He paused, leaned close to the empty void, lowering his voice to clandestine menace.

"Now salute this flag!"

Henry reached for the rope holding the banner, yanking it down in a dramatic tug. The flag swung, brushing the stage and rattling the lights. He saluted the flag, the shadows, and himself, wobbling slightly as the oversized boots betrayed him.

"…And that, my fiendish troops, is how victory is performed!"

For a long moment, he stood there, chest heaving, medals jangling, bugle still at his side. Then he shuffled off. The shadows remained silent, and Henry's grin lingered in the empty light.

He closed the lid on the disc and his trembling finger found and pressed the play button.

The boombox scanned the track to be played, the digital number blinking.

The black curtains parted. A strutting figure emerged, face down. Henry waited, still as stone, head lowered, face glowing in the footlights. His reflection stared back at him from the mic's chrome ball —hollow-eyed, jittering faintly in the hum.

He adjusted the stand, tapped the mic.

Nothing but feedback and the faint phlegmy throat-clicks and drooling hisses of the dark.

The background music started: a loose, funky, Herbie-Hancock-style groove slipped out of the boombox, rubbery and low.

Then came a whisper—faint, feminine—seeping in from backstage, or maybe from somewhere deeper inside his skull. Henry's head ticked with rhythmic whispers of "Uh-Huh…"

Soft, rhythmic, perfectly synced to the bassline.

NORA'S VOICE
(*slow, ghostly, almost tender*)
Ain't no music but my
heartbeat… beatin' in the
dark…

Henry twitched. A grin broke the stillness, wide and wired. He rolled his shoulders, snapped twice, found his tempo.

Henry (under breath): "Alright. Showtime."

Three spotlights illuminated the warped wooden stage. Henry, staring wild-eyed in purple high-top sneakers, stood at the mic stand. He wore a faded long-sleeved black T-shirt with the words "Original Gagster" painted across the chest in slanted white letters; mid-calf jean shorts; and his black NY cap now reading: "NOT YET." The air hummed with static from the old generator. Somewhere, rats skitter-scattered. Chairs sat empty, standing-room only tonight.

```
               NORA'S VOICE
          (distant, ghostly, feminine
          whisper)
     Ain't no music but my
     heartbeat... beatin' in the
     dark...
               (repeat, slow and rhythmic
               under Henry's verse)
```

HENRY

(rapping, animated, cracked,

defiant)

Well, I been crip-walkin' to de
karaoke crunk,

Smellin' my feet formulatin' da
funk,

Crossin' my toe-jams on an
ankle-crampin' krimp—

A krimp, of course, is a krump
with a limp!

Slidin', knee-slappin', on a
Seussian slip,

Killin' Krispy Kremes, glazin'
on my lip,

Like I's chompin' on crack-
cubes while snorkelin' my Coke,

Tryin' to recollect dis dirty
joke about a pimp!

And I crumple and I crawl, cuz
ya don't just fall,

When you're trippin' from a
clip,

At the corner of Hop and Hip!

(bouncing in his tempo,

rolling his shoulders)

And I guess I shoulda *known—
known,*

In a world all *alone—lone,*

Why I'm talkin' on the *phone—
phone!*

Just chillin' to da *bone—bone,*

At the growlin' on the *dial—
tone!*

NORA'S VOICE
(rising)

Ain't no music but my
heartbeat... beatin' in the
dark...

HENRY

I got one eighty-seven to the
nth degree,

With de wiggidy-wack bluh all
over the street,

Where dey's retchin' on de rats
cuz we all got to eat,

But that ain't no eater that I
wanna meet!

Opp, hoop dat brick and shoot a
laugh in de can,

So, pop a cap on that half
tank,

And stick to da plan!

Become a coma coma coma coma
coma-comedian,

And keep washin' up de jiggy I
apparently am!

I'm a one-comic band,

Band, stand,

Stand up wavin'-hand fans,

I'm a Stand-up Man, Man, Man,

I'm a Stand-up Mayyuunn!

Nora's back-up faded into silence.

Henry held his pose.

The last echo of "Stand-up Mayyuunn!" hung in the thick air.

Henry stood frozen in the light, chest heaving, eyes, glassy, on the darkness where laughter should have been.

His hand lifted, trembling slightly, accepting the applause that would never come.

A moment passed—too long, too hollow.

Then he turned slowly toward the dark curtains, the bassline fading.

Henry (softly to himself): "Curtain call."

4

The stage lights were up early.

Henry liked that. He liked arriving before the darkness settled fully into the city, before the shadows gathered themselves into shapes that pretended to be an audience. He stood at the edge of the stage, hand shielding his eyes, watching the lights warm and buzz awake like obedient suns.

"You pacing or rehearsing?" Nora asked.

She stood near the mic stand, one foot hooked around the cable, arms folded loosely. She wore one of his jackets—too big, sleeves rolled, collar brushing her jaw. The light caught her face just right. Not perfect. Real.

"I'm rehearsing my pacing," Henry said. "It's a very demanding role."

She smiled. Beautiful as ever, and smiling like she meant it.

The auditorium was filling.

The creatures slipped in the way they always did—carefully, respectfully, as if Henry's rules of the club mattered. Rows of dark forms arranged themselves beyond the lights, staying exactly where the brightness told them to stay. Yellow eyes blinked. A low, alien quiet settled.

Nora glanced out at them, then back to Henry.

"You ever notice," she said, "they're better behaved than most comedy audiences?"

"Fewer hecklers," Henry said. "More drool, but less commentary. I haven't read a bad review yet."

She stepped onto the stage beside him. For a moment they just stood there, sharing the light.

"You ready?" she asked.

"No," he said. "But I've never let that stop me."

She leaned in, kissed his cheek—quick, grounding—and moved to the second mic.

Henry took a breath.

Then he stepped forward.

"Good evening, everybody," he said. "I'm Henry Gorestriker. And yes—before you ask—I did take the elevator."

A ripple moved through the crowd. Not laughter. Recognition.

"I know, I know. Big risk. But in my defense, I like to live dangerously. And lazily."

He paced. The light followed him like a loyal dog.

"So I was thinking the other day—this apocalypse thing? Very inconvenient. I mean, no warning, no customer service desk. You call to complain and it's just screaming and hissing and someone eating a rat in the background."

He paused.

"Which, frankly, is how most calls with my ex-wife went anyway."

Nora stepped in smoothly.

"Let's hear it for Henry," she said, clapping lightly. "A man who survived the end of the world but still folds his jokes like he's afraid they'll wrinkle."

Henry looked at her.

"Oh, *now* you talk?"

She faced the audience.

"I've been watching him for a while. This routine. Same jokes. Same pacing. Same pauses, like he's waiting for applause that died six months ago."

Henry placed a hand on his chest.

"Ladies and gentlemen, please welcome my wife—Nora Grace Fullilove-Gorestriker—here to emotionally dismantle me."

A few creatures hissed softly. One rocked back and forth.

Nora smiled at them.

She turned back to Henry. "Tell them the truth," she said.

"The truth?" he asked.

"Yes. About why you keep doing this."

Henry hesitated.

The lights buzzed. The generator hummed faithfully in the back. The crowd waited.

"Because," she said finally, "when you stop talking, you'll hear the voice of the dark."

Nora didn't joke after that. She stepped closer, her voice calm, steady.

"And because," she said, "you believe—maybe foolishly—that laughter is a kind of light. And as long as the light's on…"

She gestured to the stage.

"…we're safe."

Something shifted in the crowd.

Not the usual twitch. Not the usual hiss.

"Nora," he said quietly. "Shall we?"

The stage lights buzzed above Henry like tired gods. One flickered. One swung slightly, like it had grown bored and was trying to leave.

He stood center stage, his hair damp with sweat, breath ragged. Nora was beside him—radiant in the same second-hand sequined dress, again, as she always was in his mind. The chairs beyond the footlights were empty, of course. But somehow, he could feel eyes. Dozens. Hundreds. Maybe just one.

"And that," Henry said, finishing his punchline, "is why you never date a woman who thinks a garlic knot is a weapon."

He smiled. Nora did too.

"They love you," she whispered.

Henry lowered the mic. The stage was quiet but warm, bathed in artificial light.

From the side of the stage came a creak.

Henry held, a man paused by bad timing. He studied Nora's face.

"Nora?" he said quietly.

He followed her gaze.

A shape emerged from the wing, slow and broken, as if it had been buried beneath the building and was only now remembering how to stand. Its limbs were stiff, coated in deep purple lividity, but strange, alien fluids coursed beneath the skin, giving each movement a sickly, sloshing pulse. The motion was hesitant, fractured—death rewritten— alien, stubborn, unwilling to stay dead.

The figure stepped into the edge of the light...

The light slowly unraveling the contours of its features...

Peeling off the likeness of...

Irwin Platt.

Or what had once been Irwin Platt.

His skin had gone gray in patches, stretched thin like damp paper. His Spanish moss beard had become more kudzu, a creepy outline clinging to his face. One eye reflected the light wrong—clouded, milk-white—while the other burned with something sharp and aware. Filthy and hunched, draped in layers of rotted clothing and newspaper, the garments hung loose, stained dark along shoulder and ribs.

The wound.

Henry's stomach dropped.

Irwin's jaw moved without purpose. His one good eye was trained on Henry, unwavering. *Or maybe on Nora.* Or maybe on something only he could see.

"Irwin?" Henry's voice trembled.

Henry moved without thinking. He stepped backward, placing himself squarely between Irwin and Nora. One arm stretched out behind him, protective, blind.

"Stay back," Henry said.

Not to Irwin.

Irwin advanced.

His foot dragged and smoked slightly as it passed through the edge of the spotlight. Smoke curled where it touched him. He did not react. He did not look away. He did not look around.

He only came forward.

Henry's heart hammered.

"Don't come any closer," Henry said, louder now.

He felt Nora just behind him—close enough that he believed he could feel her breath.

A groan came from deep in Irwin's chest, like a gravel truck stalling in a snowstorm.

Fangs dripped over his twisted lip.

"He's not here for me," Nora said gently.

Somewhere above, something squeaked. A light rig, ancient and rusted, broke loose from its mooring.

Henry didn't move. Didn't breathe.

The spotlight dropped.

It struck Irwin across the back, shattering on impact. Sparks flew. For a second nothing happened.

Then Irwin ignited.

There was no scream—only the sound of air forced from ruined lungs, a raw expulsion as his body flailed. He staggered off the stage, burning, arms reaching for balance, for nothing. He collapsed into the aisle as the creatures recoiled, scattering from the sudden brightness and heat.

Then—stillness.

Henry stood at the edge of the stage, shaking.

He turned.

"Nora?"

The stage was empty.

The second mic stood alone.

The light felt colder now.

Smoke drifted upward in thin curls.

Henry dropped the microphone. It hit the stage with a dull thud.

The silence that followed felt like the end of a joke dropped off at a funeral.

3

He finished reading his scrawl, dropped the closed notebook on the kitchen table, then lifted and placed the laptop next to it. He pulled it open slowly and stared blankly at the dark screen.

Henry licked his lips, then let his eyes wander gradually, finding purpose, to the closed door of the guest bedroom.

He opened the door to the walk-in closet, stepped in and unfolded and secured the step stool beneath the section of shelf where the box of memorabilia had been shoved back out of reach.

Henry carried the retrieved box back to the kitchen table and placed it next to the laptop.

He stared in awe and wonder at the pink line on the pregnancy test. Finally, he set it aside.

He dug around, picking up, studying old family photos, old letters.

He read some familiar scribbling off of one newer-looking note: "'Our Memories. Saved. Go light the corners of your mind.'"

His fingers reached in and came up with a flash drive.

Henry plugged the flash drive into the port on the side of the laptop. He pressed the power button. He waited a beat. Then, his fingers ran across the smooth edge and felt the hole where no power cord was inserted.

Henry dug through the box. No power cord.

Henry sat and stared, tired, tired of feeling beat, beat and defeated, at every beat and turn.

A chuckle rose but got caught in the choke of painful tears tightening in his throat.

As the moist tips of his trembling fingers lowered from his closed eyes, Henry blinked at the laptop as the screen bloomed with life.

Oh, yes...

Yes!

Images   danced. Music   played. Voices   sang and   laughed. Memories lit up.

2

The mic stand wobbled slightly as Henry set it upright with a clink. He adjusted it without looking, his eyes drifting out past the warm yellow light of center stage into the murky dark beyond.

He couldn't see them, but he knew they were there. Felt them. A silent, twitching tension just past the edge of the lights.

"Good crowd tonight," he said, voice dry. "Real attentive. Love that."

Silence answered.

Henry cleared his throat. His jokes came slower now, like pulling nails from old wood. "I once asked my dentist if I still needed to floss after the apocalypse. He said, 'Only the teeth you want to keep.'" A pause. "Thanks, Phil. Great advice. Wherever your corpse is."

No laughter. Not even the illusion of it anymore.

Sweat traced a slow line down his face. The generator hummed somewhere behind the curtain, steady but tired—like everything else. Henry scanned the dark again. He could hear them breathing. Clawing at wood. Sliding their nails down the walls. And tonight, they were closer.

He glanced stage left, toward the edge of the black curtain.

A heartbeat passed.

He leaned on the stool. "Used to be, I was afraid of what's waiting in the dark. Now I'm just afraid of the dark itself... as it waits to take my light."

Nothing.

No heckles. No movement. Just unblinking eyes he could almost feel, like insects crawling across his skin.

Then—one of them shifted. A scrape. Close.

"Nora?"

Henry twitched but forced himself still. The stool creaked beneath him as he stood up. His voice cracked slightly as he raised the mic again.

"You ever do something so many times it stops feeling like something and starts feeling like something else?"

Silence.

"I keep waiting for someone to clap. Just once. One idiot. One chuckle. But no. Not even a groan. Not even a boo. Which means…"

He turned slowly to face the curtain.

"…it means I've been bombing in front of the *worst damn audience in history*."

He stepped off the stool.

A growl answered this time—soft, low, guttural. Closer than ever.

Henry's voice dropped to a whisper, not for them, but for himself. "I'm outta here, folks…"

His hand reached for the curtain cord.

"…and…"

He took a breath. His fingers curled around the rope.

"…so are you."

He yanked, and kicked a switch.

The curtain tore open with a violent sweep, and the room ignited in pure, white, industrial light.

The audience screamed.

A wave of them—twenty, thirty, maybe more—fell back from the foot of the stage, their skin peeling in the sudden blaze. They were unfixable, every single one of them: humanoid but not human, with stretched mouths, bulbous burning eyes, and limbs like jointed shadows. The light didn't just expose them—it burned them.

And now Henry saw them for what they were.

They filled the theater floor, crammed like addicts in pews, writhing in torn coats and old uniforms, faces split with hunger. Their bodies twisted in every direction, scrambling for shelter that wasn't there.

Surrounding the auditorium, the walls held up positioned mirrors like an army of shields—hundreds of them—ripped from restrooms, beauty shops, and dressing rooms. They reflected the blinding light forward and back, bouncing off every angled surface until the club itself became a hall of blistering sun. The creatures were trapped in it. The few that found the exit entered a well-lit lobby. Nothing escaped Henry Gorestriker's killing performance.

It looked like a dance hall, but one from hell—every wall alive with grotesque shapes, clawing, clutching at their faces, collapsing in heaps of twitching limbs. A ballad of agony played only in indecipherable screams.

Henry stepped back, watching, heart pounding in his throat.

"They were always there," he whispered, "the whole time. I was performing for them."

A creature burst into flames at the edge of the mirror field. Another tore its own face apart trying to climb into the wall.

He didn't move.

He didn't feel brave, not even now. He felt tired. Exhausted to his bones.

But he felt sure. Finally.

"I'm not the funny one," he muttered. "The world's the joke. I'm just the poor bastard holding the mic."

The light burned on. The screaming faded.

One by one, the creatures collapsed, smoking, writhing, some dragging themselves toward corners that no longer offered safety. One tried to leap, shrieking, into the ceiling. It fell like a puppet cut from its strings.

Henry stepped back to the stool, set the mic down gently. The club smelled like scorched hair and something rotten—like burnt velvet.

He looked out into the room, now flooded with harsh, merciless light.

"Another night. Capacity crowd. All tickets are gone."

One last creature twitched near the back. Half its face was gone. It blinked up at him with an eye like a cracked marble, then crumbled into the puddle of its former self.

Henry nodded once.

"Show's over."

INT. BACKSTAGE MAKEUP ROOM - NIGHT

A single bulb burns over a cracked mirror. The room is quiet, lit only by the harsh white of a solitary stage light filtering through the open door.
HENRY sits at the makeup table, hunched, older, tired but smiling faintly.
His suit is frayed. A pencil spins slowly between his fingers.
He looks at his reflection... and begins to speak, not joking now.

                    HENRY
          Of course, it wasn't going to
          last forever.

The routine. The light. The
voice in the dark.

I guess that's the punchline.
No rimshot.

No applause sign.

He leans forward, studying himself.

                    HENRY (CONT'D)
          People always say they want to
          be remembered. But, hell...
          even memories die. Fade out
          like... a degraded videotape.

He leans closer to the mirror, voice trailing,
almost swallowed by the silence.

CUT TO:

INT. MIRROR - CONTINUOUS

We are now the mirror. Henry looks straight at
us.

                    HENRY
          I am history, folks.

He smiles — warm, strange, nearly gone.

FADE TO BLACK.

A beat.

FADE IN:
INT. TONIGHT SHOW SET - VHS QUALITY

Distorted colors. 4:3 aspect ratio. Static
rolls through the tape. A grainy camera holds
on HENRY GORESTRIKER behind the desk, tapping a
pencil on his coffee mug.

He turns to CAMERA 2.

                    HENRY
          Forgive me... We have to take
          a break. We'll be right back
          after a word from our sponsor.

He taps the pencil once more. The smile
flickers.
VIDEO STATIC overtakes the frame.
One final image freezes:
Henry's face, mid-smile, slightly askew, locked
in the quiet between laughter and goodbye.

FADE TO BLACK.

1

Sudden lightning revealed the broken blackness moving massive clouds above The Fontaine Residences. Multi-layered sheets of rain blurred the darkened tower, as the absence of powered lights within transformed the building into a looming, ghostly object.

Henry raced into the courtyard, a dissolving newspaper clinging to his head, his hair and clothes soaked, as he splashed his way to the fountain area several yards before the front entrance. The widespread black polyester wings of the Portobello met and encircled him, fending off the unrelenting drenches. As one white-gloved hand twirled the bamboo handle, casting curtains of downpour in angled designs, the tall red-haired doorman tipped his hat to Henry with the other.

"A good day to you, Mister Gorestriker!" Charles politely bellowed under the storm.

Henry nodded to Charles, then up at the Fontaine. "Erectile dysfunction?"

Charles burst into a hearty laugh, the kind Henry could almost appreciate, though the joke hung there—non-binding, disconnected.

"Yes! Good one, sir!"

Before Henry could answer, the tower's lights blazed alive. The golden glow spilled outward, making the rain itself seem to brighten.

"Ah! Excellent!" Henry exclaimed as Charles guided him toward the entrance.

"Yes," Charles agreed, glancing at the darkened neighboring towers. "That would be our natural-gas-powered generator. They say it can keep us running indefinitely."

"So I've heard." Henry smirked. "So, it was her natural gas and not the Viagra that did it for him."

Charles gave a hearty laugh, too hearty, the sound echoing strangely under the umbrella.

Together they crossed the slick stones toward the outer glass doors. Charles pulled one open, and Henry stepped into the vestibule, dripping, shivering, peeking into the empty lobby—gold and tan lighting, chartreuse LEDs gleaming over artworks. A lavish setting. Hard to believe he lived here.

"Where's our friend, Elvis?"

No answer.

He turned, half expecting Charles behind him. The doorman was back-stepping into the rain, lowering the umbrella. Blood streaked his pale face, washing away in rivulets.

"He's a beautiful boy."

Henry froze. "You're bleeding, Charles."

Charles smiled. "It rains on all of us, Mister Gorestriker. Sometimes it's good."

The umbrella spun once on the right-heel pivot, and, with a movement Henry could not pin down—walking, floating, both—Charles drifted away into the storm. His words faded with him: "Your son is waiting for you."

Henry turned and pressed through the revolving doors.

He did not emerge into the Fontaine's gilded lobby.

Instead, he stood in the entrance hall of his childhood home. The wallpaper's faint green print. The coat rack. The floorboard with its familiar creak. The hush of the rain outside.

And there, waiting in the middle of the hall, was a boy in spaceman pajamas. Rockets stitched in fading yellow on blue. Seven years old. A face Henry recognized without needing to be told.

The boy looked up at him, silent, waiting. And he smiled.

Henry blinked back tears. His voice cracked.

"I'm sorry. I'm sorry I wasn't there for you and your Mom."

The boy's answer came calm, reassuring. "It's okay, Dad. It's only pretend. You should wake up."

Henry frowned. "Huh?"

"The power is out."

The hall collapsed into black.

The darkness woke him. Not silence—darkness. An electrical-humming absence.

Henry blinked into the void of his apartment. The clock was out. The lamp, the stereo, the hall light—out.

Somewhere beyond the room, a low rustling gathered, a shuffle in rhythm, like claws on concrete, faraway but growing nearer. Becoming real.

The stairwell.

His pulse quickened. He sat up, whipping off the sheet, dropping his bare feet into his bedside Prada suede mules. He stood, tugging at the snug dark gym pants at his waist, untwisting the sleep-shifted matching pullover.

He could hear them climbing—slow but relentless, floor by floor, scraping their way upward through the black.

"They don't climb. Not happening."

He lifted the smartphone from the nightstand and unplugged the useless power cord. Fortunately, it was already fully charged.

How far from daylight?

The lit screen displayed: four-forty in the morning.

It cast a faint glow with a short reach, but it shaped a path through the dark to the flashlight in a drawer. Then, with a click, the flashlight flared, and the phone dropped deep into a pocket.

Within a few steps, he stumbled and the mules bucked his feet off their backless asses. He glared with the new beam at his twitching toes, then did a quick, panicked reliable-footwear search. Seconds ticking louder—he chased the beam to the door, unlocked and opened it; then out into the entrance hall—bare feet slapping—down toward the elevator, to the stairwell.

He removed the wedged-in broomstick, pressed into the bar, shoved the ingress wide, and stepped through. The door hung open behind him. He pointed the beam downward.

The light cut deep into the black throat of the stairwell—then caught movement. A dozen, maybe more, pale figures clinging to the railings, jerking upward in awkward bursts, their heads snapping back at the sudden glare.

Henry's breath jammed in his throat. The slightly-dimming beam trembled in his hand. The creatures didn't shrink from the light—they only blinked, jittered, and resumed their climbing, slow and patient.

He pulled the door shut and resecured the bar, but the echo followed him back into the penthouse. The thought was clear, unavoidable: they were coming. They were here. He was trapped.

In a frenzied state, he tore through his rooms, pulling at drawers, shoving aside old toys, muttering nonsense.

The gun was nowhere to be found.

As Henry's light flickered, the darkness deepened around him, the sound of hisses and scratching claws and groans spilled through the stairwell door, easily snapped the wedged broomstick, and crushed into the hallway walls. The sound was growing, booming louder, then, just outside the foyer, pounding against the entryway.

They've learned.

He staggered toward the far corner of the apartment where the maintenance hatch waited, the rusted frame, the ladder bolted into the wall. He climbed, every rung shaking under his weight, hands slick with sweat, arches straining to grip, lower-leg muscles burning.

The emergency hatch at the top groaned as he forced it, metal scraping against metal, then gave way. A blade of cool predawn air cut across his face, shocking him awake. He shoved himself through and scrambled onto the roof.

The rooftop yawned wide—the flat sprawl of tar and gravel beneath a paling sky. Henry stumbled forward, gasping, heart pounding —this was his last margin of air. The mannequins seemed to be watching. One toppled over.

Moonlight glazed the towers all around, skeletal and still, a ghost city, no comfort anywhere.

Henry ran across the tarp and gravel, measuring the boundaries of his dead end.

"Oww! Ouch! Ooh! Oww!"

Hopping more than running on the sharp, uneven surface.

He leaned against the ledge, chest hammering. Below: a plunge into blackness, the descent immeasurable. Above: sky, immense and cold.

And there—fluttering at his feet, tangled beneath a loose tarp—he found the chute. Nylon bright against the gray tar, straps unfurled, buckles gleaming in the starlight. He clutched it without thinking, teeth clenched against the absurdity. He dragged it free. Hands fumbling, he yanked it on, cinched the straps across his shoulders, and staggered to the ledge. Behind him, the hatch clanged shut in the wind—or something struck it from below.

And then he saw the creatures emerging.

No time. No alternative.

Henry leapt.

The air ripped his scream away before he could hear it. Wind clawed his face, tore at his clothes. The city rushed upward, buildings tilting, windows flashing past like teeth. His stomach pitched into his throat, but then—sudden violence at his shoulders—the chute tore open above him with a cracking bloom, yanked him back— the canopy snapping open like a flower. Falling—then caught by wind, lifted and carried. His body jerked, then floated. He swung, gasping, dangling above the dead grid of streets. Shadows stirred below, heads lifting, claws scraping against steel and stone, afflicted sucking gnawers writhing below as if they could sense his blood drifting overhead.

Henry swayed, twisting in the harness, each gust spinning him, his bare feet kicking. One frayed strap trembled against his shoulder. The whole contraption threatened to split apart. The harness cut into his ribs. Each swing threatened to smash him against the steel spires—or drop him into the black pits between the towers. His breath came short, ragged. A shape loomed briefly in the mist—dark, extended wings, demonic face laughing, jagged jaws with edges sharp and menacing— then it vanished quickly in the swirling wind. Henry shrieked.

And then, from somewhere deep inside—too clear, too absurd—a voice broke through:

I didn't plan this very well.

In fact, this might be the worst plan I've ever had.

Parachute with holes? Check. Zero idea where to land? Check. Life insurance policy? Might've forgotten to mail that in.

Descending into a metropolitan hellhole with absolutely no backup? Ladies and gentlemen, I give you: the least prepared man in the world.

The words didn't sound spoken; they were written across his skull, mocking him in his own cadence.

Pressure in his skull. Ringing in his ears. The world pinched in at the edges, like a photograph folded too tightly.

Eyes watering from wind and panic, he glimpsed his feet. Feet he'd known his whole life. Watched grow up. Grow old. Grow bunions and—

His toes twitched. Still working.

Well, that anti-fungal cream seems to be paying off.

And as he laughed—or sobbed—into the rushing air, the winds began to change. No longer dragging him down but lifting, tugging at the chute, ballooning it wider, pulling him higher, strings humming with a music that wasn't wind at all. His stomach dropped again, but this time he was rising, higher, drawn out of the canyons of glass and steel. Manhattan shrank beneath him, towers compressing into toy blocks, streets thinning to veins.

The creatures were gone now, or maybe they were never there.

For a moment, silence. Just the wind, tugging, almost singing. He soared, the rushing dark clouds above churning, drawing him higher. The rows of buildings dwindled into dark squares giving way to pale stretches. The urban celluloid seemed spliced to a new terrain. Rolling hills. Trees. Fields. Countryside.

Somewhere above him, approaching, the sound of a helicopter. But looking up he could only glimpse the round light of the moon blinking through threads of mist. And the sound was becoming more like … a film projector … like the one he had in sixth grade, watching five-minute eight-millimeter films on the drawn shade of his window at night. And he could smell the heat of the lamp, the nostalgic mix of vanilla and cherry and warm plastic.

Below, a car traced along a winding back road, headlights flicking against curves, and Henry drifted overhead, following.

He tilted his head, his arms spread wide, letting the wind cradle him. A weightlessness. A peace.

And only then did he glance down at himself:

Spaceman pajamas.

The same ones from childhood, tiny yellow rockets and white stars stitched in fading blue.

He laughed, breathless, suspended between terror and joy, carried farther from the city, into morning's glow—

And it was morning.

A rare, soft kind—the sky wearing a light gray sweater, the trees shivering just enough to whisper. Henry and Nora were driving west, somewhere just beyond the limits of cell reception, the road uncrowded, the world unstressed. A coffee craving had struck, sudden and mutual, and Henry had made a U-turn worthy of applause to chase down the promise of caffeine.

The Starbucks sat nestled by the parking lot entrance, and where its drive-thru menu display met the turn-in, Nora noticed a place called Tanning For The Soul to the right. Tropical-theme decor at the door: a potted palm plant standing guard.

"Tanning for the Soul," she read. "How much soul can you really tan?"

"I had the craziest dream last night," Henry opened up, as he rolled down his window; Nora inhaled the warm scent of freshly baked goods, letting it wash over her.

The ordering speaker crackled alive.

"GOOD MORNING!! And welcome to your best day ever!!" chirped a voice so bright it could wake the dead and then sell them on a non-dairy cremation. "What can I start for you beautiful people?"

Henry blinked. Nora immediately covered her mouth, stifling a laugh.

He leaned toward the speaker. "Uh… we weren't prepared for this level of joy. You might've just improved our marriage."

Nora elbowed him. They weren't married yet.

"Oh goodness!" the sweet voice giggled.

Henry added, "Seriously, my wife's eyes were hazel, and now they're—magically magenta!"

"We'll take a Grande Pink Drink and a Venti Pumpkin Spice Latte," Nora said, trying to keep a straight face, her eyes sparkling more green at the moment.

"Perfect! You guys are just perfect. Come on up, sunshine lovers!"

Henry pulled forward and they braced for disappointment—but no. The woman at the window matched the voice: young, wide-smiled, a comet of kindness in a green apron. She handed over the drinks like they were golden goblets. Nora beamed. Henry tipped her far too generously.

Nora whispered, as they pulled away, "I think she actually restored my will to live."

Henry sipped his latte with reverence. "I didn't even know her name," he said, a little too dramatically, gazing out the window like a man who missed the train.

Nora snorted.

They rolled up to a red light. Henry, eyes still fixed on the horizon, sucked in the sweet flavor, then added with theatrical flair, "Goodbye… my friend."

Immediately, a truck horn exploded behind them—deep, guttural, the kind that rearranges organs. Both of them jolted. Henry sloshed latte on the console. In the rearview mirror, a black Ford F-350 glared like a villain.

"Good grief!" Nora yelped. "I thought we left New York City!"

They turned onto the main road, still laughing, Henry mimicking the blaring horn every few seconds, Nora swatting him and repeating his line with increasing hamminess.

"Goodbye… my friend," she crooned, then roared like a truck.

It would be hours before the laughter stopped.

Days before either forgot that girl's smile.

Years before Henry remembered it at all.

He woke with a soft, teary-eyed chuckle—something between a sigh and a laugh—but the memory slipped away even as he tried to replay it. A memory sneaking in like a dream. Bits clung to the corners of his mind: the feel of the cup, the horn, her laughter. Sitting up, he wondered: could he relive it again?

But then—he didn't lie back down.

He rubbed his eyes, grateful to be awake, the smile lingering.

He stood.

Stretched.

Tugged on the upgraded running gear—clean, snug, perfectly fitted. Brand-new sneakers. The laces tied themselves.

His fingers brushed the cool plastic of the Walkman clipped to his waistband. Not his old one. This one gleamed. Batteries full.

He clicked it on and stepped outside.

The music played—Chicago sounding better than ever.

Henry, the man, jogged, keeping rhythm in his head and feet, knees and elbows.

Morning light draped his shoulders like an old friend's arm.

Around him—the painted city—the colors of the maze were shifting subtly, flickering shades of glass.

The city was still—breathing, maybe, but calm.

He ascended an echoing flight of shaded steps, cut right, and reached a sunlit stretch of elevated expanse.

His pocket buzzed.

He slowed. Reached in for the smartphone.

A gust of singing warmth embraced him like a lover, and he lifted his eyes.

Above the skyline across the harbor, the starship appeared—vast, iridescent—descending like a cosmic chandelier. It hovered, casting pinwheels of color across rooftops and windows, washing Broadway brilliantly and making the best of Times Square. A purifying spray of light and color swept the city, changing it... healing it. Warm vibrations poured down, and the ship was crossing the water... now floating overhead.

Then, lighter than air, he felt himself lifted. The wind—or the ship's light—took him, pulling him gently upward. The streets fell away, the buildings shrinking beneath him. He was rising, floating, caught in a current of color and sound, soaring above the city that had been his cage and his stage.

Sparkling dust swam through Henry's vision—his dampened knuckles blindly clearing it.

He was twirled gently, eyes pulled away as a lover's fingers turned his face for a kiss.

A beautifully strange alien sound wove through the air, soft but penetrating. The phone in his pocket hummed insistently.

And then—a sudden, violent tearing.

The parachute above him screamed as canopy was ripped, fibers snapping in the wind. Henry's stomach dropped. The dreamlike lift fractured. Reality stabbed in.

He rotated, eyes wide.

A gargoyle's face stared down at him. Stone eyes blank and accusing, fangs poised in shadow. The suspension lines were tangled around the creature's hybrid form, cutting across the curve of its claws, while the loose nylon draped over its carved wings flapped, making them seem alive.

And Henry's body dangled twenty feet below it, suspended absurdly in midair beneath the mounted corbel, uselessly kicking numbed feet—metatarsals lightly bruised and scraped, swollen ankles, oddly bluish toes.

The cords groaned, frayed, threatening.

Henry's clenched teeth were chattering loose.

The city spread below like a fractured toy set, and Henry realized —he wasn't floating anymore. He was hanging. Vulnerable. Terrified.

A beat. A breath. A buzzing, again.

Henry pulled the phone from his pocket. It almost slipped away.

Its glow gave him focus.

GRACE calling.

His fingers clenched around it.

He slowly lifted it, tears filling his eyes.

The gentle tug returned. The gargoyle released him.

Henry's feet were suddenly merging with warmth as the current carried him upward, higher and higher, past the gargoyle, past the city that had been his cage and stage—warmth spreading through his entire body, instilling a supercharged circuit of ebullient vibes.

His fears seemed to melt away instantly.

He smiled, lungs burning, heart full.

He laughed, eyes fixed on the sky.

Curtains parting to reunite his heart—opening softly this time, earned and real.

He brought the phone to his ear.

"Hello!"

And as he rose, hugged in color and sound, the starship brought him out of the fear, like a promise kept. Henry let it carry him.

The Manhattan stories seemed restored at last.

But somewhere Chicago keeps playing…

And, as the MUSIC continues, we FADE OUT.

And that's the director's cut.